a perfect miracle

# a perfect miracle

### JACOBS LANDING SERIES
### BOOK ONE

KATRINA ALEXANDER

Palmetto Publishing Group
Charleston, SC

Printed in the United States

Paperback: 978-1-64111-558-2
Hardcover: 978-1-64111-566-7
eBook: 978-1-64111-661-9

*For Mike and the girls, because they said, "Go for it!"*

*Special thanks to Kim, Deb, Lindsay, Shannon, and Mom for their invaluable feedback and steadfast encouragement. I couldn't have done this without your pep talks!*

Some people think a miracle is only a miracle if it happens instantaneously, but miracles can grow slowly, and patience and faith can compel things to happen that otherwise never would have come to pass.

—Boyd K. Packer

# CHAPTER ONE

It was the dog. The dog appeared on the back porch of her old Victorian home in Gabrielle Levesque's hometown of Jacobs Landing, Maine. And it was the dog who helped Gabrielle believe in miracles again.

At first, Gabrielle didn't see him in the purple dusk of evening. It was the second anniversary of her husband's death, and the loneliness of Gabrielle's life without Jean-Luc gnawed at the pit of her stomach. She was so lost in misery that Gabrielle almost stepped on him when she climbed the steps to her back door.

The dog yipped in surprise when she stumbled over him. He was medium size, with a black patch over one eye, and his sandy-colored fur was matted with dirt and debris. When she sank to her knees and offered her hand in apology, the dog licked her fingers and smiled a doggy grin. He was the loneliest and scrawniest mutt she had ever seen, but despite his dirty coat and protruding ribs, Gabrielle fell in love with him.

She dubbed him Rocky because his black patch reminded her of the iconic movie character. By the time Gabrielle had taken care of the dog's immediate needs, Jean-Luc's death anniversary was over. She made it through the day thanks to Rocky.

The next morning, despite a busy day at her shop, The Treasure Trove, Gabrielle knew she needed to have Rocky checked out by the local veterinarian. He was too underweight. Was he sick or just underfed?

Since there was only one vet clinic, Gabrielle looked up its phone number and dialed. She sipped a smoothie and waited for the receptionist to pick up on the other end.

"Jacobs Landing Veterinary Hospital, Donna speaking."

"Hello, Donna. This is Gabrielle Levesque. Last night, I found a stray dog on my porch. Can I get an appointment to see Dr. Standish today? The dog's pretty scrawny. He should get checked out."

"Dr. Standish only works on Tuesdays now. He's semiretired. Let's see…I can get you in with Dr. Leland at four thirty. It's my last appointment of the day."

"Dr. Leland?"

"Yes. Andrew Leland bought the practice a year ago. He's the doc who'll see your dog today. Didn't you and Andrew go to high school together?"

A vision of Andrew Leland's golden-blond hair, sculpted cheekbones, and white teeth flashed before Gabrielle's eyes. He was the golden boy of Jacobs Landing in appearance and standing. His father was the bank president, but Andrew's popularity was due to his friendliness and sincerity as much as his father's position.

"Gabrielle?"

"Sorry, Donna. Yes, we went to high school together, but he was two years ahead of me. He was in my brother's class."

"That's right. So do you want me to schedule that appointment for you?"

"Sure. Thanks. We'll see you at four thirty."

Gabrielle's hand shook as she hung up the phone. Andrew Leland. Scholar. Athlete. Her high school crush.

Six years ago, Gabrielle and her husband, Jean-Luc, happened to run into him and his girlfriend at a party in New York City. At that time, Andrew worked on Wall Street. How did he go from Wall Street trader to small town veterinarian?

Gabrielle groaned in frustration when she caught sight of a nearby clock. She patted her thigh and whistled to the dog.

"Come on, Rocky. We need to buy you a leash before I take you to work with me. You can hang out in the back room while I wait on customers. Phyllis, my manager, is going to love you."

The dog followed Gabrielle to the door, tail wagging and tongue dangling the whole time.

Later that afternoon, Gabrielle stared at the mesmerizing blue sparkle of the bay, just visible from her seat in the waiting room of the clinic. She checked on the dog who sat patiently next to her chair, then felt her gaze pulled back to the water.

*Jacobs Landing.* Small fishing town with hardworking New Englanders populating its confines. According to local legend, Benedict Jacobs founded the town after surviving a shipwreck. Over the centuries, the locals acknowledged their founding father by naming their male children after him. Census data showed an uncommon number of children named Jacob or Benedict over the two-and-a-half centuries of town history.

Recently, tourists had rediscovered Gabrielle Levesque's hometown. They made day trips from nearby towns such as Bar Harbor, Trenton, and Bangor to appreciate its pristine views, sample its cuisine, and shop at the unique stores along Main Street.

All these random bits of information flitted through Gabrielle's mind as she stifled a yawn with the back of her hand and gave Rocky a reassuring pat on the head. The aftereffects of yesterday's emotional day and the short night of sleep due to the dog's unexpected arrival had left her drowsy and reflective.

Suppressing another yawn, Gabrielle pondered the question of Andrew Leland's career change as she glanced around. The faint scent of paint suggested the room had been recently redecorated. Someone had chosen earth tones for the color scheme, but it was the funny photos of animals framed on the walls that caught her attention. There were no nondescript landscapes in this veterinary practice.

Did the wall art reflect the humor of the man who owned the practice? Why was she even curious about this *new* Andrew Leland?

A veterinary assistant opened an exam room door. "Rocky?"

Gabrielle stood up. She gave a gentle tug on the new blue leash she had purchased earlier. The dog trailed after her, his tongue hanging happily out of his mouth.

"Oh, he's so cute! I can see why you named him Rocky. It's the patch, isn't it?"

Gabrielle nodded.

The assistant continued, "Yeah, the patch over his eye makes him look like the boxer from that movie. Good choice. I'm Annabelle, by the way. We just need to get Rocky's weight, and then we can move into the exam room."

A minute later, Gabrielle and Rocky followed Annabelle through a nearby door.

It was the end of the day. Andrew Leland massaged the back of his neck where tension and fatigue corded his muscles. A quick check of his schedule indicated one patient left. With a double-take, Andrew reread Gabrielle Levesque's name. The quiet, curly-haired girl he barely knew in high school was waiting in room three.

Andrew remembered the girl as Gabrielle Martin. She had been two years behind him. He also remembered her older brother, Thomas. The Martins kept to themselves because they were one of the

Franco-American families in town. An imaginary line between the French-speaking families and the Anglo families still seemed to divide Jacobs Landing. It wasn't antagonistic; the line was just a simple division of two cultures. At least, that was what Andrew had told himself in high school even as he had admired her from afar. Gabrielle was beautiful. Shy. And her older brother had threatened to kill anyone who tried to approach her.

Two years ago, Andrew was finishing veterinary school when he heard about the sudden death of Gabrielle's textile-mogul husband. The town gossip went crazy. According to rumor, Jean-Luc Levesque had left Gabrielle with more money than anyone could spend in a lifetime. Andrew sympathized with her loss since he had seen firsthand how in love Gabrielle and her husband had been.

Before knocking on the exam room door, Andrew smoothed his short blond hair. Why was he nervous to talk to her? Was it because he wasn't sure if he should offer condolences? Was it because he had always found her attractive, if out of reach?

Andrew gave himself a mental shake.

*Pull yourself together, Leland. She's just a woman.*

He braced himself, then knocked on the exam room door. When Andrew entered the room, Gabrielle stood beautiful and waiflike next to an equally thin dog.

"Gabrielle, nice to see you again, and who do we have here?"

There. Businesslike. Professional. Just like any other patient.

Gabrielle's hand fluttered nervously before it rested on Rocky's head.

"Hello, Andrew. Good to see you too. I was surprised to learn you were the new vet."

Andrew grinned. "I bet. The last time we saw each other, we were hobnobbing in New York City."

Andrew's expression grew serious. "I was sorry to hear about your husband, Gabrielle."

He watched as a bleakness flashed in her dark-blue eyes. She swallowed and nodded, her dark curls swaying with the motion.

"Thank you. Sorry, I never answered your question. This is Rocky."

He nodded and moved the conversation back to neutral territory. "So how did you and this guy meet?"

While Gabrielle explained how she found the dog on her back porch the night before, Andrew crouched next to Rocky. He introduced his hand, then ran his fingers down the dog's back, sides, and underbelly.

Gabrielle followed Andrew's example and crouched on Rocky's other side. She scratched the dog's head while Andrew conducted his examination. Whether it was to comfort the dog or herself, Andrew wasn't sure.

"He is definitely underweight and has probably been on his own for some time," Andrew commented as he completed the physical exam. "I would like to draw some blood to make sure everything checks out. I'll do that, then send in my assistant to check for a microchip, if that sounds good to you."

At her nod, Andrew pulled a syringe from a nearby drawer and took the needed blood sample.

"I'll take care of this and be back in a couple of minutes with a diet plan to help him add on those needed pounds."

Andrew closed the door behind him. He leaned back and took a shuddering breath. Phew. He made it through the appointment without making a fool of himself. Gabrielle was still gorgeous, but her grief kept her just out of reach. It was like high school all over again. Andrew gave himself a mental shake, then pushed away from the door. Focus on the dog. Focus on the task at hand.

Fifteen minutes later, the vet tech flashed the microchip reader in Gabrielle's direction.

"Rocky doesn't have a microchip, Gabrielle. I've checked three times. I also checked the missing dog alerts, and there aren't any that match Rocky's description. It looks like you have a new dog."

Annabelle smiled and added dog licensing information to a folder. "Here, I'll walk you to the front desk."

At the front counter, Gabrielle juggled the paperwork, the dog leash, and her purse as she paid for the visit. She tucked Rocky's bill into the folder with the rest of her paperwork, then turned to leave.

"Gabby! Gabby Martin, is that you?"

A waft of cheap perfume hit Gabrielle's nose before she focused on the screeching female inside the clinic door. Gabrielle hated being called *Gabby*. It had never suited her. It was an adjective, not a name. But she knew whose signature scent was contaminating the waiting room. It was the same person who continued to call her Gabby, even though she knew Gabrielle disliked the term. Emily Ross. A former classmate who was just as annoying as she had been in high school.

It was times like these that Gabrielle missed living in Paris. Paris was a big city, and she didn't run the risk of meeting someone she knew, like she did in Jacobs Landing.

Gabrielle smiled weakly. "Hello, Emily. My name's Gabrielle *Levesque* now. How have you been?"

Rocky pulled on his leash. His toenails scraped the floor as he half rose on his hind legs. With his nose sniffing the air, Rocky tried to get at the pink bag Emily carried in her arms. Gabrielle scrambled to rein in her new pet.

Great. Emily had one of those small dogs in a coordinating purse. Of course she did. How humiliating for the dog.

"Oh, that's right. I guess I *did* hear you're a widow," Emily dismissed Gabrielle's loss with a wave of her hand. "I stopped to see if Andrew could take a look at Opal. She's had a little cough. I couldn't rest until I made sure she was okay."

Gabrielle eyed Emily's bleached hair, low-cut blouse, slinky jeans, and overdone makeup. Opal's cough had nothing to do with Emily's visit.

Andrew stepped into the waiting room, and Gabrielle was struck anew by the sight of him. His tall height and broad shoulders had served him well in high school sports, but now his shoulders had thickened into a man's build. His waist, however, was still narrow, unlike many other men in their early thirties. His short hair fell to the side of his forehead, and a spark of annoyance flashed in his hazel eyes.

He looked pointedly at his watch.

"The rest of my staff just left, and I have exactly five minutes, Emily. But only if Opal is really sick. Otherwise, I urge you to make an appointment tomorrow. I need to pick Jack up from the sitter's in fifteen minutes. I will not keep my son waiting."

Gabrielle's jaw dropped at the mention of a son. She eyed Andrew's hand to see if he wore a wedding ring. No ring.

"I don't know why you make such a big fuss, Andrew. It's not like Josh is really your son. He's *adopted*," she turned to Gabrielle and touted her information. "His best friend died in a boating accident, so Andrew adopted the son."

Andrew's mouth tightened. Emily had no clue she'd clinched it. Andrew would never date anyone who dismissed his child.

"His name is Jack, Emily. Not Josh. On second thought, I have to lock up. If Opal still has a cough tomorrow, you can call and make an appointment. I have to get going." Andrew glanced at Gabrielle. "If you can wait for a second, I'll help you load up Rocky and his bag of dog food. Just let me grab my coat. April in Maine can be bitter, you know."

Gabrielle read the look in his eyes. *Please don't leave me alone with her.*

Gabrielle nodded and watched Andrew disappear into the back of the building. She guessed Annabelle and Donna had left when they caught sight of Emily. Gabrielle didn't blame them. She wanted to leave too.

Gabrielle shifted from foot to foot and noted the lights shutting off in succession as Andrew made his way to the front of the building. He reappeared in the waiting room with a twenty-five-pound bag of dog food draped over his shoulder—food Gabrielle had not paid for.

Emily fell in step with them. "Well, if you have to leave, I'll walk out with you guys."

Out in the parking lot, Andrew waited next to Gabrielle's SUV while she loaded Rocky into the passenger seat. A cold wind whipped in from the bay and sliced through the lightweight jacket he wore.

As her teeth chattered, Emily called out, "I'll make an appointment tomorrow, Andrew. This wind isn't good for Opal's cough."

Before he or Gabrielle had a chance to respond, Emily sped away in her red Mini Cooper. Gabrielle closed the door of her vehicle and moved to the liftgate. Andrew set the dog food inside her vehicle.

He grinned. "That's free of charge. Consider it combat pay for running Emily interference."

Gabrielle eyed the dog food bag and then glanced back up at him. Her mouth twitched. She chuckled. After another second, she threw her head back and pealed with laughter. He watched her try to contain her amusement, but once unleashed, she seemed unable to control it.

How long had it been since she laughed? Andrew joined her in laughing at the absurdity of the situation.

As she succumbed to her laughter, Gabrielle leaned on Andrew's arm. She gasped and tried to catch her breath. He easily supported her weight and enjoyed her warmth against him. After a moment, Gabrielle wiped the tears from her eyes and struggled to stand up straight.

"I'm sorry." She patted his arm in an unconscious gesture. "It's been so long since I laughed like that. I couldn't control myself."

Gabrielle grinned up at him. Andrew froze under the full effect of her smile. She had always been such a serious girl, even in school. Never before had she directed her unfettered smile at him. His laughter died. Oh boy. He fell half in love with her that instant.

All those boyish feelings he had harbored for her in high school manifested into the feelings of a man.

Desire for her ignited quickly but to his surprise so did an almost overwhelming feeling of tenderness. Desire Andrew was familiar with but tenderness? Where had that come from?

He needed Gabrielle Levesque in his life. The timing had finally worked out. They were both single. Suddenly, Andrew could picture a future with her. Is this how love worked? One minute you're minding your own business; the next minute your focus on life completely shifts. But how did he court a widow who wasn't over her dead husband?

The wind tempted him by whipping a dark curl across Gabrielle's cheek. Andrew started to reach for it but dropped his hand when he saw wariness register in Gabrielle's eyes. She took a step back and glanced away.

He cleared his throat and fell back on professionalism to fill the awkward silence.

"I'd like to see Rocky back in a week to make sure he's putting on the weight he needs. Just call the office to make an appointment. Also, there's a new dog park not too far from here. It's a little tricky to find if you've never been there before. Here, I'll give you directions. Jack and I like to take our black Lab there on the weekends."

Why was he telling her that? Did he hope she would show up with Rocky? Of course he did. Andrew needed to see how Gabrielle and Jack interacted.

He ignored the niggling guilt in the back of his mind and wrote down the directions to the dog park. Sometimes, Andrew introduced a woman to Jack. By doing so, he could gauge the woman's reaction to having a child around. Unfortunately, most of those women never made it past the introduction stage to an actual date.

How would she react to Jack? Would Gabrielle ignore him like some women had or gush over him in order to get Andrew's attention? Why did he assume Gabrielle would be interested in either of them?

Andrew checked his watch, and swore under his breath.

"I have to get going. See you next week at Rocky's appointment."

He handed Gabrielle the directions to the dog park, then jogged to his truck. Once inside, Andrew waited until Gabrielle started her vehicle. He pulled up to the stop sign and turned on his signal. Behind his truck, Gabrielle waited for him to make his turn. He waved in the rearview mirror before turning toward the sitter's house.

After her encounter with Andrew Leland, Gabrielle felt off kilter, like her world had tilted slightly off its axis. He was more handsome than he had been in New York. His angular face and blond hair hinted at Nordic ancestry, but his kindness and genuine concern for Rocky were even more appealing.

Gabrielle frowned. The anniversary of Jean-Luc's death had been yesterday. She should *not* be thinking about another man. Even if he was her high school crush. Even if his skin glowed with a golden undertone. Even if he was unfailingly loyal to his adopted son. Gabrielle shook her head. She needed some perspective.

Gabrielle glanced at Rocky.

"Are you up for a visit with Pop and Grand-Père? I think they'd like to meet you."

Rocky smiled a doggy smile and settled onto the front seat. Gabrielle pulled into traffic and headed to her father's house. Twenty minutes later, she knocked on her only living parent's door.

"Hey, Pop. Grand-Père, I've come for a visit," Gabrielle called as she let herself in the front door.

She moved to the back of the house. They were probably in the kitchen. The room overlooked the bay and offered the retired fishermen a chance to relive their memories. As Gabrielle entered the room, the large windows painted a picture of dark water touched by the last rays of sunset.

Her father, David Martin, sat at a plank-style table with pencil in hand as if she had caught him midword. A crossword puzzle book lay on the table in front of him. Gabrielle scanned her father's appearance. He looked as steady and reliable as the tide. His gray hair and close-cropped beard were brushed neatly, and he wore a navy-blue fisherman's sweater against the cool spring night. She circled the table and gave him a kiss on the cheek.

"What kind of mongrel do you have there?" Grand-Père asked in French.

He, too, sat at the plank table and pointed the end of his unlit pipe at the dog who followed in Gabrielle's wake. Before she answered, Gabrielle crossed to the other end of the table and kissed her grandfather on both cheeks in the French custom.

"This is Rocky. He was waiting on my porch for me when I got home last night. It looks like we're meant to be."

She studied Grand-Père. His white hair and horn-rimmed glasses were the same as always, but his skin seemed more translucent. He never complained, but she knew his heart condition kept him seated more often than not. It was that same heart condition that had forced him to retire from his fishing career, although he still kept a vintage cabin cruiser moored at the dock for recreational fishing.

"His friendliness is about the only thing he's got going for him," Pop commented as he inspected the dog.

Grand-Père gave Rocky a rub behind the ears.

"You can leave him here by me while you get something to eat. There's leftover shrimp in the fridge. And salad. Help yourself."

A few minutes later, Gabrielle set her plate on the table. She slid a chair back and sat down. Pop appeared at her elbow and tilted a bottle of wine so she could see the label. He raised an eyebrow in unspoken question.

She nodded. "Only if you'll join me. There's no way I can handle more than one glass tonight without falling asleep."

With the wine poured, all three of them sat companionably around the table. Her father and grandfather were not great conversationalists. They only spoke when they had something to say, but they conveyed their love for her in other ways.

Pop cleared his throat. "What're you going to do with a dog when you go to France? He can't go with you."

Gabrielle draped an arm along the back of her chair and took a sip of wine.

"I hadn't thought about it yet. Between work and the vet today, I haven't had much time to realize I'm a dog owner. I guess I'll have to kennel him."

Gabrielle took another sip of her wine and kept an eye on her father and grandfather. To the average person, these two men were stoic and unreadable. But she knew them well. She could sense their acceptance of Rocky and their own need to have a dog in their lives, even on a temporary basis. They were drawn to Rocky, and Rocky basked in their attention.

Grand-Père spoke up. "There's no need to put him in one of those places. It looks like he's been through enough." He glanced at Pop. "I think we could keep him here during the weeks you're in Paris. Don't you agree, David?"

Pop nodded and rubbed Rocky behind the ears.

"Ayuh, that'll work." He took a sip of wine and nodded toward the stairs. "Why don't you both stay the night? You look tired. Get some rest, then drive home in the morning."

Fatigue and the aftereffects of the day weighed down Gabrielle's limbs. She nodded.

"Okay, Pop. We'll stay."

Ten minutes later, Gabrielle and Rocky climbed the stairs to the second story of her childhood home. Entering her room, Gabrielle pulled back the blue-and-white toile comforter, then slid under the covers. She fell into a deep sleep, but sometime during the night, she began to dream.

The dream began at the art gallery where she met Jean-Luc. Jean-Luc Levesque had been a magnetic Frenchmen with darkly handsome features and loads of money. He and his brother ran one of the world's largest textile companies. He had appeared unexpectedly at a weaving exhibition Gabrielle attended in New York.

Because French was her native language, Gabrielle and Jean-Luc had hit it off. In the weeks that followed, he called her regularly and flew back and forth between France and the United States. Even though he was divorced and fourteen years her senior, Jean-Luc swept Gabrielle into a whirlwind courtship. Gabrielle graduated from art school a month after they met. They were married two months later.

In the five years of their marriage, Gabrielle developed the style and social poise needed to be a wealthy man's wife. She took over the charitable functions of Jean-Luc's company and worked side by side with her husband to continue the company's success. The only thing that had been missing was a child. She and Jean-Luc had tried for most of their marriage to conceive.

One April morning, Jean-Luc kissed her and boarded a jet for Milan. Several hours later, his driver pulled the limousine out in front of a bus. The accident killed them both and robbed Gabrielle of her purpose. The love of her life was gone.

Gabrielle woke with a start. Moonlight trickled in from the window and dappled the items in the room with its silvery touch. She wiped at the wetness on her cheeks, then reached for a tissue. Rocky thumped his tail at the foot of the bed and sat alert.

"It's okay, Rocky." She sniffled. "I'll be okay."

Gabrielle snuggled under the covers and pulled a necklace out from under her shirt. She gazed at the muted shine of their two wedding bands hanging together on the chain. After a moment, Gabrielle slipped the larger one over her thumb and held it to her cheek.

*I miss you, Jean-Luc*, her mind sobbed.

Gabrielle fell asleep with her husband's wedding band still on her finger.

# CHAPTER TWO

Gabrielle parked her SUV in the alley behind her shop, The Treasure Trove. It was Saturday, and Rocky had been with her for five days.

"Come on, Rock. Let's see if Phyllis needs us to make a deposit before we head to the park."

Gabrielle's store occupied one of the various rental spaces in the historic shopping area along Main Street. Unbeknownst to the renters of these budding shops, and to most of the Jacobs Landing residents, Gabrielle owned this stretch of buildings that was the nineteenth-century equivalent of a strip mall. She loved the old-fashioned façades and the quaintness of the town's busiest thoroughfare.

Many of the shop fronts stood vacant. She hoped the renters' incentive she offered for the first five years of business would soon bring more entrepreneurs to the historic center.

Gabrielle unlocked the door to the stockroom and stepped inside. Rocky followed on his leash. Phyllis, Gabrielle's manager, caught sight of them as she opened a box of merchandise.

"I thought you and Rocky were taking the day off!" exclaimed the salt-and-pepper-haired woman as she crouched to scratch Rocky between the ears with her daisy-printed manicure.

Gabrielle smiled.

"We stopped by to see if you needed me to make a deposit before we head to the dog park. I tell you, Phyllis, renovating a home is not all it's cracked up to be. We had to get out of the house. The pounding and screech of power tools were giving me a headache."

Phyllis chuckled. "Well, you were the one who decided to buy that Victorian monstrosity. It's been neglected for so many years, you'll probably spend your whole life getting it put back together again. Here, if you watch the front desk, I'll get the deposit ready."

Gabrielle nodded and donned a black apron embroidered at the top with *The Treasure Trove* in white letters. She left Rocky in the stockroom and slipped behind the counter to watch for customers.

Six months ago, Phyllis moved to Jacobs Landing in order to be closer to her daughter, Amy, and her son-in-law, Ryan. Phyllis had approached Gabrielle about a job. Gabrielle liked her straightforward manner and her penchant for flamboyant glasses and manicures. After a month-long trial period, she made Phyllis the manager of her artisan-based gift shop. Phyllis also lived in the apartment above the store.

Ten minutes later, deposit bag in hand, Gabrielle left. She dropped the deposit at the bank and glanced at the piece of paper with Andrew's doctor-style scratches on it. Did every doctor and vet take a class on illegible writing? Fortunately for Gabrielle, she knew the general direction of the park, and she could guess the rest of his directions.

"Come on, Rock. Let's go somewhere fun." She shifted the SUV into gear.

They pulled into a parking spot in front of a fenced area. The dog park was divided into two sections. As Gabrielle and Rocky neared the gate, she saw one section was designated for smaller and less energetic dogs. Rocky did *not* qualify for that section.

Gabrielle headed inside the enclosure for large dogs. In the middle of the fenced area sat a pavilion-like structure where other dog owners congregated on Adirondack-style chairs and benches. She and Rocky took a convoluted path toward the structure since the dog stopped and marked his territory on the way. Tired of their sporadic progress, Gabrielle distracted Rocky with a game of ball.

Once Rocky tired of the game, Gabrielle ambled toward the pavilion and left him to investigate the rest of the grounds. She enjoyed the warm sunshine on her face and the peacefulness of the park. Even with the occasional barking dog, the park was blessedly quiet compared to the chaos of her under construction kitchen.

A few minutes later, Gabrielle found a seat next to a retired couple who introduced themselves as Shirley and Ralph. The older couple had a pair of Saint Bernard brothers panting at their feet. Gabrielle was impressed by the gentle giants, affectionately called Lenny and Squiggy after characters in an old TV sitcom.

As Gabrielle kept watch over Rocky's investigation of a sand pile, a slobbery tongue baptized her cheek. She yelped in surprise and found herself face to face with a panting black Labrador Retriever. Once the Lab caught her eye, he tried to crawl onto her lap. Since the dog probably weighed as much as she did, Gabrielle pushed him back onto the ground.

"Sorry, pup. There's only room for one of us in this chair." Gabrielle smiled and patted his head.

Black Dog continued to whine and inch toward her.

"No way. You *are* cute, but you're too heavy for me."

Black Dog huffed in acceptance and rested his snout on Gabrielle's knee. She smiled at his open adoration and scratched behind an ear.

"Looks like he's in love," speculated a familiar voice.

Gabrielle glanced up to see a grinning Andrew step onto the cement flooring of the pavilion. His faded jeans hugged his long legs, and a blue-and-red flannel shirt did nothing to hide his broad shoulders. Andrew's casual maleness caused a twinge of feminine appreciation to sing through Gabrielle's veins.

"Allow me to introduce Gus and Jack. Gus is the one with his head on your knee." He gestured to the dog. "And Jack is this guy next to me."

With tenderness, Andrew rested his hand on the head of the little boy next to him. Big brown eyes mesmerized Gabrielle as she gazed at the dark-haired boy of about five years.

"Hello, Jack. My name is Gabrielle. It's nice to meet you."

Gabrielle offered a tentative smile. Do people shake hands with five-year-olds? Gabrielle didn't know. She hoped she looked friendly.

Jack darted over to her chair and pushed Gus out of the way. Before Gabrielle could register his change in position, the boy threw himself at her knees.

He clung to her legs and scrutinized her face. "Are you my mom?"

Tears sprang to her eyes, and Gabrielle took an involuntary breath. She *had* hoped to be someone's mom. Once. Not wanting to upset the little boy, she blinked back the wetness in her eyes and took a shallow breath.

Gabrielle touched Jack's shoulder and shook her head. "No, Jack. I'm sorry. I'm not your mom. But I *am* a friend of your dad's."

Gabrielle noted the ashen pallor of Andrew's skin. He looked just as shocked as she was.

Andrew cleared his throat.

"That's right, bud. Gabrielle and I went to school together. Just like you go to school with your friends in kindergarten."

Rocky chose that moment to announce his presence by wedging himself in between Jack and Gus. He sniffed Jack's neck, and the boy giggled.

"Jack, this is my dog. His name is Rocky, and he doesn't always have good manners, but we're working on them."

Not a dog to sit still, Rocky took off to the other side of the park. A minute later, the dog returned. He dropped a slobbery tennis ball at Jack's feet.

The little boy eyed Gabrielle. "He wants me to play ball. Can I play with him?"

"You sure can."

Boy and dog ran off together. Gus, however, was another matter. Now that Jack and Rocky were gone, he scooted closer to Gabrielle and contented himself by sitting on her foot.

Andrew slumped into the chair next to her and ran a hand over his face. The day's growth of beard that skimmed his jawline gave him an I-just-rolled-out-of-bed sexiness.

"I'm sorry, Gabrielle. Jack's never done that before. He's never asked anyone if she were his mother. I don't know what's gotten into him."

"Maybe I look like his mom?" Gabrielle supplied.

"Nope. Julie, his mom, was blonde." Andrew sighed. "I can't understand why he'd say that to you. I'm sorry if he embarrassed you."

Gabrielle was silent for a moment.

"He didn't embarrass me. It just took me by surprise."

Intuitively knowing she could trust him; Gabrielle made the decision to share her greatest disappointment with Andrew.

"Jean-Luc and I were trying to have a baby before he died. After the funeral, I didn't think I would ever be called a mom. It just took me by surprise."

Gabrielle looked down at her hands. She felt the loneliness and disappointment anew. No husband. No baby. Just an empty house. Well, not so empty now that Rocky was in her life.

The light touch of Andrew's knee against her own brought Gabrielle out of her reverie. The contact was a conscious decision. Andrew Leland offered sympathy by the casual contact. She was grateful for the comfort of his touch.

Two weeks later, Gabrielle loaded Rocky, picnic supplies, and a blanket into her SUV. Her shop was closed on Sundays, so she and Rocky had the day to relax and enjoy the warm weather. Maine winters could be intense, so as soon as the weather turned warm, New Englanders spilled outdoors to soak up the sun. With this mind-set, Gabrielle drove to Harborview Park.

After she parked, Gabrielle grabbed her supplies and Rocky's leash. They walked to her favorite group of mature trees facing the bay. At the base of one tree, she spread out her blanket and sat down. Rocky settled next to her, his warm body heating her left thigh.

She let the contentment of the warm spring day and the companionship of a devoted dog lull her into relaxation. With a brief pat to the dog, Gabrielle rested against the tree trunk and reflected on the last couple of weeks. Rocky had gained a few pounds since he had become her dog. He was still underweight, but when she took Rocky for his follow-up appointment, Andrew had been pleased with his progress.

Gabrielle dropped her head back against the tree and continued to let her mind wander. Memory guided her thoughts. She toyed with the rings on her necklace and remembered the bleak days after Jean-Luc's death.

Gabrielle had barely left her bed after the funeral. She couldn't muster the strength to continue without Jean-Luc. He had been the center of her world. Without him, Gabrielle was like a traveler without a compass. She didn't know which direction to go.

David Martin had flown to Paris to stay with Gabrielle as soon as he heard about his son-in-law's death. For a while, he stayed with Gabrielle and kept her company in her grief. One day, her father came into her room and sat in front of her.

"Look at me, Gabrielle," he urged.

When she finally met his eyes, David spoke. "You're not the only one to go through this kind of pain. I know it seems cruel for me to tell you this, but it's true. You were just a girl when your mother died of cancer, but I felt the same agony you're feeling now. In a way, I was lucky. I had you and your brother to care for, so I had to keep going. My advice to you is to find something to live for. You are twenty-six years old, and while life may seem like it's over, you have many years ahead of you.

"First, you have to decide to live. Get up. Get dressed. Perform your daily routines. It will be difficult in the beginning, but each time you do it, it'll get a little easier. Jean-Luc was one of the most alive men I have ever met. He wouldn't like to see this shell of a wife that you have become."

Gabrielle's father brushed back a piece of her hair.

"I leave tomorrow. To go home. To Jacobs Landing. Maybe that's what you need too. Come home. I've done all I can for you. Now you must decide to live."

Gabrielle had never heard such a long speech from her father. She grasped his hand and squeezed. David squeezed back. He left the room with a soft click of the door.

That night Gabrielle dreamed of Jacobs Landing. Jean-Luc stood in the street and grinned at her. He pointed to the rundown and empty shops on Main Street.

"Your future is here, chérie. It's waiting for you," he called as he faded away.

Gabrielle returned to Jacobs Landing and tried to create a life for herself. She bought the rundown buildings along Main Street. She opened her shop and recruited new renters, but her life was empty. She was lonely.

A wet tongue licked her cheek and brought Gabrielle back to the present. She smelled the pungent odor of dog breath as she swiped drying tears from her cheeks. As her eyes flickered open, Gabrielle recognized Gus panting in her face. To her left, Rocky sat alert and on guard.

"Gus? Where are you?" Andrew's voice called from behind her.

Gabrielle swiped again at the leftover tears, then pasted on a smile in anticipation of Andrew and Jack's arrival. It wouldn't be long before they found Gus. And her.

A minute later, Jack's curly brown head peeked around one of the nearby trees.

He called over his shoulder, "I found him, Dad! He's sitting with Gabrielle and Rocky."

Andrew materialized in front of her. His broad shoulders and white-toothed grin took up what little view Gabrielle could see around Gus. He leaned down and tugged on Gus's collar. The dog slid to the edge of the blanket, and Andrew stepped closer to her.

"Sorry. He jumped out of the truck and took off when we opened the door."

Andrew chuckled and eyed her from his full six-foot-five height.

"Seeing that he found you again, his one true love, I think maybe Gus knew you were here."

Gabrielle shaded her eyes from the sun peeking over his shoulder and smiled up at him. "That's okay. Rocky and I came for a picnic. You guys can join us, if you want."

Andrew urged Gus farther off the blanket, then sat down near her. "You don't mind being the only girl with this group of motley men?"

"I've been outnumbered by The Testosterone Club most of my life. I think I can handle lunch with two guys and two dogs."

Gabrielle smiled serenely.

Jack knelt down in front of her. "Gabrielle! Look, I've got a loose tooth."

Gabrielle watched Jack wiggle one of his front teeth with his tongue.

"Wow, Jack! That looks like it's about to come out. Is it your first one?"

"Nope. I lost the bottom ones earlier this year." And with the sudden change of topic perfected by young children, he asked, "Do you have a nickname?"

"A nickname?" she asked in surprise.

Gabrielle glanced at Andrew in time to catch his amused expression.

"Lately, Jack's been interested in nicknames. Especially since he realized my full name is *Andrew*, even though my family calls me Drew."

Still on his knees, Jack scooted closer until he was almost in Gabrielle's lap.

"Dad says I don't have a nickname. I'm just Jack. It's not short for anything. There's a girl in my class named Gabriella. Her nickname is Gabby. Is that your nickname?"

Gabrielle sighed. "No. Unfortunately, *Gabby* never suited me, but sometimes my family calls me Brie."

"Can I call you Brie?" Jack asked. "It's shorter than Gabrielle."

Gabrielle noticed Andrew's smirk.

"I know. Brie is a type of French cheese." She shot him a look of chagrin and sighed. "There aren't very many nicknames for Gabrielle."

She turned back to Jack. "Sure. You can call me Brie."

"Cool! I'm hungry, Dad. Can we eat?"

Gabrielle watched as Andrew opened his cooler and pulled out a sandwich. He glanced at it, chuckled to himself, and passed the sandwich to Jack. When he pulled out a second sandwich, he chuckled again.

In the process of opening her own lunch, Gabrielle shot Andrew a questioning look.

"What's so funny?"

Andrew held up his sandwich and laughed. "It's a cheese sandwich. You know, Brie. Cheese. It just struck me as funny."

Gabrielle swatted his arm.

"Not funny, Andrew." She giggled and took a bite of her own lunch.

After they ate, Gabrielle and Andrew ran the dogs and the boy hard. They played ball and fetch until everyone collapsed to catch their breath. As the sun began to sink toward the horizon, Andrew helped Gabrielle fold her blanket. After three quick snaps, he presented it to Gabrielle in military fashion. She flashed him a grin. As a group, they walked back to their parked cars.

Andrew paused after loading the dogs. He turned to Gabrielle.

"This was fun, you know, having a picnic as a group. I think Jack gets lonely sometimes with just the two of us. Would you and Rocky want to meet again sometime?"

Gabrielle smiled. "We had fun too. Here, I'll give you my cell number, and we can do this again."

After exchanging numbers, Gabrielle climbed into her vehicle.

"See you soon."

Andrew gazed after Gabrielle's departing SUV. She had been crying before they got there, he was sure of it. When he found Gus next to her, he noticed her red-rimmed eyes were dark with grief. Over the course of the afternoon, color had come into her cheeks, and Gabrielle's blue eyes took on a sparkle. Andrew hoped it was because she had enjoyed the time with him and Jack.

They had gone to high school together, but he knew little about her. Andrew had always been curious about the beautiful girl with dark curls, but somehow, they never moved in the same group of friends. Andrew blamed Thomas Martin for his inability to get to know Gabrielle in high school. Thomas warned off any guy interested in Gabrielle, as a good brother would. Andrew had done the same thing for his sisters, Grace and Eden, even though Grace was a year older than he was.

He grimaced when he thought about Gabrielle's brother. Nobody crossed Thomas Martin. Thomas was a scrapper and had meted out his share of bloody noses during their playground years. As they grew older, Thomas's muscles also grew in proportion due to hours in the weight room. When Thomas warned guys away from his sister, none dared to cross him. Andrew hoped Thomas was not in the area at the moment because he was going to cross that line now. He was going to find a way to make Gabrielle Martin Levesque a part of his life.

There was something about her blue eyes. They were luminous, and their sapphire color burned with an internal light. He also admired Gabrielle's wavy dark hair. It beckoned for a man's fingers to run through it.

Andrew paused. A man *had* run his fingers through her hair. Five or six years ago, he had encountered Gabrielle and her husband in New York City.

After double majoring in business and biology, Andrew graduated from college and went to work on Wall Street. Adept at making money, he accumulated more money in the three years he worked there than his parents had in a lifetime. One night, he attended a black-tie event with his model girlfriend. Too late Andrew discovered that it was a fashion show, not an event he would normally attend. At the after party, his girlfriend, Chantal, dragged him over to meet one of the fashion industry's top moguls: Jean-Luc Levesque.

"Monsieur Levesque. It's me, Chantal Lamonte. It's been a couple of years since we last saw each other. I modeled in Paris. We met when one of your fabrics was featured in a clothing line I was working for," Chantal gushed as she tapped the gentleman on the shoulder.

Chantal's audacity and need for attention never ceased to amaze Andrew. It was one of the reasons he was growing tired of her. The dark-haired man in question turned and frowned in the condescending way only a Frenchman could achieve.

"Ah, yes. Forgive me, mademoiselle, but I did not remember your name," he replied in heavily accented English.

The intense gaze of this rich and powerful man reproached them for overstepping the social boundaries. Even though Andrew stood a half foot taller than Jean-Luc Levesque, the shorter man's magnetic presence made Andrew feel insignificant.

Andrew glanced at the door, but before he could make an exit, Chantal introduced him.

"This is my boyfriend, Andrew Leland. He works on Wall Street."

"Enchanté. May I introduce my wife, Gabrielle," Levesque responded, then touched the elbow of the elegant woman behind him.

At her husband's touch, Gabrielle turned and took a half step back in surprise. She recovered quickly and stretched out a slender, perfectly manicured hand. Her smile was polite.

"It's good to see you again, Andrew."

Andrew eyed the chic woman in the classy blue gown. Although the short dress was modest, her legs looked like they were a mile long in strappy heels. The expensive diamond tennis bracelet on her wrist dazzled as he took the hand Gabrielle offered.

"It's been a long time, Gabrielle. Did I hear correctly? Mr. Levesque is your husband?"

He took a deep breath. The contrast between the girl Andrew knew in school and the sophisticated woman before him was shocking.

Gabrielle's eyes feasted on her husband, then she glanced back at Andrew and flashed a million-watt smile.

"Yes. We've been married a year now."

"You know each other? Fantastic!" Chantal grasped at the budding opportunity.

Jean-Luc shot Andrew a suspicious look, then set a possessive hand on Gabrielle's waist. "Oui. Chérie, how do you know Mister Leland?"

"We went to high school together in Maine, although he was in Thomas's grade. Isn't that right, Andrew?"

Gabrielle sent him a shy smile. There. That shy look was a semblance of the girl he had known.

Andrew noted Jean-Luc's appalled expression. It probably never occurred to him that his wife had known other men before him.

He didn't blame Jean-Luc Levesque. If he had a wife like Gabrielle, he would be suspicious of every man who looked at her. Andrew scanned her dark hair styled in a twist, the poise with which she carried herself now, and the loving smile she directed toward her husband. God. Jean-Luc was lucky. Chantal's faux red hair, slinky gold gown, and heavily applied makeup didn't hold a candle to Gabrielle's elegance.

Gabrielle registered her husband's discomfort. She was smart enough to know her husband liked to be the focus of her attention. Gabrielle nodded to Andrew.

"It was nice to see you again. Please excuse us. We need to say our goodbyes before we leave for Paris."

Levesque gave a curt nod and entwined his fingers with his wife's. They strolled away.

Shortly after that meeting, Andrew broke up with Chantal. He left Wall Street and went back to school for his veterinary degree. Because he also had an undergraduate degree, it didn't take long for him to get into veterinary school. His parents had wanted him to make a lot of money. He had done that. It was time to focus on his own dreams.

Back in Jacobs Landing, Andrew shook himself out of his reverie.

"Dad?" Jack called from the back seat.

"Yeah, Jack?"

"Can we stop by Grandma's on the way home? She always feeds us if we stop by. I'm hungry."

"Again?" Andrew glanced at his watch and chuckled. "I guess it is almost dinnertime. Okay, buddy. We'll go to Grandma's."

# CHAPTER THREE

A breeze teased Gabrielle's hair as she walked with Rocky along the beach. Bass Harbor Head Lighthouse perched on rocks in the distance; a sentinel keeping guard over its populace. The weather was unseasonably warm for May, so Gabrielle wore cutoffs and an embroidered cotton shirt that hugged her narrow waist. The water was icy, but Rocky enjoyed running in and out of the surf.

"Brie!"

Gabrielle waved at Jack as he ran toward her from the nearby parking lot. Gus jumped out of Andrew's truck and passed Jack at lightning speed. Gabrielle didn't know what she had done to become Gus's idol, but she braced herself for the dog's impact.

When he reached her, Gus tried to jump up on Gabrielle. Accustomed to his adoration after a month of doggie playdates, she pushed the dog down and gave him a good scratch behind the ears. Rocky circled around Gus, then bumped him out of the way when he hogged too much of Gabrielle's attention. Gabrielle showered love on her own dog while she surreptitiously studied Andrew.

He used his key fob to lock the vehicle, his teeth flashing white as he grinned in her direction. A minute later, Jack flung himself on the ground next to Rocky. The little boy scratched both dogs behind their ears while he waited for his father. Andrew's long legs ate up the distance between them, and Gabrielle found her attention drawn, once again, to the golden Adonis striding her way.

Golden Adonis? Where had that come from? Gabrielle and Andrew were just friends. Hanging out. Right?

"Brie, can I toss the stick for Rocky? He likes to play longer than Gus does."

"Sure, Jack. As long as it's all right with your dad."

Gabrielle glanced at Andrew. Today, a light-blue T-shirt hugged his broad chest and emphasized the naturally tan tone of his skin. The robin's egg color turned his hazel eyes blue. He stood tall and erect. Narrow waist. Broad shoulders. The build of a true athlete.

Gabrielle wondered if his chest was as impressive without the shirt. She paused in surprise and guilt. She was attracted to Andrew Leland. The realization caused her gut to clench. Shouldn't she still be grieving Jean-Luc? It had only been two years since he died. It was disloyal to be attracted to another man, wasn't it?

"That's fine, Jack," Andrew's response interrupted her reflection. "Don't go in the water past your ankles. It's too cold for swimming today."

In order to recover her composure, Gabrielle bent to pick up another stick.

"Here, Gus. Go fetch."

She threw the stick out into the rolling surf, then watched the Labrador charge into the water after it. Gus was in his element.

Gabrielle grinned over her shoulder at Andrew. "I hope you don't mind the smell of wet dog."

White teeth flashed in a square jaw. "I figured both boy and dog would be wet and sandy when you asked to meet at the beach. Luckily, the truck is easy to vacuum out."

Gus dropped the stick at Gabrielle's feet, and she threw it again. When she turned back, Andrew was standing closer. Hazel eyes watched her as his hand reached out to remove a strand of hair from her face.

He took his time touching the hair, as if he enjoyed the feel of it between his fingers.

After a moment, Andrew tucked the hair behind her ear. He took another step closer. Gabrielle stood rooted to the spot. Andrew's eyes locked with hers in a look of shared awareness.

He paused and searched Gabrielle's eyes. When she didn't shy away, he stepped closer again. He skimmed his knuckles down her cheek. Heat flared between them. It ignited Gabrielle's nerve endings and sent a shiver through her body. She wondered what it would be like to kiss him. Hadn't she wondered the same thing in high school?

"Yoo-hoo! Drew! Fancy meeting you here," a voice called from behind them.

With the connection broken, Gabrielle and Andrew turned in tandem. Emily Ross strode toward them in a red string bikini, her long blond hair flowing down her back like a *Sports Illustrated* model.

*Please don't be a thong. Please don't be a thong.* Gabrielle silently begged as she watched the buxom woman's approach.

Emily ignored Gabrielle as she latched on to Drew's arm and smiled up at him. "It must have been fate that you and I were at the same beach today."

Drew extricated his arm and gestured to Gabrielle. "No, not fate. Gabrielle and I met here so the dogs could get some exercise."

With reluctance, Emily acknowledged Gabrielle. "Hey, Gabby. Look at you, all quaint in your cutoff shorts." She smiled with false congeniality.

Gabrielle forced her eyes to avoid the glaring expanse of Emily's exposed backside.

*Who wears a thong bikini in this weather? It's May, for goodness' sake. I hope it chafes.*

Gabrielle tried to distract herself by asking, "Where's Opal today?"

"These waves are too much for her. She's at the groomer. I'll pick her up later."

Emily fluttered her eyelashes at Andrew.

"I'm cooking veal tonight. I hope you, and the boy, can come for dinner."

Emily didn't even glance over to where Jack played with Rocky.

"The boy?" A tightness appeared around Andrew's mouth.

"Yeah, you know. Your son. Johnny, wasn't it?" Emily waved a hand in Jack's direction.

Andrew's mouth flattened into a line.

"The boy's name is Jack," Andrew ground out. "Listen, Emily, I met Gabrielle here today, not you.

Gabrielle and I are here *together.* Do you understand? I'm only interested in you as your dog's doctor. Am I clear?"

"Well! You don't have to get all huffy about me not remembering Jake's name." Emily used her best pout. "Fine, I'll just take Opal to a vet in Bar Harbor from now on."

"That'd probably be best."

Andrew turned to Gabrielle and held out his hand. "Shall we go see what Jack and the dogs are up to?"

After Gabrielle placed her hand in his, they strolled farther down the beach.

Once they were out of earshot, Andrew tugged her to a stop. "I hope you don't mind that I implied we're a couple."

Gabrielle glanced up at him. For a moment, she was distracted by the halo of sun behind his head, reaffirming his near-godlike status.

"I'm just tired of dodging her poor attempts to entrap me. I shouldn't have involved you. Sorry, Gabrielle."

Gabrielle touched Drew's arm. "That's okay. If it gets her off your back, let her think what she wants."

Gabrielle kept her hand in his as they ambled along in the surf. She savored the warmth of his fingers as they encircled hers. Andrew Leland's hand. Back in high school, she had dreamed of holding his hand. Ten years later, it was even better than her young heart could've imagined. As Jack and the dogs ran ahead of them, Gabrielle and Andrew followed at a more sedate pace.

After a few minutes, Gabrielle broke the silence.

"Okay, I just have to say it. Wasn't she cold? I mean, who wears a thong in this weather? It's not even eighty today. The bay is barely tolerable for wading. She better be careful or she'll freeze off some of those expensive body parts she paid for."

Andrew threw his head back and roared with laughter. "Fake were they?"

"Oh yeah. I've worked in the fashion industry for almost eight years. I can spot *fake* a mile away." Gabrielle giggled.

They followed in the wake of the dogs and the boy with the occasional chuckle interrupting their companionable silence.

As the sun began its descent, Andrew turned to her. "I'm starving. What d'you think about rounding up Jack and the dogs? We could grab some Lobster Shack takeout?"

Gabrielle examined her sand-covered feet and legs.

"We might pass the loose dress code at the Lobster Shack, but what about the dogs?"

"Like I said." Andrew smiled. "*Takeout.* We can ride together in my truck, bring the food back here, and eat at one of the picnic tables."

The warmth of Andrew's skin permeated her fingers and made its way into her consciousness. Attraction and curiosity made her want to spend more time with him. Based on his perusal of her body when he thought she wasn't looking, Gabrielle suspected he was attracted to her too. She smiled.

"Sure. That sounds good."

A few minutes later, they herded dogs and boy toward the truck. The promise of steamed lobster and fish and chips made their stomachs rumble.

A bee buzzed around her face. Gabrielle tried to swat it, but it kept dive-bombing her head. It was so close; she could almost feel the beat of its wings on her cheek. Why could she hear and feel the buzz at the same time?

Gabrielle's eyes popped open. Soft pillow under her head. She must have been dreaming. At eye level, she caught sight of the lit screen on her cell phone. Realization dawned. The buzzing sound of the bee was her phone ringing on vibrate.

She pressed the answer button. "Allô, oui?"

"Gabrielle? Is that you?"

There was hesitation in Andrew's voice. He wasn't used to her answering in French.

She rubbed the sleep from her eyes, then switched to English.

"Andrew? Yes, it's me."

"Are you okay? It sounds like I woke you up."

"You did."

Yawn.

"I'm in Paris right now, managing my part of the textile company."

Yawn again.

"God! I'm sorry. I didn't know. What time is it there?"

"Hmm? Well, what time is it there? Just add six hours. That's what time it is here."

"It's eight-thirty. I just got Jack down to bed, and I thought I'd see if you and Rocky were up for a picnic tomorrow. Shoot! It's two-thirty in the morning for you. I should let you go. Why don't you call me when you get back?"

So far, they had met just as friends, with dogs and boy in tow. But as Gabrielle talked to Andrew in the middle of the night, the stirrings of attraction reawakened. The deep timber of his voice vibrated through her. It was sexy and calming at the same time. How did he do that?

"Did you fall asleep? I should go."

"No. Don't go just yet. It's nice to hear your voice. I didn't realize how much I missed home until you called. My one-week trip has been extended, but I should be home late on Saturday."

"Did you take Rocky with you? To Paris?"

"No. He's staying with Pop and Grand-Père while I'm here. I'd better get home soon, though; otherwise I won't get him back. They love having him at the house. I think they'd keep him permanently, but Rocky's my dog. It's my first time away from him. I'll need to reassure him as soon as I get off the jet."

"The jet?"

"Yeah. The company jet is much faster than commercial flights. It has an actual bedroom, so I can catch up on sleep transatlantic style. I commute between the continents at least once a quarter, so catching some sleep on the plane keeps me from suffering too badly from jet lag."

Andrew whistled low. "Sounds pretty posh to me."

"It is. I admit it. I love being pampered once in a while. Why should I suffer traveling on commercial flights when the company jet is fueled and ready for me anytime?"

Andrew paused for a moment. She could picture him running a hand through his hair in a typical gesture.

"Listen, Gabrielle, I'll let you get some sleep. I bet you have a busy day tomorrow."

She sighed and looked at her bedside clock. It was almost three.

"I do. A fifteen-hour day, culminating in a black-tie fundraiser tomorrow night. But Andrew, I'm glad you called. It was good to hear your voice."

"It was good to talk to you too."

Andrew hesitated again, and then she heard him draw a breath. "Gabrielle, would you think about something while you're in Paris this week?"

She sensed his uncertainty.

"Sure, Andrew. What is it?"

"Would you...think about whether you might be ready to go out with me? You know, without Jack and the dogs. If it's too soon, I don't want to ruin our friendship..."

Surprise paralyzed Gabrielle for a moment. Was she capable of going out with another man? Would she feel guilty and only think about Jean-Luc? It could spoil the whole experience for the man she was with. But this wouldn't be just any man. It was Andrew, a man she had known for a long time. A man, she admitted to herself, she wanted to see again.

He cleared his throat. "You know what? Forget it. It's too soon."

"Andrew, wait. You need to understand. I haven't dated since Jean-Luc died."

"I understand. I'm sorry I brought it up."

"No, I don't think you do. Oh, I'm making a mess of this. You're the first man to make me consider dating again. I'm comfortable with you. And attracted to you. And even though it scares me, I think I would like to try it. A date. With you, I mean."

She thought she heard a murmured *yes* from the other end of the line before Andrew responded.

"At least the attraction isn't only on my part. I hoped I wasn't reading you wrong. How about the age-old dinner and a movie when you get back?"

With butterflies in her stomach, Gabrielle heard herself answer, "Sounds good. I'll call you Sunday after I've had a chance to recover from my trip."

"Okay. If you think about it this week and change your mind, I'll understand. But, Gabrielle…"

"Yes?"

"Don't change your mind, okay?"

She chuckled. That was one of the things Gabrielle appreciated most about Andrew; he always made her laugh.

"I won't change my mind. I'll talk to you Sunday. Tell Jack and Gus I said hi, okay?"

"Will do. Talk to you then. Now, get some sleep. I don't want to be responsible for dark circles under your eyes at that gala event."

"Night, Andrew," she purred just before she ended the call.

Back in Jacobs Landing, Andrew placed his cell phone on the kitchen island. He stared at it. Resting his hip against the counter, Andrew pictured Gabrielle stretching in bed like a cat. The image did nothing for his libido, which had kicked into overdrive the minute she answered her phone in that sleepy, half-awake voice. Gabrielle's good-night purr had shot all the way to his groin. God, he wanted her. Not just for her body, which was fantastic, but also for her sensitivity and honesty.

He was perched at a precipice. With the right encouragement from her, Andrew would fall in love with her. Maybe he already had. This new relationship with Gabrielle would be more delicate than any surgery he had performed. If he could just be patient, there might be a future for them. He sensed the reward would be worth it.

Andrew pushed away from the counter and began his nightly routine. The sooner this day was over, the sooner Gabrielle would return. He checked the refrigerator to see if Jack's lunch was there, then locked up the house for the night. Sleep, he suspected, would be a long time coming.

Andrew munched his sandwich while he leafed through a veterinary journal during his lunch hour. The vibration of his cell phone on his desk caught his attention. A text message had come in. Curious, he opened the message and choked when he saw the attached photo. He pounded his chest with one hand, while he zoomed in with the other.

Gabrielle stood in an ivory cocktail dress; her dark hair swirled into an elegant updo. A grin lit up her face. Next to her stood the current president of France, his arm wrapped around her waist like they were old pals. On the other side of Gabrielle was Michel Levesque, Gabrielle's brother-in-law, in a severe black tuxedo. His dark gaze was as aloof as always.

Andrew read the message.

"See? No dark circles. Hope you're having more fun than I am. Talk to you Sunday."

Andrew snapped a picture of a stack of file folders on his desk. He tapped a message on his screen, then hit send.

"You call this fun? At least you have booze. :) Looking forward to Sunday."

Over the next few days, Gabrielle sent Andrew photos and texts that gave him an insight into her quirky sense of humor.

On Wednesday, a photo showed Gabrielle in a tweed skirt and silky blouse. She stood in the center of a group of supermodels who were prepped for a photo shoot. Andrew thought she was more gorgeous than any of the surrounding women.

"Look at the whale in the middle. Oh wait, that's me. : ) I'm the largest one here. Maybe I should cut out the French food? Looking forward to our date."

Drew grunted. He shook his head and typed a response.

"You are gorgeous, and you know it! Stop fishing for compliments. :) Can't wait until you're back in the USA."

Andrew grinned. He clipped his phone back onto his belt and knocked on the next exam room door. It was time to assess the health of an overweight cat.

On Gabrielle's last night in Paris, she found herself on the overstuffed couch at her brother-in-law's upscale apartment. Michel had invited Gabrielle to dinner with the family before she flew back to the States in the morning. The evening meal with Michel; his wife, Sophie; and their two teenage children, Vivienne and Luc, was informal and relaxed after a busy week. She enjoyed being Tatie Gabrielle, *Auntie Gabrielle*, to Michel's children and always missed them when she was in Maine.

Looking forward to heading home, she read Andrew's most recent text. A smile played around the corners of her mouth as she read about an incident with Jack, Gus, and mud pies.

Michel Levesque entered *le salon*, a glass of red wine in hand.

He eyed her smile and teased, "Who's the man?"

"What?" she asked. "There's no man."

Michel quirked one eyebrow in skepticism, then slouched in an armchair across from her. He took a sip from his glass and continued to study Gabrielle. It was one of his most useful negotiation tactics: wait for the silence to become uncomfortable, and the competition would fold.

Gabrielle sighed under Michel's scrutiny and knew hiding anything from him was a lost cause. He would never let her leave tonight. Not without her giving him some information about Andrew. Michel was as bad as her older brother, Thomas. He watched over her like a guard dog, probably out of obligation to Jean-Luc.

"There is no man," Gabrielle restated. "At least, not yet. More like the promise of a friendship that could be more."

She glanced at Michel to gauge his reaction. His expression was unreadable.

"Michel, do you hate me for even considering another relationship? God knows I'm having second thoughts."

Michel stroked his goatee, which was salt and pepper colored like his hair. He was older than Jean-Luc by seven years, which made Michel closer to her father's age.

"You are more alive this time than I have seen you since Jean-Luc's death. Jean-Luc loved your vibrancy and enthusiasm. It is time for you to live again."

Michel's words were a benediction. The tension in Gabrielle's shoulders relaxed, and they conversed amiably until she left for her own Paris lodgings.

The next morning, Gabrielle boarded the company's private jet and reclined in one of the comfortable armchairs. Before takeoff, Gabrielle grabbed her cell phone and checked last-minute messages. After she resolved a few company issues through email, she sent a text to her father.

"On my way home. See you soon!"

After sending the message, Gabrielle sat back. An image of Andrew Leland flashed in her mind. Was she crazy to go out with him? She wasn't over Jean-Luc yet, was she? But Andrew was handsome and caring. And sexy. He made her laugh. That was the thing that most drew her to him; he put her at ease.

Gabrielle snatched her phone again. She found her previous text to her father, then forwarded it to Andrew. Phew. It wasn't sentimental, but the text showed Andrew she was thinking of him.

Relief and fatigue caused Gabrielle to sit back in her chair and close her eyes. All her men were waiting for her in Maine. Lacking the energy to move to the plane's bedroom, Gabrielle pulled a blanket over her shoulders and fell asleep.

# CHAPTER FOUR

On Monday, Gabrielle whistled as she opened her store. After almost two weeks away, Gabrielle loved being back at The Treasure Trove. It held all the delights she rescued from flea markets and thrift shops and purchased from local artists.

Gabrielle was packing a customer's purchase into an ecofriendly bag, when the doorbell chimed. With a start, Gabrielle recognized the two men browsing at the front of her shop. One of them was the mayor of Jacobs Landing, and the other man was Bob Leland, Andrew's father. The intimidating pillars of Jacobs Landing society perused the displays until the customer left. Once the store was empty, the two men ambled toward the counter where she stood. Their casual manner didn't fool Gabrielle for a moment. These men were in her store for a purpose.

All the insecurities she had about being a Franco-American rushed back. In her grandfather's day, French speakers were ignored or given second-class treatment. In her father's era, the two groups coexisted in town but rarely mingled. During her school years, there were polite interactions between the two groups, but both sides kept their distance, wary of the unknown.

Did Andrew's father know about their date Friday night? Was he here to warn her away from his son? If so, why did he bring the mayor with him?

"Gabrielle, I'm Bob Leland, the bank president. I believe you went to school with some of my kids."

He smiled and held out a hand.

"Yes, Mr. Leland. I remember you. Nice to see you again."

Gabrielle shook hands with an older replica of Andrew. She imagined Andrew in twenty or thirty years, complete with silver-sprinkled blond hair and bright intense eyes, just like his father.

"Let me introduce you to Jacob Hartwell, the town mayor."

"Mr. Hartwell, it's a pleasure."

She shook the hand of the balding, barrel-chested man in front of her.

"What can I help you with, gentlemen?"

Gabrielle rested an arm against the counter and tried to convey an ease she did not feel. What did they want with her?

Both men glanced around the store, as if to make sure there was no one else there. They shifted from foot to foot. They, too, were not as at ease as they seemed.

"Well, you see, Mrs. Levesque, it has come to my attention that you are more than you seem."

Mayor Hartwell raised an eyebrow as he settled his weight against the counter.

"I understand that you're not only a shop owner in this town, but you're somewhat of a real estate mogul. You've bought the empty storefronts up and down most of Main Street."

Gabrielle shot an accusing look at Bob Leland. Before she bought it, the bank had owned most of the defunct property. Gabrielle knew where the mayor had gotten his information.

Bob had the grace to look sheepish.

"It's a matter of public record, Gabrielle. Anyone who wants to look through the town records is able to access that information."

With arms crossed, Gabrielle raised her chin a notch and looked them squarely in the eyes. "Is there a problem, gentlemen? Are you here to accuse me of something underhanded? Or is it something more subtle? Perhaps something to do with me being a Franco-American, perhaps?"

"Gosh! No," the mayor reassured her. "I see we're handling this badly. We've heard of your incentive program for new renters, and we're impressed with the vitality it's breathing back into our town."

Gabrielle eyed them both with skepticism.

The mayor continued, "You see, we need someone like you in this town. Jacobs Landing was slowly dying. But your investment in the downtown area has given the commercial zone a rebirth."

"We want you to be on the town council," Bob explained with a smile of pride. "We like your ideas, and we hope your new perspective will be just what this town needs."

Pleased with themselves, both men beamed at her.

Speechless for a moment, Gabrielle rubbed her forehead. This would be a first. She would be the first French-speaking resident of Jacobs Landing to sit on the town council. It wasn't that there were any laws barring French speakers; there just had never been one before.

"I don't have any experience with this sort of thing, gentlemen."

"Sure, you do, Gabrielle. How many board meetings do you chair when you're in France running your other company? How many charities do you sponsor through the textile company? This would be a much smaller scale than what you're used to. You might even find us quite rustic," Bob assured her.

"We meet the first Wednesday of the month. We'll plan on seeing you next week at seven," Hartwell called over his shoulder as he made his way to the front of the store.

Just like that, both men were gone.

Gabrielle was dumbfounded. How had they railroaded her into a town council meeting without her agreement? It was a rookie move on her part. She let the element of surprise get the best of her. Gabrielle shook her head. She would just have to be smarter about negotiations at the meeting next week. Wait. She was going to the meeting? Of course, she was. She couldn't let the opportunity to represent her people's interests pass her by.

Phyllis stuck her head out of the back room, light reflecting off her hot-pink eyeglasses.

"Did I hear that right? They want you to attend the town council meetings and become part of the boys' club?"

Speechless, Gabrielle nodded.

"Well, wonders never cease. Do you think he found out about your date with Andrew, and that's why they came in here?"

"Mr. Leland didn't seem to know anything about it, Phyllis. I guess, for once, I earned this dubious honor on my own."

Gabrielle shrugged.

"This is an honor I'm not sure I want. But, for now, I guess I don't have a choice."

Gabrielle eased past Phyllis into the stockroom.

"I'm going to open some boxes for a while. Will you hold down the fort?"

"No problem. You go tear apart some cardboard; it might make you feel better."

On Friday night, Gabrielle's hand shook as she locked the shop's front door. It was Date Night. She thought about it in capital letters because it was a milestone in her stages of grief. Rocky followed her around as Gabrielle turned off display lights and checked windows. At the counter, Phyllis counted down the till, her rhinestone manicure winking in the overhead light.

Gabrielle sighed. Her stomach was jittery.

"Phyllis, tell me again why I'm doing this? Maybe it's too soon. Maybe I should just call Andrew and tell him I can't do this yet."

Phyllis bundled the bills, then turned her vibrant purple glasses toward Gabrielle.

"How long has Jean-Luc been dead?

"Two years."

"Do you like Andrew? Do you find him attractive? Do you think about what it would be like to kiss him?"

"Yes. Yes. And yes."

Phyllis came around the counter and draped a comforting arm across her shoulders.

"Then go out with him. Have a fun time. Enjoy being in the company of a man who finds you attractive. You don't have to sleep with him, marry him, or have his babies."

Gabrielle glanced at Phyllis in horror.

"Do you think he'll expect me to sleep with him? I mean, I've never...not with anyone but Jean-Luc. Maybe I should cancel."

Phyllis chuckled.

"I'm telling you, go out and have a good time. You're already friends with the man, just enjoy his company. Besides, he probably already has a babysitter lined up for that little boy of his. It wouldn't be nice to cancel now. I bet he's just as nervous as you are. I don't think he dates much, not with Jack depending on him. Plus, he knows your story. He's probably scared he'll do something wrong and you'll never want to see him again. Now scoot."

Phyllis shooed Gabrielle through the back door.

"It's almost five thirty. Didn't you say he was picking you up at seven? Go home. Shower. Gussy up. Remember, he said casual. But it's *date* casual. Not *lounge-at-the-house* casual."

Phyllis patted Gabrielle's cheek and gave her one last fortifying hug.

"Good luck, hon. Don't forget to tell me all about it tomorrow."

Before she knew it, Gabrielle was standing outside the back door of the shop, keys in hand and Rocky at her feet.

"Come on, Rocky. Let's head home."

The doorbell chimed downstairs. It was one of those old-fashioned crank ones that turned in your hand—an original to the house. Rocky took off for the stairs and barked a warning to the trespasser below.

Gabrielle took a deep breath. She checked her reflection one last time in the vanity mirror. Wavy dark hair. Deep-blue eyes. Rosy lips, shiny from a touch of lip gloss. She hoped she would do.

The gold chain around her neck hung loose, and she noticed Jean-Luc's wedding band. It rested in the modest neckline of the sleeveless navy-blue linen dress she wore. It wasn't right to go on a date with one man while her dead husband's ring rested in full view.

Could she do it?

Slowly, Gabrielle reached behind her neck and unfastened the chain's clasp. She brought Jean-Luc's ring to her lips and kissed it. After she stashed it in her jewelry box, Gabrielle headed into the hall.

She came down the stairs in tan wedge sandals, a small clutch in her hand. The doorbell chimed again. Rocky recognized Andrew on the other side of the window and jumped off the floor in excitement. She nudged the dog out of the way with her knee, then unlocked the ornate stained glass door with leaded pane windows.

The first full view of Andrew on the porch took her breath away. A casual blue buttoned shirt and khaki pants didn't sound sexy, but on him they emphasized his broad shoulders and athletic frame. The pull of attraction wound its way through her as she admired the physical aspects of the man before her.

"Hi." She smiled with a calm she didn't feel. "Can you come in for a minute? I need to feed Rocky before we go."

"Sure." Andrew grinned.

Gabrielle's stomach did a flip. No person should look that good.

Gabrielle thought he was completely at ease until she noticed the tremor of his hand when he placed it on the doorframe next to her. Andrew Leland was as nervous as she was.

As he followed her inside the entryway, Andrew paused and looked up in awe.

"Wow! I've always wanted to see the inside of this house. The entry is amazing. Is that the original fresco on the ceiling?"

"Yep. The frescoes are one of the reasons I fell in love with this place. You'll have to excuse the mess. I've only begun to renovate and restore the house. If a room isn't missing walls, it's probably in need of a face-lift."

She began to move toward the back of the house. At the kitchen archway, Gabrielle glanced back. Andrew wasn't behind her. A quick scan found him studying the carved lion heads of the main staircase. His intense examination of the carvings would have been comical if she wasn't so nervous.

Gabrielle strolled back to Andrew and stood for a full minute before he glanced at her.

"Sorry." He shot her a sheepish grin. "I'm just amazed at the detail in these carvings. The lions are very realistic."

He pointed at the wood trim in the rest of the room. "I can't believe the woodwork in this room. Is the whole house like this?"

"Most of the downstairs has the ornate carving and detailed trim work."

Gabrielle slid her hand through Andrew's arm and conducted him toward the kitchen. Along the way, she pointed out some of her favorite features of the house.

"The house was in such bad condition when I bought it. Hopefully, I can restore it all someday. Here's my current project. I love to cook, so the kitchen seemed the best place to start. As you can see, I haven't been doing much food prep in the last few months."

Gabrielle led Andrew into the partially renovated kitchen, which included tasteful countertops and traditional white cupboards. There were gaps where appliances belonged, and the new drywall was unpainted.

Andrew eyed the blank spaces, and she grimaced.

"I know it's a mess. But you should've seen it two months ago. The appliances will be installed next week. In the meantime, Rocky and I have access to the fridge in the mudroom."

Gabrielle picked up Rocky's water bowl. "I'll just be a minute."

Andrew watched Gabrielle's graceful movements as she moved to an outdated powder room off the kitchen. With bowl in hand, she filled it with water from the sink. After setting the bowl on the designated dog mat in the kitchen, she dished kibble into the food bowl. The bag of dog food was the same one he had given her at Rocky's initial veterinary visit. After washing her hands, Gabrielle stood before him with purse in hand. How did she make every task sexy and appealing?

As she gazed up at him, the features of the house faded into the background. They were alone. It seemed like they were the only two people on earth. Andrew stood close to Gabrielle but hesitated to touch her. It would only take a few inches for him to lean down and brush his lips across hers.

Instead, he reached out and rubbed the pad of his thumb over her cheekbone. Across her lower lip. He watched her eyes dilate. In them he saw awareness. Need. Fear. It was the fear that checked his actions. He refused to do anything that scared her.

"I haven't told you how gorgeous you look tonight. After all these years of knowing each other, but never quite getting the timing right, I can't believe you agreed to go out with me. I'm the luckiest man in the world right now."

Gabrielle smiled at his statement. He saw the fear recede. She skimmed her fingers along the buttons of his shirt, her movements shy and tentative. After a moment, Gabrielle glanced up at him through her lashes; a slight blush colored her cheeks.

"I had such a crush on you in high school. I can't believe you're actually taking me out tonight. Back then, I would've never thought it possible."

Andrew grinned at Gabrielle and cupped her cheek with his hand.

"You were pretty hot back then yourself. I couldn't get near you, though. Your brother would've made me eat my teeth if I'd asked you out."

His bluntness startled a laugh out of her.

"Thomas has always been hyperprotective. Especially after our mother died. He's always felt the need to look out for me."

Andrew smiled a little but gazed into Gabrielle's eyes. He let her see his desire. His need.

"Gabrielle," he sighed. "Do I have to wait until the end of the night? Or can I have that *good-night kiss*, now?"

He saw her hesitate.

"The awkwardness would be gone," he urged gently, "and I've been wondering what it'd be like to kiss you. For years, even—"

He broke off when she pressed her lips to his. After the initial contact, Gabrielle let him take the lead. He explored her lips, her cheek, and even her neck before he returned to her mouth. Andrew pulled back when he tasted something salty. His fingertips brushed away tears.

"Ah, love. We'll take it slow. I promise. I won't rush you. Please don't cry, honey. I'm sorry, Gabrielle."

He pulled her against his chest. She clung to him with one arm and swiped at the tears with her other hand. Andrew spotted a nearby tissue box. One handed, he grabbed some tissues. What a loser he was! Always thinking about his own needs. He shouldn't have rushed her.

Andrew pushed some of the tissues into her hand. Gabrielle used them to dab at her eyes. After a moment, she drew a shaky breath and turned away from him.

"I'm sorry." She sighed. "I don't blame you if you don't want to go out anymore. Who'd want to deal with my emotional baggage?"

"Don't want to go out? I wouldn't blame you if you called off our date. After all, I rushed you. I pushed when I shouldn't have. I know you loved Jean-Luc. It was crazy of me to think that I could compare with him."

He turned away from her and took a step toward the front door.

"Andrew."

He paused. She stood behind him. He could sense her heat and the essence that was only Gabrielle. Her fingers brushed against his back.

"Drew, don't go."

He inhaled. She had used his nickname. It was a gesture of familiarity. Maybe there was still hope?

She rested her head against his back.

"How do I explain it to you? It felt good. You know, to be held. And kissed. And appreciated as a woman. My tears were happy tears. Yes, I loved Jean-Luc. In many ways, I still do. But I wasn't thinking of him when we were kissing."

Hope sprang up inside of him. Drew swung around to face Gabrielle. She stepped closer and rested her hand on his cheek.

"I was thinking of you."

She smiled.

"Can we try it again? I promise I won't cry this time."

Her honesty and openness hit Drew like an aphrodisiac. He wished he could pull her to him. He wanted to ravage her mouth until they tore each other's clothes off. Instead, he lowered his lips and kissed Gabrielle with aching gentleness.

Andrew let her set the tone of the kiss. Of her own accord, she pressed her body against his. He moaned with the pleasure of her warmth and slipped his arms around her back. Drew pressed Gabrielle closer and let her explore his mouth. The passion between them began to escalate.

They pulled back at the same time. Andrew knew she could feel his desire pressed between them. He was surprised when she didn't move away but gazed up at him, blue eyes dark with need. For a minute, Andrew struggled with the urge to sweep her into his arms and find the nearest soft surface. He took a shaky breath and released her.

"Gabrielle," he groaned, stepping back. "Now isn't the time. Someday soon maybe. But not tonight. Tonight is about getting to know each other. To find things in common. To see if this'll work for us."

He ran a shaky hand through his hair before he smiled.

"How 'bout we get that pizza?"

She nodded.

Andrew glanced at his watch.

"We might have to see a later movie since we've spent a little more time here than I originally thought. Not that I'm complaining."

Gabrielle scooped up her purse from the floor where she must have dropped it earlier. She looped her hand through his arm.

"Pizza sounds good. I'm suddenly starving."

He grinned at her and drew her closer to him. "Then let's go. Can't keep a hungry woman waiting."

They locked the house and wound their way down the sidewalk toward a sleek black sports car parked out front.

"I thought you had a truck," Gabrielle commented as he helped her into the car.

After he shut her door, Andrew moved around to the driver's side and got in. When he started the engine, it purred like a contented kitten.

He wiggled his eyebrows at her.

"You're not the only one who is wealthy, my dear. It just so happens I made more than my share of money on Wall Street. This honey of a car is one of my indulgences. I wanted to take you out in the style in which you are accustomed."

Gabrielle laughed. "You're joking, right? About Wall Street?"

"Nope."

He smirked, but he kept his eyes on the road. "Huh."

She leaned her head against his shoulder and stared at the road ahead.

"I think I might've liked you better before. At least I *knew* that Andrew Leland. Who is Andrew Leland the millionaire?"

She glanced up at him, and he shook his head. With a grin, he jerked his thumb in an upward motion.

"More?" she asked.

He nodded.

"Multimillionaire?"

"Yep."

"Wow! You were right. We really *do* need to get to know each other better."

He laughed outright. With a quick pat to her knee, Andrew returned his hand to the steering wheel. He focused on the road instead of the woman next to him. She stirred up powerful emotions he couldn't voice yet.

*I'm in love with you*, he wanted to tell her. But she wasn't ready to hear it.

By unspoken agreement, their first date was away from the prying eyes of their small town. They drove to Bar Harbor and ate pizza at an Italian restaurant not much larger than a postage stamp. After dinner, Andrew took Gabrielle to a funky movie theater in town. They snuggled on one of the theater's unique couches and watched a lighthearted comedy.

It was raining when the movie let out. Neither Andrew nor Gabrielle had an umbrella, so they held hands and dashed for his car. Their laughter trailed behind them.

Once in the car, Andrew turned to her. "Do you want to go for a drink before I take you home? Or are you tired?"

She smiled. "A drink sounds good."

In a secluded booth at the back of a local pub, they faced each other. This night was a dream. Andrew was sure he would wake up and none of the last few hours would be real. The waiter placed Drew's beer in front of him, startling him out of his reverie.

Touching his bottle to Gabrielle's glass of wine, he grinned.

"Cheers."

"To a fun evening," Gabrielle agreed and took a sip out of her glass.

"Well, hello there. Drew. Gabrielle. We didn't expect to see you here tonight. *Together.*"

Both Andrew and Gabrielle froze. A glance at the speaker confirmed Drew's parents stood at the end of the booth.

They were dressed for a casual evening out. Bob wore khaki pants and a melon-colored shirt. His gray-blond hair was brushed in the side-part style most men of his generation wore. Andrew's mother was still pretty in her autumn years. Her gray hair was cut in a layered bob that rested just below her jaw. Hazel eyes mirrored the porcelain-blue blouse she had paired with white capri pants.

"Here, darling. Slide over. We won't stay long." Andrew's mother tapped his shoulder.

With a grimace, Andrew did his mother's bidding. Gabrielle also slid to the inner wall of the booth. Bob took a seat next to her. Could this night get any more awkward?

"Mom. Dad. We're on a date here, so if you don't mind—"

"On a date? How wonderful!"

Andrew's mother cast Gabrielle a speculative look.

She turned back to her son. "Where's Jack, honey? We would've watched him for your date."

Andrew shot Gabrielle an apologetic look.

"He's at home with a sitter, Mom. You don't have to babysit every time I go out. Besides, this is our *first* date. We wanted to keep it low key."

Andrew's mom reached across the table and patted Gabrielle's hand.

"I did hear about your husband. I'm so sorry for your loss. Bob tells me you've been asked to be on the town council. Let me know if you need any pointers dealing with all those stuffy men. I've been doing it for years!"

"Really?" Andrew glanced between his father and Gabrielle.

Bob shrugged his shoulders.

"Hartwell and I stopped by Gabrielle's store this week. We asked her to come to the meetings. She owns at least two blocks of retail space on Main Street, plus some harbor property. We need fresh ideas in this town."

He raised an eyebrow at his son.

"I didn't know you two were an *item*."

"It's a *first* date, Dad."

Andrew saw their evening crash and burn before his eyes. Up to this point, the night had gone so well—especially the kissing before they left her house. But in the worst scenario he could've come up with, Andrew could not have predicted this scene. The idea that his parents would join them for a drink tonight would have been inconceivable ten minutes ago. Mentally, he shook his head.

Andrew risked a glance at Gabrielle. She was watching him from across the table, but instead of anger or fear, he saw amusement in her eyes. He thought she might run from the pub, but it seemed she was taking this in stride.

"Well, Gabrielle, since no one has thought to introduce us, I'm Elaine Leland. If things work out for you two, tell Andrew to bring you over for Sunday dinner. I'm sure his sisters will want to meet you."

Andrew dropped his head into his hand and muttered an expletive. He had no idea how to repair the damage done by his parents tonight. He couldn't even stand to leave because his parents had boxed them in. It took years of married teamwork to orchestrate the strategy his parents had just pulled off. Just when he thought the night was lost, Gabrielle rescued him.

"I'm sure they are lovely. Andrew? You said Jack has a sitter? Is there a certain time you need to be back?"

Andrew lifted his head and shot Gabrielle a look of gratitude. Years navigating corporate boardrooms had given her ease in sticky social situations.

"Yes. Unfortunately, we need to get going. Mom. Dad. The sitter needs to be back by a certain time."

He threw a couple of bills on the table to pay for their drinks and eyed his father.

Bob took pity on him.

"Come on, Elaine. Let's go so these young people can continue their evening."

The look Bob gave Gabrielle was stern, but the joking tone of his voice belayed the severity of his expression. "I expect to see you at the council meeting on Wednesday."

Gabrielle nodded. "See you then."

Bob guided Elaine out the front door while Andrew helped Gabrielle out of the booth. Watching his parents pass in front of the bar window, his lips compressed in consternation.

Gabrielle leaned in toward him.

"Quick! We better get out of here before they come back. Do you have any more relatives lurking about?"

He glanced at her and tried to gauge her mood. She flashed him a smile and touched his arm.

"Come on. It wasn't that bad. I'll remind you of this when you meet my family."

She paused at the implications of her words.

"I mean…that is…if you meet them."

He covered her hand with his.

"Gabrielle, does this mean that despite everything that's gone wrong tonight, you'd still go out with me again?"

She smiled again.

"Well, first you'd better meet Pop and Grand-Père. Now that *your* parents know, I better tell them right away. There are no secrets in a small town, and I don't want them to find out I've started dating again from someone else. They'll want to inspect you and make sure you're 'up to snuff,' as Pop would say."

The rain had stopped by the time they got outside. Andrew held open the passenger door of his car and admired the bare expanse of Gabrielle's legs as she slid onto the seat.

On the way back to Jacobs Landing, Andrew picked up the line of their previous conversation.

"I don't mind meeting your father and grandfather. Isn't Thomas around?"

"Thomas joined the Coast Guard right out of high school. He isn't on leave right now, so you won't have to worry about him. Or losing your pearly whites."

Andrew chuckled at the reference to their earlier conversation about Thomas and his threats. They drove in silence for a while. Andrew replayed the whole night in his head and tried to figure out if there was something he could have done differently.

The purr of the car was the only sound as Gabrielle sat in the passenger seat. She watched chagrin and confusion play across Andrew's face. It was amazing how in tune she was with him.

"Come on, Drew. It wasn't that bad. Your parents didn't disapprove of me, which is a plus. And there were some real highlights to the evening."

Drew frowned again. "Why would they disapprove of you?"

Gabrielle shrugged.

"You know, my French-speaking background. Franco-Americans and Anglos don't usually mix in our town."

Drew waved a hand in dismissal.

"My parents aren't like that. All they worry about is a person's character. Not ethnic or religious backgrounds. Besides, that *no mixing* philosophy is so fifty years ago. I don't think anyone in Jacobs Landing feels that way anymore."

Hazel eyes gave her a quick glance before they returned to the road.

"At least, none of us *Anglos*," he teased.

Gabrielle felt the paradigm shift. Could it be that it was her own people's fears about being rejected that kept them from mixing with the rest of the Jacobs Landing population? A fear that kept them from mixing with the rest of the world? She'd have to think about this more on her own.

By the time they reached her house, the moon was a lighthouse guiding them up the back-porch steps. Rocky barked a greeting. His shadow flashed repeatedly in front of the window as he jumped to get their attention.

"Go ahead and let him out, Gabrielle. I'll wait to make sure you're safely inside."

When she opened the door, Rocky flew down the steps to do his business in the yard. Gabrielle discovered Andrew stock still on her darkened porch. She walked up to him.

"You'll have to come over sometime. I'll give you the full tour of the house. It's much better in the daylight."

He frowned down at her from his full six-foot-five height. Did he know how intimidating he could be when he wasn't smiling? Luckily, Gabrielle had experience with brooding, moody men.

She offered him a soft smile. "A penny for your thoughts?"

Drew ran a hand through his hair.

"I had everything planned out in my head. You know, how to make this date one to remember. Now I'm afraid you'll remember it for all the wrong reasons."

"It's not over quite yet. Maybe we can end on a high note?"

Gabrielle led Andrew to her porch swing. They sat in the moonlight. The swing rocked slowly back and forth. Crickets and the occasional tree frog called to their mates.

Andrew turned to her. "I didn't know you owned most of the buildings on Main Street."

"I didn't know you were a multimillionaire."

"Well, I didn't know my father asked you to be on the town council."

She searched for an adequate rebuttal.

"I didn't know your kiss would make my knees go weak."

He rested his hands on her shoulders, his gaze intense. Searching.

"I could always give you a repeat performance."

He waited. It had to be her choice.

For a moment, Jean-Luc's face flashed before Gabrielle's eyes. She still loved him. But Andrew was alive. He stirred a complex web of emotions inside of her. His tenderness and his masculine charm caused desire to pool in all the right places.

Gabrielle leaned forward until her lips met Andrew's. He tasted of mint, man, and the promise of slow, sensual lovemaking. Just as the kiss began to heat up, she pulled back and rested her head on his chest.

Andrew's heart pounded under her ear. If she stayed any longer, Gabrielle might do something she would regret. There had been enough change for one evening. With one last peck on his cheek, Gabrielle got up and headed for the back door.

"Give me a call if you, Jack, and Gus want to meet at the dog park Sunday. I have to work at the store tomorrow," she called over her shoulder.

"I will. Good night, Gabrielle. "

"Night, Drew."

She called Rocky into the house and locked the door.

# CHAPTER FIVE

Panic. Gabrielle awoke with it churning in her stomach. She was uncomfortable in her own skin. What had she done? She had gone out with Andrew. They'd had a nice time. That wasn't so bad, was it? Gabrielle groaned in embarrassment when she remembered the kisses from the night before.

Oh God! How could she do that? She had loved Jean-Luc. How could she be so easy?

Well, okay. Gabrielle gave herself the benefit of the doubt. Kissing Andrew a couple of times wasn't really easy, at least by today's standards. But she had vowed *for better or for worse* to Jean-Luc. Yeah, but what came next in the vows? *Until death do you part.* And Jean-Luc had been dead for over two years.

Gabrielle continued to argue with herself as she showered and dressed for work. She fed Rocky, locked up the house, and drove to the store.

In general, Saturdays were steady with customers. But this was prime tourist season, and sales were brisk all morning. Phyllis worked alongside her. Hailey, a teenage girl Gabrielle had hired part time, filled in wherever needed. Gabrielle kept an eye on the door all morning and hoped Andrew wouldn't stop by. Before she saw him again, she needed space and time to get her head on straight.

A lull around lunchtime gave each of them an opportunity to step into the small break room and eat. While Gabrielle munched on a sandwich, Phyllis sat down at the table across from her.

"So how did it go?" Phyllis beamed.

Much to her consternation, Gabrielle burst into tears.

"It was wonderful," she sobbed.

Phyllis flung an arm around her shoulders. "Then what's the problem, hon?"

Gabrielle told Phyllis about the kisses in the house and snuggling with Andrew during the movie. She explained Drew's embarrassment when his parents joined them at the pub, and she admitted she had a great time despite it.

"But now that it's the next day, I guess I'm having buyer's remorse, so to speak. I feel so guilty, like I cheated on Jean-Luc. Even though I didn't feel that way last night. Do you think it's possible to be drunk on a man? I swear looking back, I acted so out of character. I almost think I was a little tipsy."

Phyllis patted her gray hair and adjusted her red-framed ladybug glasses.

"You know my husband died. Irv was his name. He dropped dead mowing the lawn one day. For the first few weeks, I walked around like the air was knocked out of me. I went through all the stages you're going through. I was numb for a year or two, then I started dating again. The pain you're feeling now, it's the pain of coming alive again. Think about when you're sitting too long and your foot goes to sleep. When you get up and start walking on it, it hurts like hell. Then suddenly, it's working just fine. It'll be the same for you."

Phyllis dabbed a tear from her own eye, then smiled at her.

"And yes, I *have* been drunk on a man a time or two. If Andrew Leland can make you feel that way with just a look, and you're comfortable with him already, then he's worth it. Cut yourself some slack. Don't overanalyze this so much. Just let it happen how it's supposed to happen."

Phyllis kissed Gabrielle's cheek and passed her a couple of tissues.

"Take your time coming back to the floor," she called before she went back into the shop.

Thank God, she had Phyllis! Her own mother had died while she was in elementary school. Gabrielle spent her teen years raised by three New England men whose lifelong philosophy was *just suck it up*. It wasn't that they didn't care about her; it was just that they were *men*. When a subject was uncomfortable, they refused to talk about it.

But it was those gruff men who also loved and treasured her. They were her safe haven when she was confused or scared. She needed them now.

She took out her cell phone and dialed a familiar number.

"Hey Pop, how're you? I was thinking Rocky and I would come out after work and stay overnight tonight. Do you and Grand-Père have any plans? No? Good. See you around six. Love you too. À bientôt!" *See you soon.*

Gabrielle sighed. She would go home tonight. To her grounded family. She'd leave behind her guilt.

On Sunday, Andrew and Jack got home from church around noon. While Jack went up to his room to change clothes, Andrew glanced at his cell phone. Yep. Plenty of battery. Plenty of reception. He'd hoped to hear from Gabrielle before now, but she hadn't sent a text or called. Well, neither had he. He was giving her time to process their date.

Andrew missed her. He needed reassurance that Friday night hadn't been a bust. At the end of their date, Gabrielle had mentioned the dog park. It was as good excuse as any to contact her.

"Jack, Gus, and I are heading to the dog park around 1. Hope you and Rocky can make it."

He waited for a few minutes. When no response came in, Drew shook his head. Gabrielle was probably having second thoughts. His shoulders slumped as he climbed the stairs to change his own clothes.

The woman in question was sitting in the hammock chair on her grandfather's porch. She watched the waves gently lap the shore and allowed the rhythm to sooth her jumbled thoughts. Her cell phone chirped, but Gabrielle ignored it and continued to stare at the bay. A paved path ran from the porch down to the dock, where Grand-Père's boat bobbed next to it.

"Aren't you going to check that, Brie?" Grand-Père asked in French.

"Pas aujourd'hui," she responded. *Not today.*

"What? You've sworn off that blasted contraption?" her father asked from behind the grill where scents of cedar mingled with cooking salmon.

"You go out with a man on Friday and then don't respond to him? He's going to think you're not interested," Grand-Père commented from the chaise longue where he chewed on the end of his unlit pipe.

"It was only a text that came in. Besides, I don't even know if it's from him," Gabrielle replied.

"Well, you won't know until you check," Pop grumbled as he flipped a fillet.

She glanced at two of the men she loved the most in the world. The two men who had opened their door to her and Rocky last night, no questions asked. Two men who had also lost their wives, she reminded herself.

"Well, what's this? The lonely spouses club?" a deep voice called from the door.

Belatedly, Rocky wolfed at the visitor. Gabrielle turned to see a muscular, dark-haired man leaning against the kitchen doorframe. She launched herself from the chair and threw herself into her big brother's arms.

"I swear he can smell salmon cooking from fifty miles away," Pop grumbled to Grand-Père.

"Oui," Grand-Père grunted as he pushed up from the chaise and swung his legs over the side.

"You know, I'm right here."

Thomas approached his father. They shook hands, and Thomas gave him a one-armed man hug. Next, he moved to the chaise longue and leaned down to shake hands with his grandfather.

"Sir. It's good to see you."

"Oui." Grand-Père eyed his grandson over the horn-rimmed glasses he had worn for ages. "Did you stop by for salmon then?"

"I heard Gabrielle's dating again, so I thought I'd stop by to get the scoop. Got to be back on duty tomorrow, though."

Thomas punched Gabrielle lightly on the arm and raised an eyebrow.

"Andrew Leland? I thought I told him to stay away from you, back in high school. I turn my back for a few weeks, and he swoops in while I'm gone. 'Course I'd given up hope you'd ever start dating again, so my guard was down."

Gabrielle sighed. The wonders of the small-town grapevine. Only modern conveniences like social media could begin to compare with the speed of gossip in Jacobs Landing.

Pop slid salmon fillets onto a platter.

"Come. We've already heard this story, Thomas. Talk later. Now it's time for food. Let's eat before this gets cold."

They settled down at the outdoor table. Conversation was random and lighthearted while they consumed the succulent meal.

It was almost dusk when Gabrielle and Thomas found themselves on a bench near the dock. Rocky sniffed along the water's edge. Occasionally, he ran back to his mistress for a pat on the head.

Gabrielle told her brother how Rocky showed up on her porch on the anniversary of Jean-Luc's death. It was through Rocky that she'd met Andrew again. She also recounted an edited version of their date.

"So now you're feeling guilty because you had a good time, right?"

Gabrielle nodded.

"Well, I liked Jean-Luc. You know that, right?"

Again, she nodded.

"But Jean-Luc was a selfish bastard."

Gabrielle gasped and whipped her head around to stare at her brother.

"What? How can you say something like that about my husband?"

"He was, Brie. I know you loved him. And he loved you. But *you* had to become part of *his* life. He didn't make any major changes for you. You're the one who moved to France. You became the figurehead for the company's charitable organizations, and he groomed you to be a rich man's wife. You gave up your design career. For him."

Gabrielle frowned at the picture he painted. On some scale, Thomas was right. But it made her sound like a weakling. A pushover.

"Don't get me wrong. You also gained confidence in yourself and social poise, but there were sacrifices, and Jean-Luc wasn't the one making them. Now, it sticks in my craw to say this about Andrew Leland. But if you like him, if he gives you space to be *you*, then give it a chance, Brie."

Gabrielle mulled that over for a while.

"Why do you hate Andrew so much, Thomas?"

"Hate him? God, I wished I *was* him in high school. He was a chick magnet, although he didn't play the field. He only had one girlfriend during that time. But he was athletic, handsome, nice, and everyone looked up to him. Why wouldn't I envy him?"

Gabrielle eyed her brother. He was broad shouldered, had dark hair given to wave, and piercing blue eyes.

"I don't think you have to worry about female attention, Thomas. You could be the spokesperson for Coast Guard Hunk of the Month. Hasn't there ever been anyone in your life? Anyone special?"

"We're not talking about me," Thomas play growled. He got up.

"Come on, let's see if there's any dessert before we have to leave."

Gabrielle followed her brother into the house. They joined their only living parent and grandparent for chocolate chip cookies. It was late before Gabrielle and Rocky drove back to her Victorian house in town.

In bed, Gabrielle drifted toward sleep. She thought about what Thomas had said earlier. He was right about Jean-Luc. Jean-Luc's magnetic personality attracted everyone around him. He attracted their interest, and sometimes their greed, but he was always the center of attention. There was only room for one person in the spotlight, so Gabrielle had orbited around him. Like everyone else.

Jean-Luc had loved and spoiled her, but her goals and ambitions were swallowed up by his. Their love for each other had been so intense, Gabrielle hadn't noticed how much of her essence had been consumed in the process.

With Andrew, things were different. She enjoyed being with Andrew. She relaxed with him and found an ease with him that hadn't existed with Jean-Luc. Gabrielle was a different person than the young girl who married Jean-Luc fresh out of art school. With Jean-Luc's death, Gabrielle had found strength and a sense of self that hadn't been there before. Maybe Andrew Leland was the person the *new* Gabrielle needed.

Andrew. Oh shoot! She had forgotten to check her text messages!

Gabrielle scrambled out of bed and flew down the back stairs. In the dark kitchen, she stubbed her toe on a sawhorse but didn't let the injury stop her from limping toward the counter where her purse sat. She pawed through it until she found her cell phone. It was dead.

Back in her bedroom, Gabrielle plugged it in to a socket near her nightstand. When her phone finally booted up, she read Andrew's message about the dog park. During her weekend of misery and self-loathing, she had forgotten about her offer to meet them today. Hopefully, Jack wasn't too disappointed. Gabrielle hoped Andrew wasn't either. She tapped out a response to his text.

"Drew, just got your message. Thomas was home today. Phone was dead. Talk to you tomorrow?"

There. She'd texted him back. It wasn't the whole story, but the rest could wait until tomorrow. She climbed back into bed. A quick flick of the light switch and she was asleep.

# CHAPTER SIX

It was almost lunchtime, and Drew paced the length of his office. It had been a mistake. He had given Gabrielle too much time to think about their date. Disappointment coursed through his veins, but he was also angry with himself for waiting too long. Yeah, he had gotten her text when he woke up this morning. He would *not* let her put him on hold any longer. He needed to remind her of their attraction because Andrew feared she would retreat inside her shell.

A look at his schedule told him there were no more patients until after lunch. Andrew told his secretary he was headed out, then walked down the street to The Treasure Trove.

Gabrielle glanced at the clock. Eleven forty-five. She had a twelve thirty appointment with a potential renter for one of her retail spaces. A café. It would be nice to have another place to catch a sandwich in town. Besides fast food, there was The Lobster Shack, but after living in Paris for five years, she craved variety.

The doorbell jingled. Gabrielle's eyes widened in surprise as Andrew came through the door. If someone could emit testosterone, it was him. Drawn to him, she moved out from behind the counter. His hazel eyes had a determined glint as he strode toward her.

Phyllis whistled under her breath. "That's one tall drink of water."

Andrew strode up to Gabrielle and grasped her elbow. Without breaking his stride, Andrew nodded to Phyllis, then steered Gabrielle toward the stockroom.

"We need to talk," he murmured.

He was disgruntled. She could tell by his firm grip on her elbow and the straight line of his mouth. Despite all of this, her happy synapses fired up as soon as he touched her arm.

"I've got the front, Gabrielle, but don't forget you've got to leave in half an hour for your meeting," Phyllis called after them.

Andrew closed the door to the stockroom. After he greeted Rocky, he stood up and glowered at Gabrielle.

What should she say? She knew she needed to apologize, but it was so good to see him. It had only been two days. How had she missed him so much?

Because she didn't know where to start, Gabrielle followed instinct. She threw her arms around his neck and kissed him with all the turbulent emotions from the past few days.

Andrew froze. After a brief hesitation, he crushed Gabrielle against his chest and took out his frustrations on her mouth. He pushed Gabrielle against the wall. His hands ran from her cheeks down to her breasts, then back up again. His mouth never left hers.

Before either of them realized what he was doing, Andrew had half the buttons of her blouse undone. With a shaky breath, Andrew paused and took a step back from her. He groaned and turned his head away.

Whoa! What just happened? With her free hand, Gabrielle pushed her mussed hair away from her face. Her other hand, she realized, still cupped his hard backside.

"Drew."

She raised her hand from his butt to his chest.

"I'm sorry I didn't call or text this weekend. It was rude of me. I'm also sorry I didn't respond earlier to your text about the dog park."

Steely eyes turned toward her. A muscle ticked in his jaw. "I told myself to give you space. I tried to wait for you to come to me, but here I am. Were you going to call? Should I just walk away now? If you aren't going to be there for him, I can't risk Jack getting attached. I have to protect my son."

Gabrielle read between the lines. If she wasn't going to put forth some effort to make their new relationship work, Drew wasn't going to get attached either.

She sighed. "I was scared after our date on Friday."

He raised an eyebrow.

"I woke up Saturday morning feeling guilty and all shook up instead of excited and happy, like I was when we were together. I had to step back and work some things out this weekend."

"Jean-Luc." He grunted and turned away from her.

"Yes, Jean-Luc. But also things about me."

Gabrielle put a hand on his shoulder.

"Drew, please look at me."

His face was a mask of stone when he turned back to her.

"I promise you, I will follow through on my word. And if I can't, I'll call you. Please be patient with me. I want this to work between us; I'm just not sure how to make it happen yet."

"Yesterday, at the park, Jack kept asking if you were coming."

Tears welled up in Gabrielle's eyes at the little boy's disappointment. She glanced down in shame.

"I'm sorry." She sniffed. "I didn't mean to let either of you down. Can you forgive me?"

She glanced up through the filter of her tears and saw Drew's shoulders relax.

"That depends on you. Can you see a future for us? I'm not asking for a lifelong commitment. I'm just asking if all you see is grief, or do you actually see *me*?"

Gabrielle gazed into Drew's ever-changing eyes. She traced his high cheekbones and skimmed her fingertips over his lips. His nostrils flared.

"I see you, Drew. I can't guarantee the grief is gone because that doesn't happen immediately. I'm still finding my way on that one. But after this weekend, I realized that if I let you walk out of my life, I would regret it forever."

"Gabrielle, please don't disappear on me like you did this weekend. If you're sad, tell me. If you're happy, tell me. If you need space, tell me. I might not like what you have to say, but tell me anyway. Don't leave me wondering where I stand."

"I promise, Drew. Is there any way I can make this up to Jack?"

Phyllis cracked the door open and called in, "Five minutes, Gabrielle. It's almost twelve fifteen."

The door closed as quickly as it opened.

Andrew ran a hand through his hair in frustration.

"Crap. I've got surgery in half an hour. What kind of meeting do you have?"

Drew eyed her silky top, gray pencil skirt, and high heels. Gabrielle flushed at the gaping blouse and began to refasten the buttons.

"I have a meeting with a potential renter for one of the storefronts."

Drew stilled her hands with his own. Gabrielle tipped her head back to look up into his eyes.

"Are you free tonight? Can you and Rocky come over for dinner? It would just be steaks on the grill, but it would go a long way toward making up with Jack."

*And me.* It hung unspoken between them.

"What time should Rocky and I be there? What should we bring?"

Andrew grinned.

"Six o'clock? Does that give you enough time to close the shop?"

"Six sounds good."

"Oh, and there's something else."

She was surprised to see a light flush spread across his cheeks. Was he embarrassed?

"I hate to ask this."

He hesitated.

"What is it, Drew?"

"Well, tomorrow Jack is in charge of snack for day camp. He tells me it can't be store-bought cookies again. The other kids' moms make something *cool*. Can you cook? Or bake? Or anything that will save Jack from being embarrassed by my poor attempt at parenthood?"

That's what was bothering him? Gabrielle beamed.

"How many kids?"

"Twenty-four."

"Healthy or sweet snack?"

"Um…both?"

"Sure. Rocky and I will swing by the grocery store to pick up supplies. It might be closer to six fifteen before we get there, but I *will* call if it's any later."

Gabrielle glanced at her watch. She blanched, then hurried to finish the buttons of her shirt.

"I really have to go. Tell Jack I'll need his help making the treat for tomorrow, okay?"

Andrew rested a hand on her shoulder.

"How 'bout a makeup kiss before we go?"

He flashed Gabrielle his signature white-toothed grin.

At her nod, Andrew leaned in and nipped her lips.

Gabrielle pressed a hard, fast kiss to his lips.

She called over her shoulder on the way out the back door, "Good luck with the surgery. Hope everything goes well. See you tonight."

She snagged her purse from a nearby hook and flew out to her SUV.

Could life get any better? Andrew wondered as he cleaned the patio grill later that night. A glance through the sliding screen door showed Gabrielle and Jack at the kitchen island. They sat on stools and threaded fruit and giant marshmallows onto wooden skewers. Gus, as always, leaned as close to Gabrielle's leg as he could get. When it came to Gabrielle, Andrew decided he and Gus had way too much in common.

"Jack." He heard her laugh. "You're supposed to put them on the stick, not eat all the fruit and marshmallows. We still have twelve more to go. Your dad is going to kill me when he sees the stains all over your face and shirt."

Andrew grinned. He would buy Jack twenty new shirts if this scene was the outcome. After all, he *could* afford it. He grinned again and looked at his middle-class condo.

Besides Andrew, his accountant and the IRS were the only people who knew how much he was worth. That's the way he liked it. Money complicated things. He'd rather have it be a nonfactor when people met him. Andrew suspected Gabrielle felt the same way. He wasn't sure how much Jean-Luc left her, but just her stock alone in the textile company must be worth millions. He couldn't care less. Neither of them found happiness through money.

Inside the house, Jack giggled.

"Dad won't mind, Brie. I'm eating fruit, and fruit is healthy."

"Well, young man," she replied with mock seriousness. "We're running out of fruit. We need to get these kebabs done because your bedtime is just around the corner."

Andrew watched as Gabrielle smiled at Jack and tousled his hair. Jack patted her cheek with sticky fingers and beamed. Miracle of miracles, Gabrielle didn't flinch away from the boy's gooey hand. She just laughed.

"Race you," the boy dared.

Jack threaded fruit and marshmallows as fast as he could. Gabrielle laughed again, then matched the boy's pace. The scene filled Andrew with an intense longing to make this a nightly occurrence. They were so like mother and child; it took his breath away.

God, he loved her. She never overlooked Jack. She understood the responsibility of a relationship with his son, and Jack thrived from her attention. Maybe Jack had been right at that first meeting. Maybe Gabrielle was his mom. Andrew hoped so. He wanted Gabrielle. Forever. But she wasn't ready yet. He would have to tread with care.

When Andrew entered the kitchen a couple of minutes later, Gabrielle smiled up at him. He washed his hands at the sink, then turned to watch as Jack and Gabrielle packed their carefully prepared snacks into Ziplock bags.

"Jack, why don't you head upstairs and find your pajamas? I'll be up there in a minute to start your bath," Andrew urged.

"'Kay, Dad. Brie, will you read me a story tonight?"

"Jack, I think Gabrielle's tired—" Drew began.

Gabrielle held up a hand and stopped him.

"I don't mind, but," she turned to Jack, "I only read to clean boys, fresh out of the bathtub. Better hurry up. If you take too long, I might have to leave before you get done."

She smiled to soften her words.

Jack grinned at both of them, then whooped up the stairs like little boys do. Gabrielle cleared her throat, then rose from the stool. She padded over to the refrigerator in her stocking feet. Andrew leaned against the counter so she couldn't get the door open to the refrigerator unless he moved.

"'Scuse me, sir, I need to put these in the fridge."

She bumped her hip against his and reached over the island to grab the plastic bags.

Andrew encircled her waist from behind.

"Let me help you," he murmured in her ear.

She turned in his arms and laughed up at him.

"I'm not sure the help you're offering will get the job done."

He rubbed himself lightly against her. "Oh, it will get the job done. I promise."

Gabrielle laughed in astonishment at his not too subtle innuendo. Andrew knew he had the advantage. Gabrielle was pinned between him and the kitchen island. In her hands, she balanced two bags of fruit kebabs; helpless to move without his cooperation.

"Come on, just one kiss," he urged.

"One kiss. *Right.* Look where one kiss got us today in the stockroom."

The memory of her partially bared breasts and the intensity of her kisses flashed before him. He groaned.

"You know, you really shouldn't kiss a man like that just before he performs surgery. It took walking back to the clinic, changing into scrubs, and washing up before I got my libido under control."

Gabrielle's laugh turned into a sigh when Drew nuzzled her jaw.

"I didn't know my kisses had that effect on you." She breathed. "I'll have to use them more sparingly if they're so distracting."

*Marry me and put me out of my misery*, he urged silently.

But he knew Gabrielle would bolt if he voiced his thoughts. After their first date, Gabrielle had avoided Andrew for two days. If he told her he was in love with her, he would never hear from her again.

Andrew leaned in to kiss her rosy lips, but Jack called down from the level above.

"Daaad. I'm ready! Can you start the water for me?"

Drew sighed.

"Saved by the boy, for now. Can you stay for a few minutes and read that story? He'd really like it."

"Sure. I'd like it too. While you take care of bath time, I'll finish cleaning the kitchen."

Fifteen minutes later, the kitchen was clean. Gabrielle grabbed her tote bag from the floor near the back door. In the downstairs powder room, she changed into more comfortable clothes. Nylons, skirt, and blouse were not her idea of cozy. She sighed in relief when the nylons came off. A soft cotton T-shirt slipped over her head, then came a pair of shorts. Gabrielle washed her face and looked in the mirror above the pedestal sink.

Who was that woman looking back at her? Three months ago, she was wan and underweight with eyes full of sorrow. The woman in the mirror had a flush on her cheeks, her mouth was slightly swollen from stolen kisses, and her blue eyes sparkled with anticipation. She looked like a woman in love.

The woman in the mirror's expression changed to one of horror. She couldn't be in love with Andrew, could she? She wanted to deny it, but Gabrielle suspected it was true. Terror gripped her, and she bent over the sink. *Do not hyperventilate!*

Gabrielle had loved before. When Jean-Luc died, she was devastated. She couldn't go through the pain of losing someone again. She didn't think she was strong enough. Panic caused her stomach to contract. Would she be sick?

She should leave. Just go. Gabrielle picked up her discarded clothing in quick, jerky motions. She shoved the pieces into her tote bag.

"Gabrielle?" Andrew knocked on the bathroom door. "Are you okay in there? Jack's in bed, waiting for his story."

Jack. The thought of the darling dark-haired boy stopped her in midpanic. She had promised to read to him. Gabrielle would *not* let the little boy down again.

Gabrielle eased out of the powder room and dropped her tote near the back door. Andrew took one look at her drawn face and pulled her to him.

"Hey. Hey, what's wrong?" he murmured.

His hand soothed her as he ran it down her hair.

"I'll read Jack his story, and then I've got to go."

"Okaay. But what's got you so upset? I left you down here with a sparkle in your eyes. Now you look like somebody died. Oh…"

She watched comprehension dawn. Then a flash of resentment as Drew realized Jean-Luc's specter stood between them. Again. Andrew schooled his expression into one of understanding—but not before she saw the hurt in his eyes.

Gabrielle ran a shaky hand through her hair. She didn't want to hurt Drew, so she searched for words to explain.

"The feelings between us. They're just so sudden. And intense. I'm not coping very well with that," she admitted.

Her body relaxed. It felt good to tell Andrew how she felt.

Drew draped Gabrielle in a one-armed hug. He rubbed her other arm with his hand.

"It's okay, honey. If you're overwhelmed, then we step back a little. What I feel for you is pretty intense, but I can do gentle too. Why don't you go up and read Jack that story? While you're up there, I'll microwave some popcorn. We can watch a movie on the couch. You don't have to run away. I'll just back off a little. How's that?"

With a small shudder, Gabrielle looked up at Drew.

"Okay. I'll stay for a movie."

She moved toward the stairs.

"And Drew, thank you."

Ten minutes later, Gabrielle and Andrew were munching popcorn on the couch. A movie played on his big screen television above the fireplace. Drew sent her a curious look when Gabrielle yawned for the fifth time.

"Movie boring you?"

"Huh?" She yawned again. "Oh, no. I just haven't slept very well, and it's catching up with me."

"Why don't we lie down on the couch? No funny business, I promise. It's extra wide because I'm a big guy, so there's enough room for both of us. Just cuddling."

Drew crossed his heart with his finger.

Before she could answer, Drew took their bowls and set them on the straight-legged end table. He slid down behind her with his back to the couch. He extended his arm and waited while Gabrielle curled in front of him. His arm became her pillow, and Drew curled his other arm around her waist. He pulled her closer so she wouldn't fall off the couch.

"Okay?" he asked.

"Yeah. This is nice." She smiled against his arm.

Curled up against Drew, his chest warm behind her back, Gabrielle felt safe and cherished. How long had it been since she had this sense of security? Maybe not since her mother died. Her father and grandfather weren't much for cuddling. Jean-Luc desired and loved her, but he always needed something from her. Andrew made her feel safe. He nurtured and took care of her. Cocooned in his arms, Gabrielle's eyes drifted shut.

Rocky's whine registered before Gabrielle was fully awake. A wet cold nose nudged her arm in urgency. When Gabrielle opened her eyes, she realized she was still on Andrew's couch. The room was dark except for a light over the sink, just the way they had left it before they started the movie. She could feel Andrew's chest rise and fall behind her. Gabrielle rubbed the sleep from her eyes and looked at her waiting dog.

Rocky's eyes apologized as he tapped his tail on the floor. He got up and went toward the sliding door. The dog looked back to see if she got the message.

"Okay, Rock. I'm coming," Gabrielle whispered as she removed Andrew's arm from her waist and slid off the couch.

"Everything okay?" he rumbled behind her.

"Rocky's gotta go out."

Gus appeared from behind the couch. He whined and moved to stand near Rocky.

"Gus too."

Andrew groaned as he sat up. He moved his left arm up and down, then rotated his shoulder.

"I think my arm is numb."

As she opened the sliding door, Gabrielle watched Andrew over her shoulder.

"Sorry, I think that's my fault."

He shook his head, then ran his hands over his face.

"What time is it?"

Gabrielle pulled her phone out of her pocket.

"Three thirty. I need to get home. You need to get to bed. Didn't you say you were double-booked tomorrow? I mean today."

"Yeah. Dr. Standish is on vacation, and he usually takes patients on Tuesdays. I'm covering his and mine. Luckily, no surgeries scheduled."

Gabrielle let the dogs back inside. She moved on wooden legs to the back door. While she slipped into her shoes, Andrew attached Rocky's leash.

"This has been nice. I know we're both exhausted, but I like waking up to you."

He rubbed Gabrielle's arm and gave her a quick peck on the lips.

"Will you be okay to drive?"

"Yeah. Luckily, it's not too far."

"Text me when you get home so I know you're safe, okay?"

"I will. Drew, I'm hitting a couple of flea markets today, and I have to see a few artists. I'll be on the road most of the day. I won't be home until late, but I'll text you when I'm back for the night, okay?"

Still half asleep, he smiled at her.

"Fine, no problem. I'm just glad you let me know."

She hugged him and gave him a quick kiss.

"Come on, Rocky. Morning's going to be here before we know it."

Gabrielle drove home. After she checked her house, she fell into bed. Face down, she slipped her cell phone from her pocket and sent the promised text to Drew.

# CHAPTER SEVEN

On Wednesday evening, Gabrielle paused to steady her nerves. She pulled open the door to city hall. Inside, the front desk was as empty as a church on Friday night. Voices echoed from a hallway to the right. Gabrielle followed a sign indicating the conference room; her low heels clicked on the polished floor.

For her first meeting with the pillars of Jacobs Landing society, she'd chosen her outfit with care. Linen pants and a coordinating blouse gave her a casual but polished look. As Jean-Luc's wife, she knew appearances were important, especially when making a first impression.

"Ah, Mrs. Levesque. You made it." The mayor ambled over to her. "Let me introduce you, although you probably know almost everyone."

Mayor Hartwell made introductions to the seven local businessmen who sat on the council. He pointed to Andrew's father.

"Bob, of course, you know."

She nodded after each introduction. If she were at a job interview, she would be more comfortable.

"Please everyone, call me Gabrielle. We've known each other for years. Let's not stand on formality."

"Well, let's get down to business."

Mayor Hartwell sat at the head of the conference table. After the men filed into their chosen seats, an empty chair stood open to the right of the mayor. Great. The hot seat. Everyone could watch Gabrielle make a fool of herself.

Once the meeting got underway, Gabrielle sat and listened. She'd learned from experience that jumping in with suggestions and changes wasn't always appreciated from a newbie. It also gave her the opportunity to get a feel for the political undercurrents in the room. The main topic on the agenda was how to encourage more tourism and shopping in Jacobs Landing.

"We've already done fundraisers and concerts, Jacob," Puck Canon, the owner of The Lobster Shack commented to the mayor. Canon was a burly man with wiry gray hair scraped back into a ponytail.

Halfway down the table, a gaunt man with a comb-over spoke up. "Let's ask the *new girl* what she thinks."

All eyes turned to Gabrielle. Sweat broke out on her palms. Gabrielle reminded herself this situation was just like the boardrooms of Paris. Except that here, in Maine, she was Gabrielle Levesque, not Jean-Luc Levesque's wife. Those were two different people. This time Gabrielle had to prove her worth; her last name meant nothing.

She cleared her throat and tilted her head at the pallid man.

"My suggestions might be biased, Mr. Franz, because my interests and businesses are rooted in art."

Gabrielle paused. Bob Leland caught her eye and gave a quick nod of encouragement. Gabrielle took a breath.

"Several years ago, a town in Michigan started an art festival. Artists from all over the country take their work to Grand Rapids for an exhibit. Residents and tourists view the pieces and vote for their favorite artist. It's become so popular that other cities are considering their own versions of the festival."

Complete silence. Was that good or bad?

Gabrielle continued, "Our town is nowhere near the size of that city, but we could run a smaller version of the competition. It could be a weekend event."

Still no one spoke.

"It would bring in artists and tourists, which would boost sales in our restaurants, stores, and lodging..."

The mayor pointed a chubby finger at her.

"Answer me this. Where would we display the art?"

Gabrielle focused on the mayor and warmed to her subject.

"Well, that's the beauty of it. The art is displayed inside local businesses and community buildings. Tourists and locals have to enter these buildings to see the exhibits. If the art is large, like a sculpture for instance, then it's displayed outside in a central location."

Bob Leland asked the next question.

"So the voters purchase a pass—let's say for the weekend—which allows them free entrance into any of the buildings displaying art for the competition. Does this include buildings that would normally charge admission?"

Gabrielle nodded.

"What do we award the winner?" Puck asked.

"It's usually a cash prize."

"Well, that's a bust," Franz interjected. "The town is near broke."

"The tickets fund the prize money," she replied. "We just have to project ticket sales and weigh them against a large enough prize to encourage artists to participate.

You'd be great at figuring the projections, Mr. Franz, since you're an accountant. Once we have our numbers, we advertise like crazy."

Dead silence. The men considered this last piece of information before all heads swiveled to the mayor. Mayor Hartwell sat back in his chair and clasped his hands over his pudgy belly.

"I think it's a brilliant idea."

He leaned forward.

"Let's call for a vote."

Two hours later, fatigue weighed down her limbs as Gabrielle trudged to her SUV. The council had decided to hold Art Fest the first weekend in October. Somehow they had designated Gabrielle to be the project manager, but final decisions needed the mayor's approval. The town council would meet every Wednesday until the festival.

At home, Gabrielle let Rocky out. Feeling sweaty after the stressful meeting, she headed for the shower.

Her cell phone was ringing when she shut off the water and pulled back the shower curtain. She wrapped a towel around her wet body and dashed into her bedroom to answer it. Gabrielle glanced at the screen. Drew.

"Hello." She breathed.

"You sound out of breath. Did I catch you at a bad time?"

"Just got out of the shower. Had to run for the phone."

He groaned.

"You're killing me here. Just tell me one thing, towel or no towel?"

"I'll do no such thing." She giggled. "Give me five minutes. I'll call you back."

"So no towel, huh?"

"You wish."

Gabrielle hung up and dashed back to the bathroom before she left a puddle on her bedroom floor. Ten minutes later, Gabrielle called Drew back and told him about the council meeting.

"Yeah. Dad was pretty impressed. He called me on his way home to brag about you. I think he likes you, and that's saying something. My dad's a shrewd businessman, and he doesn't like very many people. By the way, I'm supposed to invite you to the Fourth of July next week."

"I'm invited to the Fourth of July? I don't understand. Aren't all Americans invited?" she joked.

Andrew laughed. "We have a family cookout, then take the boat out at night to watch the fireworks. Mom and Dad want me to bring you this year. They want to get to know you better."

"Oh no. It's time to meet *the family*, isn't it?"

"Hey, I've had a terrible time holding them off until now. Somebody drove by my house the other night and saw your car there. Late. Somehow, Mom found out about it. I can't say for sure, but I suspect the culprit is my older sister, Grace. Mom showed up at work today. She informed me that now that you and I are sleeping together, it was time I introduced you to my sisters."

Gabrielle gasped in dismay. "But we never…"

"I know, but I couldn't convince Mom of that. She has complete faith in my masculine charm. Little does she know…" He paused. "I'm sorry, Gabrielle. If you're not ready, I can push it off for a while."

"No. I'm glad you warned me. Sometimes, it stinks living in a small town. I better take you out this Sunday to meet Pop and Grand-Père. Even though they live twenty minutes from town, gossip reaches them quickly."

"Really? You want me to meet your father?" His voice perked up. "Can we bring Jack along? I'm sure he'd love it. He's been asking for you, by the way."

"Of course Jack can come! He's such a charmer. He'll have my father and grandfather wrapped around his finger. You *do* know that once we meet each other's families, they're going to have us married and producing offspring."

"And that would be a bad thing?"

"*Andrew.* I'm just saying this is going to put more pressure on us from both families."

"It's a pressure I'm willing to bear. As long as you compensate me in kisses and the occasional groping."

Gabrielle burst out laughing. Disturbed by the sudden noise, Rocky sat up and woofed. God, it felt good to laugh. Andrew always knew when to lighten the mood. He made her laugh often, but he never let her forget his physical attraction to her.

"So it's a plan then?" he asked, his slight insecurity coming through.

"Okay. You've persuaded me, especially if kissing is involved. I'll call Pop and find out details for Sunday. Then we make an appearance at your family cookout on *the Fourth.*"

"Sounds good. But, Gabrielle? Do I get to see you before Sunday? What's the rest of your week look like?"

Gabrielle ran through her mental agenda.

"Are you guys up for a picnic tomorrow night? We could head to the harbor and watch the boats."

"What about your place? You said the appliances were installed today. How about that tour you offered?"

Except for dinner at Drew's condo the other night, Gabrielle had restricted their interactions to public places. She wasn't sure if she could cope with Andrew and Jack in her personal space yet.

Gabrielle inhaled. Andrew tested the limits of her commitment to their budding relationship. The Victorian, torn up as it was, was her sanctuary. She rarely let anyone inside because it was the one place where she found peace. If things didn't work out with Andrew, she would be haunted by him and Jack.

"No can do," she responded with a lightness she didn't feel. "There are literally floor boards missing in all the downstairs rooms right now."

*Which was true.*

"I'd be terrified Jack would trip or fall through one of them."

At Andrew's silence, Gabrielle continued, "I promise. Once I have floors in all the rooms downstairs and my kitchen set up, I will have you both over. *And* I will cook for you. I *am* quite a good cook. I just haven't had the chance to prove it since I've been eating out of a microwave for months."

"All right, Gabrielle," Andrew replied quietly. "I understand you're not ready yet. I'll be patient and wait until you are."

How did he always read her with such accuracy? Everything she had told him was true, but he still saw the motivation behind her words.

Gabrielle kept her voice cheerful. "So I'll pack a picnic for us and meet you tomorrow night at the harbor?"

"Yeah, sure." He sighed. "Hey, remember, Jack—"

"I know," she interrupted him. "Jack only likes peanut butter on his sandwiches, no jelly."

"That's right. You remembered!"

"Ayuh. I'll see you tomorrow."

"Night, Gabrielle."

"Night, Drew."

Thursday, they met at the harbor with the dogs. Jack squealed when he saw Gabrielle and launched himself at her legs.

"I missed you!" the boy exclaimed.

Two grandmotherly women stopped and smiled at the scene.

They nodded at Gabrielle.

One of the women commented, "Your little boy looks just like you! Isn't he just precious, Elsie?"

Andrew ambled up just then. The other woman, Elsie, regarded him with wise eyes.

"You have a wonderful family, young man. Take care of them. She's a treasure. And so is this little man."

Appalled at the ladies' misinterpretation of their relationship, Gabrielle looked to Andrew for his response. He grinned and wrapped his arms around both her and Jack.

"Believe me, ma'am, these two are the most precious people in the world to me."

Gabrielle peeped up at him. Though he was smiling, his eyes were grave.

*Don't love him. Don't love him*, she told herself.

Gabrielle worried that she already did. She watched Andrew wave goodbye to the Grandmother Twins, then turn to her. Why did she feel so exposed, like he could read her thoughts? Andrew's mouth tightened for a minute, then he lightened his tone as he pointed to the basket.

"Here, why don't you let me carry that picnic basket? It looks heavy."

He lifted the basket from her like it was a pillow. Jack ran ahead of them with the dogs.

"You know what I think?" Andrew asked after a moment. "I think you care about me and that terrifies you."

Gabrielle blinked.

"I'm going to believe that until you tell me differently. I'm going to say it first. I care about you, probably more than you want to hear right now. The ball's in your court."

Andrew lengthened his stride and caught up with Jack. A few minutes later, Gabrielle met up with them at her own pace. The rest of the evening was strained. Gabrielle and Rocky left earlier than planned. As he buckled Jack into his truck, Andrew watched her and Rocky pull away.

Gabrielle shook her head. She didn't know how to give him what he wanted. She just wasn't ready to admit she might be falling for Andrew Leland. At least, not out loud.

On Friday, Andrew shuffled through the files on his desk. He didn't expect to hear from Gabrielle or see her before Sunday, if the strained picnic last night was any indication.

He took a bite of his sandwich. While Andrew was in midchew, a knock sounded at the door. It cracked open, and his vet tech peered through the gap.

"You have a visitor, Dr. Leland."

Annabelle swung the door wider to show Gabrielle shifting from foot to foot behind her.

Drew nodded and swallowed.

"Gabrielle? Come in."

Dread pooled in the pit of his stomach. What if he'd pushed her too far? Was she here to call everything off?

Annabelle closed the door behind Gabrielle.

"Am I interrupting anything? I hate to barge in at your work. I never know if it's a good time or not."

"No, it's good. I'm finishing my lunch. Come in, sit down."

Andrew moved a pile of books off a nearby chair. He motioned for Gabrielle to sit. She hovered near the chair but continued to stand.

"Drew, I want to apologize for last night. You're probably wondering if I need to be on meds or something."

Gabrielle took both of his hands in hers. When she looked up at him, her face held a greenish pallor. She took a shaky breath.

"You were right. I do care about you. More than I want to. More than I think is wise."

Wow! Andrew registered the strain in her face. It was painful for her to admit her feelings, but inside he soared. He schooled his face into a bland expression even though he wanted to grin like Gus with a new bone.

"And I'm *not* saying that because I need a place to stay," she continued.

Drew shook his head. "Excuse me?"

"The contractor stopped by the shop this morning. I'm banned from the house—at least until sometime next week. They found asbestos when they began the HVAC overhaul."

"Let me get this straight. You care about me *and* you need a place to stay for a few days?"

"Yes. But think of it as two separate conversations."

Gabrielle swayed on her feet and gripped his arms.

"Hey, honey. You don't look so good. Sit down."

"No." Tears welled up in Gabrielle's eyes. "If I sit, I'm not sure I can get back up again. On top of everything, I'm sick as a dog. I think I have the flu."

She sniffled.

"On second thought, I don't want you or Jack to get sick. I wasn't thinking clearly when I came here. I'd better go to Pop's."

Gabrielle swayed again. Andrew wrapped an arm around her waist and pulled her against him. He rested his hand on her forehead and jerked it back quickly. She was burning up.

"Let's get you to my house. You can stay in the guest room."

He took the keys from her hand and half supported Gabrielle against him.

"Where's Rocky?"

She rolled her head up to look up at him. "He's in my car."

They passed Annabelle in the hallway as they headed out the back door.

"Gabrielle's sick. I'm going to take her home, Annabelle. When's my next appointment?"

"Not until two."

"Okay. I'll be back by then."

At his condo, Drew unlocked the front door and greeted Gus. He ushered in Rocky and turned to help Gabrielle up the steps. Her pallor was ashen, but her cheeks were decorated with poppy-red blossoms of fever. Gabrielle swayed on her feet.

As soon as she was inside the house, Gabrielle dashed to his powder room and slammed the door. On the other side of the door, Drew heard her retching.

He wasn't disgusted. It must be his dad training or his medical background, but Andrew waited a few minutes for her to finish. After he heard the toilet flush,

Andrew cracked open the door. He found Gabrielle sitting on the floor with her head against the wall. Her teeth chattered.

"Come here, sweetheart."

He lifted her up to a standing position.

"Let's get you into bed."

Andrew swept Gabrielle into his arms and carried her up the stairs. In the hallway, he changed his original plan and carried her into his own bedroom.

"This is your room, Drew. I can't take your room. Just put me in the guest room," Gabrielle urged with glassy eyes.

Andrew set her on the bed and removed her shoes.

"No. And I'll tell you why. There's a bathroom right through that door over there. It's much closer than the one near the guest room."

Andrew pulled one of his clean T-shirts from a dresser drawer and handed it to Gabrielle.

"Here." He grinned. "Do you need help putting this on?"

She swung her head up to look at him, then sprinted for his bathroom.

Andrew decided it would be a good time to get her a drink, and some aspirin, from downstairs.

Five minutes later, Drew returned to find Gabrielle's clothes in a pile on the floor next to his bed. She shivered beneath his comforter. With his foot, Andrew nudged the pile out of the way and placed a big plastic bowl on the floor near her head. Jack called it the puke bowl, and although it was clean, that was its only use.

"Do you think you can drink a little something to get this medicine in your system?"

He wiped the damp hair off her forehead.

"It'll help with the fever."

Gabrielle accepted the water and pills without comment. She swallowed them, then rested her head back on the pillow.

"I hate being sick. Thanks for taking care of me, Drew."

Andrew stroked Gabrielle's cheek.

"I know, love. I'll have to take your car back to work soon, but if you need anything, call me. I can be back here in five minutes."

He set her cell phone on the bedside table and turned back to her.

Gabrielle's eyes drifted shut. "I'll just sleep for a while."

Andrew hated to leave her, but when he was sick, all he wanted to do was sleep. After making sure anything she might need was in reach, Drew stroked her forehead. Then he returned to work.

Gabrielle lay in bed and waited for the roiling in her stomach to stop. This was the end of their relationship; she knew it. If Drew wasn't turned off before by her vacillating attitude, her flu symptoms would do it. He probably couldn't wait to get her out of his house.

The next few hours were pure misery for Gabrielle. Eventually, there were no more mad dashes to the bathroom. She slept. When she woke next, the room was dark except for a soft light from the doorway.

"Is Brie going to stay here *all* night, Dad?" she heard Jack ask.

"Yep, but remember, she's sick, so we want to let her rest, okay? You can see her in the morning. Maybe she'll feel better by then."

"All right, Dad."

Gabrielle dozed again. She woke later when a cool hand touched her forehead. "Drew?"

"Yeah. I think your fever is spiking again. If I prop you up, can you take more medicine?"

Not sure if he could see her in the dim room, Gabrielle nodded anyway. The next instant, Drew's arm slid under her shoulders and lifted her into a reclining position. Gabrielle sipped from the straw he pressed to her lips, then swallowed the pills he offered.

With her head on the pillow and her mind groggy from the fever, Gabrielle spoke, "You know, in pioneer days, sometimes all they had was a veterinarian for a doctor. You'd make a good doctor, Drew."

He chuckled. "I *am* a doctor, Gabrielle."

"You know what I mean."

He brushed her cheek.

"I'll try not to be offended. It's nice to know you think I might make a good doctor—*someday*."

"I think you're a great doctor *now*. Just for people I mean, not pets."

She heard Andrew chuckle again. A rustle came from the direction of his closet.

"What're you doing?"

"I am getting undressed," he responded.

"But you're not going to get into bed with me, right?"

"Of course, I am. I'm tired. And you're in my bed."

"But I might get you sick."

He slid into bed next to her and kissed the back of her neck.

"I'll take that risk. Besides, I need to stay close in case you need more medication during the night."

"What'll Jack think?"

"Jack is asleep in his own bed, Gabrielle."

He put his finger over her lips.

"Just relax, honey. Sleep. Tomorrow's Saturday, so we can sleep in."

Andrew listened to Gabrielle's steady breathing next to him. She had fallen asleep. Good.

Mentally, he groaned. This was the second time he had slept with her and neither time had involved naked bodies or lovemaking. Maybe he'd lost his touch.

Gabrielle rolled over and rested her head against his shoulder; fever radiated from her skin.

"I love you, Drew. Don't give up on me," she sighed.

He froze. Had he heard right?

"Gabrielle? Gabrielle?" he whispered.

She sighed, and he realized she wouldn't remember this in the morning.

"I love you, Gabrielle. Someday, I'm going to convince you to marry me."

It felt good to say it out loud even though she was asleep. Exhaustion took over. Drew also slept.

# CHAPTER EIGHT

"My daughter is *living* with you, Mr. Leland?"

David Martin shot Andrew a look of steel. Andrew cringed inside.

"No, sir. She's just staying with me until they get the asbestos cleaned up in her home."

"She stayed overnight. In your bed?" Gabrielle's grandfather inquired next.

Andrew glanced at Gabrielle's grandfather. Under Pierre Martin's glare, he resisted the urge to squirm. Pierre reminded Andrew of Jacques Cousteau in horn-rimmed glasses. But, unlike the photos Andrew saw of Jacques Cousteau, Pierre was *not* smiling.

"Well, sir. You see, she was sick with the flu. She had a fever. I had to wake her up throughout the night to give her medicine. To keep the fever down."

"Hmph."

How did he do it? He conveyed disbelief and disdain in one syllable.

"When's the wedding?" Gabrielle's father asked.

Andrew swung his head back to David Martin. They had arranged the seating on purpose, Drew was sure of it. He sat on the Martin's back deck in a chair that faced both David at the grill and Pierre on an outdoor settee. Salmon was not the only thing being grilled today.

Andrew answered with honesty. "I would've married her last week or last month, but she's not ready. I love her. And I hope she'll marry me someday. But there's a ghost between us."

"Hmph." Pierre grunted again, moving his unlit pipe to the other side of his mouth.

This time, Andrew detected a slight change in tone. Was there a hint of approval and understanding now?

"Jean-Luc." David nodded. "He was like a drug to her. He used her spirit to feed his own ego. Don't get me wrong, I think he loved her. I even think he was faithful to her, which was something he wasn't known for. But if the marriage had lasted for decades, instead of a few years, I'm not sure how she would've ended up."

David glanced at the side yard where his daughter threw a ball to Jack. Rocky and Gus circled the boy's legs. Love. Pride. Fierce protection. All those emotions flashed across David's face until he glanced back at Andrew.

"So, Andrew, what kind of man are you? Do you tend the garden? Or do you pick flowers?"

How did a man respond to that?

*I'd love to tend her garden for years to come.*

He couldn't say that without sounding perverted. Hands resting on both legs, Drew leaned forward.

"Gabrielle is an intelligent and resourceful woman. She is brilliant in business and doesn't need any man to support her. I hope I can prove to her I am a worthy partner. The fact is I'm desperate for her to be a permanent part of my life. But I can't rush her. If I do, I'll lose her."

"What kind of partner?" Pierre questioned. "Everyone knows she is wealthy. Are you hoping to cash in on her money?"

Andrew roared with laughter.

Pierre pointed his pipe at him. "This is no laughing matter, son. We are here to make sure you have my granddaughter's best interests in mind."

Andrew choked back the last of his laughter. "Sorry, sir. I own a flourishing veterinary practice. Not to mention I'm independently wealthy from the years I worked on Wall Street. I don't need her money. Heck, I don't even need most of *mine*."

Pierre and David eyed him in disbelief.

"I don't like to talk money, gentlemen, but I will make an exception in order to put your minds at ease. When I graduated veterinary school, I set up a trust at the University of Maine. It funds three full-ride scholarships for students interested in pursuing the veterinary sciences. That trust is self-sustaining."

"Hmph." Pierre sat back against his chair and clamped the pipe between his teeth again.

"Like I said, I don't need her money. I just need Gabrielle."

The noise of dogs and child gave a few seconds of warning before Gabrielle and her entourage climbed the steps to the deck.

"Hey, guys," Gabrielle called.

Andrew sucked in a breath at Gabrielle's beauty. She looked like a woodland fairy today. Her hair curled around her shoulders and a cotton sundress flowed around her knees. Her illness had left her slightly gaunt around the eyes and cheekbones, but flushed cheeks promised the return of good health.

"Dad! Look, I found a feather. I told Brie we had to come and show you," Jack exclaimed holding up his prize.

"Brie?" Gabrielle's father questioned.

"He always calls me that, Pop. Jack likes my nickname since he doesn't have one of his own."

Grand-Père surprised them all when he leaned forward. "What kind of feather do you have there, Jack? Come show Grand-Père."

He pronounced Jack the French way: *Jacques*. But the boy brought the feather to him anyway.

Gabrielle glanced at her father and mouthed, "Grand-Père?"

Pierre looked up to find everyone's eyes on him.

"What? I'm so old I could be grand-père to almost everyone in town."

He turned his attention back to Jack.

"Now, Jack. Do you like fishing? Maybe next time, you and your dad can come along on my boat."

Just like that, he was accepted. Andrew doubted it was the money that convinced them. He hoped it was his honesty.

Gabrielle pulled up a chair next to him. Gus appeared at her side and begged for her attention. She sat down and gave the dog a good rub behind his ears. Rocky showed up for his turn, then scampered off to explore. Andrew noticed the slump of fatigue in Gabrielle's shoulders. She still didn't have her stamina back. After a moment, Gabrielle rested her head against the back of the chair and raised her face to the fading sunlight. She closed her eyes.

What a picture she made! All three men froze, spellbound for a moment. How did something so lovely and delicate exist within this realm of men? The sun bathed her hair in a halo of light, and for a moment, she looked like an angel incarnate.

Gabrielle broke the spell by laughing. Her eyes popped open when Gus scooted onto her foot.

She smiled at Andrew. "I guess I'll appreciate this when the cold weather hits. At least I'll always have one warm foot with Gus around."

Andrew marveled at the woman before him. Gabrielle was more relaxed than he had ever seen her, maybe because she was in her family home. It was one more element of her personality he needed to digest.

"What?" She smiled again. "Why're you looking at me like that?"

Andrew linked his fingers through hers. He brought her hand to his lips and kissed the back of it.

"It's good to see you feeling better."

After dinner, Gabrielle and Andrew herded the dogs and child in front of them as they walked out to Andrew's truck. Andrew buckled Jack into his car seat while Gabrielle opened the passenger door. Before she slid onto the seat, she waved to her father and grandfather. A minute later, Andrew started the truck and turned it toward town.

David and Pierre Martin watched Andrew Leland's truck head down the driveway. The setting sun highlighted Gabrielle's profile before the truck turned the corner.

"Qu'est-ce que tu penses?" Pierre asked David. *What do you think?*

"Ils ressemblent comme une famille." *They look like a family.*

"Do you think she'll come around? Or will she push him away?"

"Only God knows the answer to that one."

On the Fourth of July, Andrew pulled into his parents' driveway. He glanced at Gabrielle and smiled with reassurance. They had left the dogs at home since the boat would be full later. Gabrielle got out of the car and took a deep breath. She tried to prepare herself for Andrew's family cookout.

Jack appeared next to her and took her right hand. Gabrielle was surprised by the little boy's sensitivity to her discomfort. When Andrew appeared next to them, Gabrielle looped her free arm through his.

She leaned over and murmured, "Remind me again. You know. Your sisters' names, their kids, etc."

Andrew grinned, his white teeth flashing in the sunshine.

"My older sister is Grace. She's married to Adam Wolfe. They have two kids. Sara is two, and Robbie is six. Grace is a first-grade teacher. Adam is a marine biologist."

"And Eden?"

"Eden is my younger sister. She's an artist. And as far as I know, she's unattached right now. I think you'll like her. I mean, I think you'll like Grace too. But you might have more in common with Eden. Just to warn you, when Grace and Eden get together, they can be a little juvenile. But it's usually in good fun."

The front door of the sprawling cedar shake house opened. Andrew's mother stepped onto the white wrap-around porch and waved them toward the house.

"Grandma!"

Jack released Gabrielle's hand and took off running. He threw himself into Elaine's arms.

Gabrielle glanced at her sundress and hoped she looked okay. When she had questioned him about appropriate attire, Andrew said to go patriotic. She wore a sundress printed with the stars and stripes. The stripes ran at a diagonal, and the blue and white of the stars rested at the neckline of her dress, setting off her blue eyes. Silver sandals completed the outfit. Had she gone overboard?

Gabrielle allowed Andrew to steer her to the porch, where Elaine extended her hug to include both of them.

"Welcome! Welcome! I'm so happy you came today, Gabrielle."

In midhug, Gabrielle caught sight of Elaine's firecracker-shaped earrings, blue shirt, and red-and-white plaid shorts. Phew! Her dress was fine!

Gabrielle smiled. "Thank you for inviting me."

Elaine ushered them inside. They made their way toward the back of the house and into a large kitchen. Three huge picture windows framed a view of the yard, dock, and harbor.

"What a fantastic view!" Gabrielle exclaimed.

Elaine paused beside her.

"Yes! It's my favorite part of the whole house. When we built this house years ago, I insisted on the windows. Think about how much time a mother and wife spends in the kitchen. I wanted a fantastic view to break up the daily drudgery."

Jack stood at one of the windows. He turned to Drew. "Dad, I see Robbie! Can I go out?"

"Sure, kiddo. Just don't go down to the water without an adult."

Elaine picked up a tray with various raw meats on it and handed it to Andrew.

"Here, son. Take this out to your father so he can start grilling. Make sure he doesn't burn every burger he cooks."

"I'll do my best, Mom."

He grinned at their shared joke, then glanced over at Gabrielle.

"She's fine, Andrew. I'm not going to bite. We'll just get these other things and be right out."

Elaine pointed at a pitcher of lemonade and a tray of cups. Gabrielle nodded to Andrew. He left through the sliding door.

"I hope you don't mind, but I wanted to get you alone for a minute before you meet the rest of the family. Once the girls see your dress, I'll never get a chance to talk to you one on one."

Gabrielle looked down at her attire.

"My dress? Is there something wrong with it?"

"It's fantastic. And so chic. You'll put the rest of us to shame."

*It's a sundress. How chic could it be?*

Gabrielle decided not to ask the question out loud.

"Now, Bob tells me I'm quite a whirlwind. He says I'm too nosy, but I have to ask, Are you living with my son?"

Gabrielle laughed in relief. This question was easy to answer.

"Well, I *was* staying with him temporarily while I had the flu and asbestos was removed from my house. Yesterday, once the contractor gave the all clear, I returned home. Drew got the same questions from my family, so I guess you're entitled to ask yours."

Gabrielle eyed Elaine Leland. It would be easy for someone to dismiss her carefree ways and straightforward attitude as a sign of small intellect. But Elaine had shrewd eyes. Gabrielle sensed that only after she gained Elaine's approval would she be accepted by this family.

"Okay. Question number two, and this one is much harder. Do you love my son?"

The pain was instant. Gabrielle's eyes welled up with tears, and she gasped. It stabbed below the solar plexus. It cleaved her in two, yet Gabrielle knew it wasn't physical pain. It was a pain of indecision, a pain rooted in her soul. Elaine reached out and patted her arm.

"What is it, Gabrielle? Why does that question hurt you so much?"

Gabrielle inhaled.

"I want to love him, but it terrifies me. I loved my husband. When he died, I lost half of my soul. I'm not sure I can go through that again. It's much easier to tell myself not to love Drew. But when I do that, I let him and Jack down. What if I can't ever love again? What if I hurt both of them in the process?"

"Oh, my dear girl." Elaine's hand soothed her back. "I think you already love them. Only by surrendering to it will it stop hurting. Once you understand you can't fight love, you'll be free from this torment. Forgive yourself for loving again."

Elaine handed Gabrielle a couple of tissues.

"Drew has never brought a woman home to meet the family before. Not even that good-for-nothing fiancée, who left him when he adopted Jack. He loves you. I'm his mother; I can tell. Just trust the strength of his love. Now, if you need to freshen up, the bathroom is that way. Come outside when you're ready."

Elaine carried the drink tray out to the back deck while Gabrielle found the hall bathroom. She took five minutes to splash cold water on her puffy eyes, then refreshed her makeup. When she opened the door,

Andrew was leaning against the opposite wall, arms across his chest.

He was so handsome in his navy polo and red shorts. His natural tan contrasted against the cream-colored wall behind him, and his sandy hair begged for her fingers to run through it. Desire pooled in her belly. A fantasy of them making love against that wall flashed through her mind.

He advanced slowly.

"Don't look at me like that unless you expect me to take you against the wall right now."

Her eyes widened in surprise.

"I see. We're having the same fantasy," he commented in a neutral tone.

He pulled her against his chest, then claimed her lips. She opened her mouth and let him explore. His tongue was teasing hers when a voice interrupted.

"Holy cow! I'm so sorry to interrupt, but Sara needs to use the potty."

They jumped apart. Gabrielle turned to see a blond-haired woman in the hallway. Grace. Andrew's older sister. It had to be. The woman pointed to the bathroom door. Andrew's two-year-old niece held Grace's hand and shifted from foot to foot. A flush crept up Gabrielle's neck. She turned away in embarrassment.

"Uh. Sorry, Grace. Here, we'll just move out of your way," Andrew replied.

He grabbed Gabrielle's hand and pulled her into the kitchen.

"Thanks." Grace ushered Sara into the bathroom and shut the door.

Gabrielle stood a couple of steps in front of Andrew, her back to him.

"How embarrassing," she murmured. "I haven't even been introduced to her yet, and now your sister probably thinks I'm a slut."

She shook her head. "Me, making out with her brother in the hallway."

Andrew chuckled.

"No. She's probably thinking *payback*. I accidentally walked in on her and Adam in that same hallway a few years back. Similar situation, fewer clothes."

Despite her embarrassment, Gabrielle giggled. "I guess we should head outside."

"Not just yet." Andrew turned her around and pulled her into his arms.

"Why?"

"Because if I walk out there just now, I'll embarrass myself in front of my family."

"Oh."

He smirked. "*Oh*. That's all you have to say?"

"Yep. Pretty much." Gabrielle blushed.

He traced around her cheekbones and then her eyes. His touch was gentle and soothing. After a moment, his eyes turned serious.

"Why were you crying earlier? And don't tell me it was nothing. Did my mother say something to hurt you?"

"No. Not really. She said I was hurting myself."

"You are? How?"

"I need to *give in to love*. Only then will I be free."

Rather than laugh like she expected him to, he paused to consider the statement.

"What do you think? Is she right?" Andrew asked.

"Who *are* you? Dr. Phil?"

"No deflecting, Gabrielle. What do you think?"

Jack appeared inside the slider door.

"Dad. Are you and Brie going to come out and eat?"

Gabrielle turned toward the boy. "We'll be right there, Jack."

Grace and Sara squeezed past them. They took Jack outside with them.

"We should go and join everyone," Gabrielle suggested and started to follow the others.

Andrew grabbed her hand and stopped her.

"Not yet, Gabrielle. I'm not letting you avoid this question. We'll stay here until you give me an answer."

She sighed and ran a restless hand through her hair.

"I think she may be right. I just don't know how to do what she suggests."

Tugging her hand free, Gabrielle slipped out the door.

Later that evening, Grace and Eden rested against a stone wall. They watched Andrew, Gabrielle, and Jack as they played with sparklers.

"What do you think, Grace?" Eden whispered. "Are they sleeping together like everyone says?"

"No."

"No? Why do you say that?"

Grace pushed a blond strand of hair out of her eyes.

"Drew wouldn't be so frustrated right now if he was getting any. Look how he hovers near her but doesn't touch."

"You think she's a cold fish? That's why she won't put out?"

"God, Eden! You can't have it both ways. You can't assume she's loose one moment and a saint the next."

Eden turned green eyes and red curls toward her older sister.

"I don't think she's a slut. I think she's nice. She's coming to my studio next week to see some of my pieces."

The two sisters watched their brother for a while.

Eden picked up the conversation where it left off. "So why don't you think she's a cold fish?"

"I saw them together in the *hallway*."

"You mean *the* hallway. The one Mom and Dad say at least one of us was conceived in?" Eden clarified.

"Ew, Eden. Yeah. That one. The same one Sara was conceived in a few years back when Adam and I were house-sitting for Mom and Dad."

"Ugh. Now it's my turn to be grossed out. Not a picture I needed, Grace."

"Yeah, I know. But there's something about that hallway. It brings out the pheromones or something when you're with *the one*. You haven't experienced it yet, Eden, but someday you might conceive a child in that same hallway."

"Wow! Something to put on my bucket list. *Conceive a child in Mom and Dad's hallway.*"

"Hah. Hah."

"She wasn't immune to him in *the hallway*?"

"No. They both were having the do-it-against-the-wall fantasy when I walked in with Sara to go to the bathroom. I tell you the heat between those two would melt butter."

"It's easy to melt butter, Grace."

"Well, I couldn't come up with a better analogy off the top of my head."

"She spent the whole weekend at his place. Why do you think he's still *frustrated*?"

"I heard she had the flu."

"Do you think she's pregnant?"

"No, silly. I just told you: they aren't doing it. God, Eden. How do I get into these conversations with you? I'm thirty-two years old, but when we talk, it's like I'm in middle school again."

"I'm a people watcher. I like to watch. To wonder. To speculate."

"You need to get a life of your own. Then you won't have to watch other people. What are you? Twenty-five now? Don't you have a boyfriend or something?"

"I've sworn off men for a while, thank you. The last idiot I dated ran off with my rent money."

"I thought you weren't living with anyone," Grace commented.

"I'm not. I wasn't. He took the cash out of my cookie jar while I was changing in the bedroom."

"You keep your rent money in a cookie jar?" Grace's blue eyes shot up in disbelief.

"Hey. It was a good spot. Until Jeff discovered it."

Eden twirled a red curl around her finger. She focused her attention on Gabrielle.

"She looks sad to me."

"Well, her husband died. What do you expect?"

"Wait! Watch, Grace! Look at her looking at Drew when he's not looking. Oh, you know what I mean. She looks like she could eat him up. She's got it bad. She only turns away from him when he looks at her. That is some messed up courtship ritual! What if she breaks his heart?"

For a while, the sisters watched in silence.

Grace bit her nail. "I think she's torn. Torn between the past and the future."

It was almost dusk. Jack went inside with his grandmother to get a sweatshirt before everyone took the boat out to watch fireworks. Gabrielle moved closer to Andrew. She ran her hand up his muscular arm, then stretched up on tiptoe.

Gabrielle whispered in Andrew's ear, "What do you think your sisters are talking about over there? Do you think they wonder what you see in me?"

Andrew chuckled. "No, they're wondering if we're having sex. Especially after you stayed at my house last weekend."

Gabrielle huffed with injured pride. "I had the flu."

"Yeah. But half the town assumes you're pregnant."

"God, don't people have anything better to do?"

He draped an arm across her shoulders and pulled her against him. Gabrielle could smell the masculine scent of him as he rested his chin on her head.

"It's kind of fun to keep them guessing, isn't it?"

"Well, your sisters probably *do* think we're sleeping together."

Drew detected something in her voice.

"Why? Did you have a conversation with them about it earlier?"

"Well, sort of. After lunch, while you were playing tag with Jack, they asked me what I liked best about you."

Andrew pulled back. Curiosity flashed in his eyes.

"What'd you say?"

"I told them I liked your rock-hard butt."

Drew threw his head back and laughed. She giggled up at him.

"What? I thought they knew I was joking. Now I'm not so sure."

He continued to chuckle. "Oh, we're definitely having sex now. You confirmed it for them. Come here, and let's give them something to talk about."

He cupped her face and gave her a tender kiss right in front of his family. Gabrielle was surprised, but she wasn't embarrassed. She kissed him right back and enjoyed it.

Andrew grabbed her hand.

"Come on. Let's go find Jack. Those fireworks won't wait."

# CHAPTER NINE

Gabrielle moved about her room and tossed items into her suitcase. As she packed, Gabrielle thought about her relationship with Drew. The rest of July and August had fallen into a comfortable pattern. She saw Drew and Jack at least twice a week. Every other weekend, they spent Sunday with either her family or the Lelands.

A week after the Fourth of July, Gabrielle visited Eden's studio. Eden Leland, she discovered, was a talented sculptor who worked in a variety of mediums. Before she left, Gabrielle had taken a few of Eden's pieces on consignment and put them in her store. Two of them had already sold.

But now, the warmth of summer was gone, and fall had descended on Jacobs Landing. The September temperatures were colder at night, and it was time for her quarterly trip to France. Gabrielle stopped at the bedroom window and watched leaves swirl in the gusty wind. Normally, she looked forward to her Paris trips but not this time. Gabrielle wished she could stay home. Only two weeks remained until Art Fest, and she was swamped with last-minute details. If she were honest, she would admit she didn't want to leave Drew and Jack. Would the separation put too much strain on their budding relationship?

After a quick glance at her clock, Gabrielle scurried into the adjoining bathroom to collect her toiletries. The car would be here in an hour, and she wasn't quite packed. Thank goodness she had dropped Rocky at Pop's house earlier in the day.

Gabrielle paused in the process of flipping through dresses in her closet. Had she heard the door chime? She flipped through a couple more dresses but paused. There it was again: the chime from the front door. Gabrielle frowned. She didn't have time for interruptions.

On the third chime, Gabrielle hurried down the partially restored main staircase. When she got to the bottom of the stairs, she could see a familiar outline through the stained glass panels of the front door. Drew stood on the front porch.

With a smile of gladness, Gabrielle ushered him into the house. Drew brought the gusty wind inside with him before Gabrielle could latch the door.

"Phew, you haven't left yet." He grinned in relief.

"Why? Did something come up? Is Jack okay?" Gabrielle bit her lip.

Drew shook his head and stroked her cheek. "Everything's fine. I just needed to see you one more time before you go."

She grabbed his hand and pulled him toward the stairs. "The car service will be here in less than an hour, so you better come upstairs and talk to me while I finish packing."

"Upstairs." He wiggled his eyebrows. "I've never been allowed upstairs before."

Gabrielle pulled him after her. "Come on, silly. I'm going to be late if I don't get the rest of my stuff packed."

He followed her down the long hallway and paused in the doorway of her bedroom.

"Well, it's not what I expected from one of Paris's fashion icons. Plain bed. 1970s floral wallpaper. Wood floor in need of refinishing," Drew commented.

Gabrielle grimaced. "I know. It's old and dated, but I haven't had a chance to renovate the master yet. Getting a functional kitchen, and a working HVAC system, was priority. I've only lived here for a year. There's decades of neglect—and bad decorating—to make up for."

"I wasn't criticizing, Gabrielle. Somehow I always pictured you in a lavish boudoir with gilt furniture and satin bedding."

She pushed past him and headed toward her closet.

"That's my Paris apartment. In my other life," she called over her shoulder and grinned, before disappearing inside.

In her closet, Gabrielle flipped through more clothing, choosing outfits and formal wear for her weeklong trip. The screech of metal hangers against the iron rod grated on her nerves, but she didn't have time to slow down.

"Big enough suitcase?" Andrew called from the bedroom.

She stuck her head out the door.

"I know. It takes up one whole side of the bed, but it's the one I usually take." At his raised eyebrows she chided him, "Come on, Drew. Don't stereotype me. I'm usually in Paris for at least a week, sometimes more. My schedule during that time barely gives me time for a bathroom break, let alone laundering clothes."

Gabrielle rushed back into the closet and resumed her scraping. When she came out of the closet, several hangers in hand, Drew had paused in front of her suitcase. A black bustier and matching garter belt dangled from one finger. A vein ticked in his jaw. He swallowed once.

"What do you need these for?" he ground out.

Ah, crap. She didn't have time for this.

Gabrielle grabbed the lingerie out of his hand and shoved it back into the suitcase. "I'm trying to pack here, not *unpack*. What were you doing going through my stuff anyway?"

When she glanced up, the vein had popped out even farther. His eyes were steely, but otherwise he exuded control. What would happen if he ever lost that temper?

Gabrielle dumped the extra clothes into the suitcase. Now that her hands were free, Gabrielle reached up and stroked Drew's cheek. He flinched away from the contact.

"Don't be angry, Drew. In your eyes, that bustier is for bedroom play. In the world of fashion, it's just underwear. The bustier is great because many of my gowns are strapless or halter style. By wearing it, I don't have to worry about bra straps showing or a little belly pudge."

"And the garter belt?" There was no inflection in his tone.

"It keeps my pantyhose up. I wear them for sixteen-plus hours a day. But if I wear the garter belt, I don't have to hike them up every fifteen minutes. It's all about utility."

"Hmph."

"Now you sound like Grand-Père. I think you're picking up some of his bad habits."

Drew slumped onto the side of the bed. Gabrielle inched closer to him and ended up in his lap. She placed a peck on his stiff lips, then pulled back.

"Seriously, Drew. Do you think I could manage another man? Half the time, I completely mess things up between *us*. If I were to wear that bustier for any man, it would be you. I swear."

His hands gripped Gabrielle's upper arms. "Once I saw that bustier, I thought maybe you had someone in Paris. And that's why you always pull back from me, the reason you don't want to make love with me."

She gave a half laugh. "What makes you think I don't want to make love with you?"

He raised an eyebrow sardonically. "I don't know, maybe because we've never actually made love, despite my multiple attempts to let you know I'm interested?"

"Drew, can I be blunt with you?"

He grunted. "I thought we *were* being blunt. But if you need to be *more* blunt, go for it."

Gabrielle took a shaky breath. "Every time I'm in the same room with you, I want to get naked with you.

You make me tingle in all the right places, and I haven't felt that with any other man."

"Except Jean-Luc?"

"With Jean-Luc it was different, but let's not talk about him. I'm talking about you. About us."

"*Let's not talk about Jean-Luc?* When have you ever pushed your dead husband out of the conversation?"

"I'm doing it now. Right now." She swiped a hair out of her face with frustration. "I haven't pursued lovemaking with you because I know the minute we do make love, everything changes. We're still getting to know each other. It's easier when sex doesn't cloud things. Lovemaking is just that for me. It's a commitment and a promise, not just a release of bodily urges."

She sighed and skimmed his lips with her fingertips.

"I'm not quite ready for that commitment. But I think I'm getting closer. I do know I'm going to miss you and Jack like crazy."

Andrew released a sigh and ran his hands down her face, then through her hair. He pulled her against him for a searing kiss that stole her breath.

When he pulled back, he was already talking. "God, I'm going to miss you. Promise me you won't go off to France, find another Frenchman to marry, and leave me and Jack in the dust."

She saw the anxiety in his eyes and tried to lighten the mood. "Well, there's always the president of France. But if anyone else asks, I'll tell him I'm committed back home."

Gabrielle smiled at Andrew and wrapped her hands around his neck. "We've got fifteen minutes to make out before I need to zip those clothes into my suitcase and dash for the door. What do think?"

Gabrielle was on her back before she knew what hit her. He kissed her with a hard urgency. Lying on top of her, Drew braced his weight on his elbows and nudged her legs apart. Even though they had clothes on, his heat branded her. Gabrielle could feel him pressed against her. She moaned and arched her back. He kissed down her neck to her collar bone, then licked the pulse at her throat.

With a hand on the buttons of her blouse, he paused. "Something for me to remember while you're gone?"

She nodded as her breath came in short, quick gasps. The next instant her shirt was open and her bra undone. Drew froze, his gaze fixated on her bare breasts. He swallowed. Once. Twice. When he still didn't move, she wondered if something was wrong.

"Is there a problem?" she breathed.

Hazel eyes gazed at her from unfathomable depths.

"Perfect." He shook his head. "I just needed to make sure I wasn't dreaming. Who has perfect breasts like that? Obviously, you do. I'm the luckiest man in the world."

He bent his head and worshipped each breast. Through his actions, Drew let Gabrielle know how lucky he felt. Gabrielle was in a haze of passion when the doorbell chimed below. She shook her head and tried to gather her thoughts. The doorbell chimed again. Gabrielle nudged Andrew's head.

"Drew."

"Huh?"

"Drew, the doorbell. The car's here."

He raised his head and looked at her without comprehension. His eyes were clouded with passion and need. The doorbell chimed for a third time.

"Ah, shit." He groaned, then slid off her.

Drew pushed himself into a sitting position on the edge of the bed. He panted and tried to calm his raging hormones. Next to him, Gabrielle flung off the remnants of her open shirt and bra. He groaned again at the sight of her nude torso. She grabbed a T-shirt from her suitcase and pulled it over her head.

At the doorway, Gabrielle called over her shoulder, "I'll tell them I need five minutes. Be right back."

When Gabrielle returned to the room, Andrew was still sitting on the edge of the bed. His eyes were closed, and he breathed in and out through his nose. Gabrielle bustled over to her suitcase. She ripped the clothes off the hangers and zipped them inside one of the compartments.

"You okay?" She shrugged into a zip-up sweatshirt and a ran a quick brush through her hair.

"Just give me a minute." He grimaced.

Her toiletry bag thumped into the suitcase. Gabrielle closed the final zipper. Her laptop landed on top of the suitcase. Then her purse. A second later, Gabrielle sensed Drew standing behind her. She turned into his arms.

"Gabrielle…"

She looked up at him and nodded. "I know."

"Come back to me." Drew's hand shook as he caressed her cheeks. Pain and doubt hovered in his eyes.

"I will. Tell Jack that I'll miss him. I want him to call me every other day. Even if it's two a.m., I want to hear from him. To hear from both of you. I promise I won't fall off the face of the earth while I'm in Paris. I'll send you funny pictures, and text messages, just like last time, okay?"

He gave her a crooked smile. "Okay."

The doorbell chimed.

Drew pointed at Gabrielle's suitcase.

"Here. I'll get that for you. You get the rest."

Five minutes later, Gabrielle's limousine pulled away. Andrew hung his head and trudged over to his truck. A cool wind kicked up, and the weak sun went behind a cloud. Gabrielle took the sun with her when she left. Andrew grimaced. He drove back to work, a black cloud hanging over his head.

At eleven o'clock that night, Andrew was reading in bed when a text came in on his phone. Gabrielle had kept her promise. He opened the message and read it.

"Made it to Paris. Imagine how embarrassed I was when I went through customs, realizing I had no bra on. Luckily, it's 5 a.m. here and not too many people around. TTFN."

Drew smiled at the Winnie the Pooh reference. TTFN: ta ta for now. Jack's favorite movie was *Winnie the Pooh*, although Drew imagined he would outgrow it soon.

"Glad to know you're safe. Get some rest. Talk soon."

A minute later, another text came in.

"Oh no, bubba. No rest for the wicked. Costume change at the apartment. Board meeting in 2 hours. Won't sleep again until tonight, Paris time. Kisses."

Andrew shook his head. He wasn't sure how she managed this kind of schedule every three months. Andrew turned to his bedside table and made sure his alarm was set. One day done. One day closer to Gabrielle's return. Curled around a pillow, Andrew fell asleep. It was a poor substitute for the woman he loved.

The next morning, Drew's father was waiting for him when he pulled into the veterinary clinic parking lot. As Andrew got out of his truck, Bob strolled up to him.

"Heard from Gabrielle yet?"

"Yeah. She got in late last night. What's up, Dad? You never track me down at work."

"Well, we've run into some issues with Art Fest. Did Gabrielle talk about the plans with you? We're trying to clarify some things."

"Dad. Just call or text her. She's so organized, she probably has all her notes and plans for Art Fest with her."

"Well, I don't want to bother her if she's in meetings. I know her schedule is over the top while she's in Paris."

"She gave you and Hartwell her contact info, right?"

"Yep."

"Then she's expecting you to call her with questions. Knowing Gabrielle, she'll worry if you don't contact her."

"You sure, Drew?"

"Positive, Dad."

A quick beep signaled an incoming text. Drew looked at his phone. No text. Bob pulled out his phone and touched the screen.

"Well look at that. Your lady just sent me a message asking how Art Fest preparations are going."

Drew smiled.

"See, Dad. I told you she was on top of things. Tell her I'll talk to her tonight."

Andrew entered his building.

On Friday, Gabrielle stood outside one of the boardrooms at the company headquarters. She was on a video call with Jack while he explained his recent trip to the emergency room.

"And Brie, sthee my stitches. Dad had to pick me up in the middle of the day and take me to the hospital because I fell on the playground after Tommy kicked me. I hit my mouth on the slide."

After spending several months with Jack, Gabrielle was getting used to resequencing the order of events in Jack's stories. The scenario made complete sense even if the order he told it in did not.

As Gabrielle watched, Jack flipped up his lip so she could see the stitches inside.

"Sthee?"

"Yep, Jack. I see. I bet it hurt a lot, didn't it?"

Jack shrugged his shoulders in little boy bravado. "Maybe a little. I cried 'cause of the blood."

"Well, you were very brave. I'll have to give it a kiss when I get home."

"When're you coming home, Brie? I miss you."

"I miss you too, Jack. I'll be home soon, maybe even with a present for you."

"A present? Really! What is it?"

"It's a surprise. Tell you what, you call me again tonight. Before bed. I'll read you a story okay?"

"Dad says when we're eating dinner, it's the middle of the night for you."

"That's true. But for you, I would definitely wake up in the middle of the night to read a story. Especially since you were so brave getting stitches today. Now, is your dad there? I'd like to talk to him before I go."

"Yep, here he is."

Jack disappeared, and Drew's face materialized a second later. His skin was gray and haggard.

"Hi. How're you holding up?"

He ran a hand across his eyes. "It's been a day, and it's only ten a.m. When I got the call from his school…"

Drew shook his head.

"Are you going to stay home with him for the rest of the day?"

"Mom said she'd do a better job fussing over him than I will. I think she's just saying that because she knows I've got a surgery scheduled this afternoon. I'll get him a clean change of clothes since there's blood all over his current ones, then drop him at mom's house for the afternoon."

"Madame Levesque," an aide called from the conference room door.

She glanced up to see the squirrelly little man beckoning.

"Madame Levesque, nous sommes prêts," he called again when she didn't answer right away. *We're ready.*

"Un moment, s'il vous plaît. Je viens." she responded, then looked back at Drew. *One moment please, I'm coming.*

"You've got to go, don't you?" he asked with resignation.

"I do. I'm sorry, Drew. I miss you and Jack. I'm sorry you both had a rough morning."

"We miss you too. Do you know when you're coming home yet?"

She hesitated. "We've run into a snag. I probably need to stay into next week."

"Next week." He frowned. "That's right before Art Fest. Are you going to make it back in time for the festival? *You* are the mistress of ceremonies for the awards banquet."

"I'm disappointed, too, but I *will* be home for Art Fest. I promise."

"Good. Because my friend Quentin Shaw will be in town. He's entering one of his pieces in the contest. You might remember him from high school. He was in the same grade as Thomas and me. I'd hoped to reintroduce you guys."

"Madame Levesque!" The aide's tone was more strident this time.

Gabrielle closed her eyes. She prayed for patience. "Un moment."

She shot the aide an impatient look, then turned back to Drew. "I promise to be there for the awards ceremony next Sunday. I can't guarantee anything else right now. I've got to go, honey. Give Jack a hug for me. Don't forget to call me tonight so I can read him his bedtime story."

Gabrielle hung up and pocketed the phone in her blazer. She slipped into business mode and strode into the boardroom.

Back in the United States, Drew gazed at his blank phone screen. She'd hung up on him. He shook his head, then ran his fingers through his hair. Well, at least she had called him *honey*. That was something.

Memories surfaced of those last few minutes in her bedroom before she had left. Another week before they could pick up where they left off. Andrew compressed his lips into a grim line. God, he hated being separated from her.

At the tug on his sleeve, Andrew glanced down at his son.

"I miss her, too, Dad." The little boy leaned his head against Andrew's leg.

Andrew sighed. "Come on, Jack. Let's get you changed. You can stay with Grandma for the rest of the day."

# CHAPTER TEN

The city hall conference room dividers stood open to accommodate the large crowd of Art Fest contestants and their dates. Many people wore tuxedos and evening gowns. The artists stood out in the crowd, their outfits matching the bold styles of their art pieces. It was the first formal event Jacobs Landing had hosted in Andrew's memory.

Across the makeshift ballroom, Drew's father caught his eye, then tapped his watch. Drew nodded and checked his phone again. No message. The awards ceremony started in ten minutes, and Gabrielle wasn't there yet. He looked back at his father and shrugged his shoulders.

When his phone vibrated, Andrew snatched it from his pocket.

"Engine problems with jet. Landed in London. Took commercial flight back to Bangor. Be there in five minutes. Don't worry."

Andrew held up five fingers to let his father know when Gabrielle would arrive. Bob Leland's shoulders relaxed.

At seven o'clock, Andrew stood next to his friend Quentin Shaw. Mayor Hartwell strode onto the stage and thanked everyone for their patience.

"Please find your seats everyone, and we will get started momentarily."

Seconds later, everyone in the crowded room paused. Something drew their collective attention.

"Ho-lee shit," Quentin exclaimed next to him. "Is that Gabrielle Martin? From high school? Wow! How'd she get so hot?"

Andrew's breath caught when he saw Gabrielle glide onto the stage. She wore a filmy black halter dress that hit just above the knee and dipped low in the back. The dress boasted a glittery buckle that emphasized Gabrielle's slender waist. Her hair was piled on top of her head in an elegant updo, and she wore glittering earrings that emphasized her long neck. Desire slammed into him like a freight train. Under it all, he was pretty sure she was wearing that black bustier and garter belt.

Quentin nudged his arm. "Dude, are you okay? You look like someone just kicked you in the nuts."

"Gabrielle and I are dating. I haven't seen her in two weeks."

Quentin shot him a knowing look. "Feeling the absence, are you?"

Drew sent him a quelling look. Quentin turned his dark head back to the stage.

At the podium, Gabrielle greeted everyone. "Good evening ladies and gentlemen. My name is Gabrielle Levesque, and I would like to thank you for participating in our town's first annual Art Fest."

She was a natural. Drew marveled at her ease in front of such a large crowd. As the ceremony progressed, her professionalism and poise never wavered. He was the only one in the room that knew she'd probably been up for more than twenty-four hours. No one else suspected anything amiss because she never gave an impression of fatigue. She was in complete control of the proceedings.

"And now I would like to turn the proceedings over to Mayor Hartwell for the moment we've all been waiting for: the revelation of Art Fest's first winner."

Gabrielle backed out of the spotlight, and Hartwell stepped forward.

"The winner of this year's Art Fest prize is..."

He opened the envelope and pulled out a slip of paper. Hartwell adjusted his reading glasses.

"One of our homegrown alumni, Quentin Shaw, with his piece entitled *Back to Basics*."

Andrew clapped his friend on the shoulder in congratulations. Quentin made his way to the stage to accept the award. After Quentin received the prize check, he shook hands with all the city council members, including Gabrielle. Andrew's eyes narrowed when Quentin leaned in to say something in her ear. Gabrielle's smile shifted, and she glanced out at Andrew in the audience. As their gazes connected, the impact was physical.

Holding his over-sized presentation check, Quentin made his way to the microphone.

"Thank you everyone who voted for my work. Thanks to Jacobs Landing for the prize money and for hosting this event. Now let's get this party started!"

He strode off the stage. On cue, the DJ started up the dance music, and the lights dimmed. Andrew searched for Gabrielle on stage, but she'd disappeared.

Ten minutes later, the first slow song of the night came on. Andrew listened to the chorus and scanned the crowd. A tap on his shoulder drew his attention. He turned, and there was Gabrielle. His Gabrielle.

Before he could say anything, she leaned toward him. "Dance with me, Drew."

She pulled him toward the dance floor. Drew pulled her into his arms. "You're really here. It's been so long," he murmured in her ear.

"Shh, just listen to the song."

She wrapped her arms around his neck and swayed to the music. Andrew held her against his chest and absorbed the feel of her closeness. Gabrielle was in his arms. The world was right again.

"What did Quentin say to you on stage?"

"He told me, 'Drew's a lucky guy,'" she replied. "And I told him I was lucky to have you in my life."

After the song ended, he pulled her out into the quieter hallway. Drew skimmed his hand along her cheek and noted the dark circles nearly camouflaged by make-up. Fatigue hovered in her eyes, turning them to a dark sapphire blue.

"You were fantastic tonight, love. A real pro. I know Dad and the other council members were impressed. Heck, the whole room paused in admiration when you walked in. But when was the last time you slept?"

"Um, maybe two days? Well, except for an hour nap on the flight back. The guy next to me woke me for dinner. I was so tired I didn't want any food. But after he woke me up, I couldn't get back to sleep."

"What's this about your jet having engine problems?"

She sighed and put a shaking hand to her forehead.

"We hadn't been in the air very long when one of the engines died. Since we were already over the English Channel, the pilot chose to land in London for repairs. Because I had to be back here for the ceremony, I paid someone a thousand dollars to take their spot on the next commercial flight from London to New York. I just barely made a connecting flight to Bangor. The car service met me there, then drove me the rest of the way."

"Car service?"

"Yeah. I didn't want to rent a car; I'm too tired to drive."

"Gabrielle!" Hartwell's voice boomed behind them. "Fantastic event! It was a success. And to think, you orchestrated the last-minute preparations from Paris. We were brilliant when we chose you as project manager!"

Andrew and Gabrielle turned to greet the mayor. The rest of the council members moved toward them in his wake. Gabrielle straightened her spine. Boardroom Gabrielle was back in place. She accepted their handshakes and congratulations with her usual charm and humility.

Bob Leland leaned in to murmur in her ear.

"Cutting it close, weren't you, my dear?" He grinned. "You must be dead on your feet. I'll run interference. Why don't we have Drew drive you home?"

Gabrielle gave Drew's father a weary smile. "Thanks, Bob. I think I'll take you up on that offer."

They retrieved Gabrielle's luggage from the small office where the driver had deposited it.

A few minutes later, Andrew parked his sports car in Gabrielle's driveway. He came around to the passenger side. When Gabrielle stood up, her legs shook from fatigue. He took the keys from her hand.

"Here, I'll open the house for you."

Inside, Andrew dropped Gabrielle's luggage in the mudroom, while she made her way up the back stairs. He did a thorough check of the whole house to make sure it was safe. As Drew climbed the stairs to her bedroom, his pulse accelerated in anticipation. They could finally pick up where they left off two weeks ago.

At Gabrielle's bedroom door, Drew paused. His shoulders slumped at the scene before him. Gabrielle lay passed out on the bed, her foot bent up behind her in an awkward position. One hand was on her shoe, as if she had fallen asleep in the process of unbuckling it.

Drew pawed through her dresser drawers, until he found an oversize T-shirt that looked comfortable. Mouth clamped in a straight line, he began to undress her. It was agony to run his hands up her legs and unhook her stockings.

Self-loathing gnawed his gut; he was aroused over a sleeping woman. Despicable. Throughout the process of undressing Gabrielle, he gritted his teeth and worked as fast as he could. When he reached the black bustier, he tossed the T-shirt on the bed next to Gabrielle in surrender. The bustier clinched it. He could go no further. He couldn't trust himself.

"Gabrielle." He shook her shoulder. "Gabrielle?"

"Mmm." She sighed and rolled away from him.

Dammit! He was not a saint.

Andrew scooted Gabrielle into a more comfortable position, then threw a blanket over her. The bustier and garter belt were her problem. If he stayed in the room a minute longer, he was afraid instinct would take over.

Andrew stomped down the back stairs. He pulled the locked door shut and trudged out to the car that was as black as his mood.

On Monday, tension still remained coiled throughout Drew's shoulders and rested in his stomach. Was it sexual frustration? Disappointment? Drew didn't know, but if he didn't get some air, he was afraid his usually contained temper would erupt. He left the clinic at lunch and strode down to the new Saltwater Café. The owner of the café was the same renter Gabrielle had met right after their first date.

While Andrew sat in a booth and picked at his sandwich, his sister, Grace, slid onto the seat across from him.

"Why so glum, sugarplum?"

She snatched one of his fries and ate it.

"Don't you have children to tend to or a class to teach?" Drew grumbled.

"I'm taking a personal day. Adam and I are working on baby number three. We thought today would be a good day."

"Ugh. Not something I needed to know, Grace."

"Why? Because I'm getting some, and you're not?"

He smiled grimly at her. "You're not getting any either. You're here talking to me. Where's your husband by the way?"

"He worked a half day, so we're meeting at home after he gets out of work."

Grace grabbed another one of his fries and popped it into her mouth.

"You sure you're not already pregnant? You keep eating my fries."

Grace's smile held a mysterious air. She swallowed. "Could be. Why're you so down? Didn't Gabrielle get back last night? I thought you would've had a big romantic reunion or something."

"Thought so too," he mumbled.

"Ooooh. What happened? Did she say, 'No way Jose'? Or did she get mad at you and kick you out of her house?"

"What's with all the rhyming today? You're driving me nuts." Andrew rubbed his forehead, then murmured, "She fell asleep."

"Fell asleep?" Grace snickered.

"Yeah. I took her home and checked her house to make sure there wasn't anyone lurking about. When I got upstairs, she was dead to the world. I mean, I understand, because she hadn't slept in days…"

"But your body didn't understand. Which is why you're grouchy today," Grace finished for him.

"You know, you're really annoying."

"That's what big sisters are for. Whoa, look at the time! I need to get going if I'm going to beat Adam home."

She stood and rested her hand on his shoulder.

"Hang in there, little brother. Things are changing between you and Gabrielle. I can see it."

Drew hung his head. "Changing for the better? Or for the worst?"

"Absolutely for the better. You'll see."

She kissed his cheek and disappeared out the café door. Andrew paid his bill, then wandered back to work.

Gabrielle woke around three in the afternoon. She showered, then slipped into comfortable jeans and her favorite soft sweater; it was the shade of periwinkles. Around four o'clock, she threw in a load of laundry and puttered in the kitchen.

Seated on a stool at her kitchen island, Gabrielle jotted a grocery list and tried to shake off the fuzziness of jet lag. Usually, jet lag didn't hit her so hard, but then she normally slept in the bed on the jet. She was spoiled. She knew it. Most people had to take commercial flights all the time and deal with the jet lag that followed.

Gabrielle arched her stiff back and admired her brand-new kitchen. Custom white cabinets, high-end appliances, it couldn't get any better. She was happy, she realized. Even if every muscle ached with a dull throb and her head felt like it was stuffed with cotton. Earlier, she called and asked Pop if she could pick Rocky up in the morning. Her reflexes were still lethargic, so she didn't trust herself to drive.

At five o'clock, Gabrielle threw some cheese and crackers on a plate and returned to the island to eat her makeshift dinner. A knock on her back door caught her attention. Drew stood on her back porch. She waved and came over to unlock the door.

"Hi." She smiled. "I was just having cheese and crackers. Want some?"

"No, thanks. I've got to pick up Jack in half an hour, but I wanted to stop by and check on you. You were out cold when I left."

Gabrielle detected an edge to his voice. "I know, I'm sorry. I can't believe I passed out like that. Thanks for tucking me in and locking up when you left."

Drew prowled around her kitchen. He touched a dish towel and eyed the coffee maker. He fidgeted with an empty fruit bowl on the counter. Why was he so restless?

He paused in front of the stove and stared blankly at the professional range hood. Gabrielle pushed away from the doorframe and came up behind him. She wrapped her arms around his waist and rested her head against his back. Tension drained out of Drew's shoulders.

"I missed you," she murmured against his back.

Drew turned, pulled her into his arms, and possessed her mouth. Before she registered his actions, Drew lifted Gabrielle into a sitting position on the island and wedged himself between her legs. His hands and mouth were everywhere.

"When I saw the black bustier and garter belt last night…" he murmured against her neck.

"Yes?"

"I about lost it, Gabrielle. Even though you were sound asleep, all I wanted to do was tear them off and bury myself inside you. My control was that close to snapping."

Based on the frantic movements of his hands, Gabrielle was pretty sure his control was in the same condition right now. Physically, he had always been patient with her, but today he was wild with need. Her pants were already unzipped, and his hands were under her sweater.

"Make love with me, Gabrielle. Put me out of my misery." He breathed into her neck.

Drew bombarded her senses with his mouth and his hands. Even his scent filled her nostrils. Gabrielle froze in panic. Jean-Luc had used his sexual experience to overwhelm her with physical passion. He had seduced her before she was ready. That wouldn't happen again.

"I can't," she croaked.

Drew's body went rigid. Hazel eyes glittered at her. "What do you mean you can't?"

"I want to, but I'm just not ready yet."

Andrew turned his back to Gabrielle.

"When do you think you might be ready?" he ground out.

"I don't know, Drew. I think I'm getting closer, but I'm not sure. You're ready to pick up where we left off two weeks ago. I'm trying to clear the jet-lag-induced cotton from my head."

With barely controlled fury, Drew snatched his coat from the stool where he had left it. He strode to the door.

Gabrielle's rare temper flared. Hopping off the counter, she grabbed his arm.

"I'm sorry," she replied with a sarcastic undertone. "I don't put out whenever you have the urge."

Instantly, she regretted her words.

Drew paused. Then his control snapped. He grasped her shoulders and held Gabrielle against the side of the refrigerator. His face was inches from hers.

Gabrielle's heart pounded in her ears. Even though she knew Drew would never physically hurt her, his anger was magnificent in its intensity.

When he spoke, the quiet tone was unsettling. "You said making love was a promise. A commitment, right?"

"Yes," she breathed.

"Well, that's what I want. It's not just about the sex. You keep me dangling after you, occasionally meting out affection, like I'm some puppy. Well, I'm through with that. I want the commitment. Show me you're as committed to this relationship as I am."

Gabrielle bit her lip.

Releasing her, he stepped back and ran his fingers through his hair. He paced back and forth, then stopped in front of her.

"I'm in love with you!" Drew roared. "I have been. Ever since the first day you brought Rocky into my office. Maybe even before that."

Her face jerked up in shock. Gabrielle registered the desperation in his eyes.

Drew cupped her elbows. "I want the whole package, Gabrielle. I want to marry you, make babies with you, grow old with you. Don't you feel any of those things for me?"

"I care about you..." she began.

"I don't want *care about*, Gabrielle. I want you to love me as desperately as I love you."

She was not ready for marriage. Not yet. She resented the way he continued to push her.

"You keep saying you won't rush me. But every time we're together, you ask for more than I'm ready to give," Gabrielle accused.

Drew loosened his grip on her elbows and stepped back.

"You know what I think? I think you love me, but you're too terrified to acknowledge it. If you ever find the courage to face love, find me. Maybe Jack and I'll still be around."

He had the back door open when she called out, "Drew wait."

Gabrielle rushed to him and pushed a package into his hand.

"Here. It's the gift I promised Jack."

With disgust, he snatched up the package and stomped out the door.

Gabrielle moved to one of the front windows and watched Andrew Leland climb into his truck. In an abnormal display of recklessness, he gunned the engine as he took off. Gabrielle slid down to the floor and gave into tears of fatigue and sorrow.

# CHAPTER ELEVEN

A week later, Gabrielle slumped in one of the Adirondack chairs at the dog park. Shirley and Ralph were there again with their Saint Bernards, Lenny and Squiggy. The couple kept up a lively chatter while Gabrielle watched Rocky sniff a nearby post.

He raised his head. Woofed. Then took off. Following the dog with her eyes, Gabrielle saw familiar figures approaching from the parking lot. She had just enough time to brace herself, before a black Lab threw his weight against her leg and a little boy threw himself into her arms.

"Brie! I missed you so much!" Jack hugged his little body against hers.

Gabrielle closed her eyes and inhaled his little boy scent of paste, sand, and sweat. She snuggled him and cleared her throat.

"I missed you too, Jack. Did you get the gift I brought you?"

Out of the corner of her eye, she saw Drew. He leaned against the farthest post of the pavilion, clad in a tweed fisherman's sweater and jeans. He refused to make eye contact. Instead, he stared out over the dog park.

"I did! A Formula One toy race car. Brie? Why're you crying?"

"I'm just happy to see you, Jack," she croaked.

She felt Drew's eyes on her, but when she looked up, he glanced away. At least he didn't plan to keep Jack away from her. For half an hour, Gabrielle visited and played with Jack and Gus. Drew remained at his post, his face impassive.

After a while, Drew called out, "Jack, say your good-byes. It's time to go."

Jack threw his arms around her neck in a quick boy hug. "Bye, Brie. You're coming to my Halloween parade, aren't you? I'm going to be a superhero. You *have* to see my costume."

Gabrielle glanced up at Drew and asked permission with her eyes. He stared back at her.

*It's your call.*

"Sure, Jack. I'll come. I wouldn't miss it."

"Cool! It's the Friday before Halloween, at one o'clock."

Drew called dog and boy over to him. They left the park. Part of Gabrielle's heart went with them.

Shirley patted her arm. "Did you two have a spat, dear?"

"You could say that."

"Well, don't worry. Every relationship has its rough patches. You'll find a way to smooth things over."

Gabrielle gave her a bleak smile. "Thanks, Shirley. I hope so."

The day before Halloween, Gabrielle arrived at Jack's school fifteen minutes before the parade started. She stood in the gym doorway and looked for a place to sit in the already crowded room. Next time, she would arrive earlier. If there was a next time.

She spotted Elaine and Bob wedged onto some bleachers. Gabrielle ambled over to them.

"Gabrielle, come sit by us. We've got great seats, and you'll be able to see Jack better," Elaine suggested.

Before she could answer, Drew appeared and slid onto the bench next to his mother. He refused to meet Gabrielle's eyes.

"Um, no thanks, Elaine. It's already crowded. I'll just stand against the wall by the other late arrivals."

"Well, don't forget to look for Robbie too. He's dressed as a dinosaur. Grace should be leading her own class of first graders. Not sure what her costume will be but she's always so creative. Isn't that right, Drew?"

Drew nodded and stared straight ahead. Gabrielle gave Drew's parents a weak smile, then edged over to the nearest wall.

For the next half hour, she watched children file past in a variety of colorful costumes. They waved to parents, grandparents, and younger siblings. When Jack caught sight of Gabrielle, he waved and raised his plastic hammer to show off his muscles. Robbie's costume was *not* the typical fuzzy dinosaur. Somehow, Grace and Adam had constructed Robbie's costume to look like it had actual scales.

Grace smiled at Gabrielle when she walked past with her class. She was dressed as the Tooth Fairy, complete with actual toothbrushes strung on a necklace. Gabrielle detected a note of sympathy in Grace's eyes.

After the parade, Gabrielle pulled her purse strap onto her shoulder and turned to leave. Elaine touched her shoulder.

"Gabrielle, everyone goes back to the kids' classrooms now. We watch the Halloween parties. It's a lot of fun."

"Oh. Well, I should get going."

"He'll be disappointed if you don't show up," Drew rumbled behind her. "Or are you afraid to *commit* too much time?"

Bob and Elaine glanced at their son, surprised at his barbed comment. Drew ignored them. His eyes drilled into Gabrielle's.

Her throat went dry with hurt and anger. Gabrielle raised her chin a notch.

"I'll stop in for a few minutes, but then I need to get back to the store."

Leaning against the wall in Jack's classroom, Andrew paid marginal attention to the Halloween festivities. Most of the time, he watched Gabrielle. When she gave Jack a high five after he won a prize, Andrew's hands ached to touch her. To hold her. This separation was tearing him apart.

Since their argument, his anger had cooled enough to think more objectively. In some ways, Gabrielle was right. He had pushed her. He couldn't help himself.

Now that he knew Gabrielle was the one for him, the instinct to make her his mate was strong. Primitive. If they lived in a different century, he would kidnap her, marry her, and deal with the repercussions later.

Andrew frowned. He suspected Jean-Luc was the culprit for Gabrielle's reluctance. Was it because she still mourned her husband? What if Jean-Luc had manipulated Gabrielle into a relationship? After all, Gabrielle had been much younger than Jean-Luc. Perhaps Jean-Luc had done the equivalent of emotionally kidnapping her? Could that be the reason she pulled back from Andrew when he got too intense?

Damn. He had made a mess of things. How was he to repair their relationship without pushing her? Andrew grimaced as he thought about his snide comment in the gym. The first step would be to stop insulting her.

As Andrew watched, Gabrielle gave Jack a quick hug and waved at Andrew's parents. She slipped her purse strap over her shoulder, then headed to the classroom door. Gabrielle glanced at Drew over her shoulder; hurt and anger flashed in her eyes. She was gone.

Andrew rubbed at the tightness in his neck. Pride warred with need. His pride told him she needed to come to him. His need urged him to do anything to repair their relationship.

"Looks like you're in a tough spot, son," his father murmured next to Andrew.

"You could say that, Dad."

"What're you going to do to fix it?"

"Hell if I know. I can't seem to figure anything out right now."

"In my experience, flowers work pretty well. That and a sincere apology."

"I think it's going to take a lot more than flowers, Dad. Besides, part of me thinks she should be the one to apologize."

Bob Leland laughed and clapped a hand on his son's shoulder.

"You've got a lot to learn, son. You want to smooth things over, you apologize first."

Six o'clock. Her alarm clock glowed with the time when Gabrielle checked it on Halloween morning. Gabrielle lay in bed thinking over her encounter with Drew the day before. She chafed at his accusation. Was she too much of a coward? Is that why she couldn't commit to him and Jack?

She climbed out of bed and wandered over to her vanity. When she opened her jewelry box, the weak light from the windows illuminated the chain strung with the two wedding bands. Gabrielle flopped onto the vanity stool and took the rings off the necklace. She slipped her own ring onto her finger, then put Jean-Luc's over her left thumb.

She waited to feel *something*. Sadness. Nostalgia. Something. Gabrielle only felt the pinch of her old wedding band, like it no longer fit. Had she gained weight? No. She'd lost weight since Drew stormed out of her life.

Wryly, she pulled off both rings. She put them back in her jewelry box. The wedding band Jean-Luc gave her chafed now. If Gabrielle were a psychoanalyst, she would point out the significance of this revelation. Was she ready to put Jean-Luc to rest?

Unable to sleep, Gabrielle figured she might as well go to the shop and get some bookwork done. She dressed in her normal Saturday work attire: jeans, button shirt, and comfortable shoes. She and Rocky ate an early breakfast, then left for work.

In the back alley of the shop, Gabrielle let Rocky out the passenger door of her SUV. A noise drew her attention to the door of Phyllis's private lobby. The door opened, and her father stepped out of the entrance to the upstairs apartment. Phyllis stood in the doorway. She wore a fuzzy blue robe.

"Pop?" she asked in surprise. "What're you doing here?"

David caught sight of her and flushed. Gabrielle had never seen her father embarrassed before.

"Phyllis and I have been keeping company for a while now."

"You and Phyllis?" she asked in disbelief.

"I'll not answer to you, girl. I'm still your father." David pointed a finger in her direction.

Phyllis put a hand to her throat in distress.

To their surprise, Gabrielle laughed. "I think it's fantastic you've found each other. It just took me by surprise. Well, I've got work to do. You go ahead and do... whatever you were going to do before I got here."

Gabrielle entered the back room and shut the door behind her. She giggled as she made her way to the small office where she placed orders and kept the books. Her father had a girlfriend. It was Phyllis. There was still hope for love.

Later in the morning, Gabrielle sighed. There was finally a lull in the Saturday influx of customers. By silent agreement, she and Phyllis didn't discuss the early-morning scene outside Phyllis's door.

Gabrielle stuck to professionalism so she wouldn't embarrass her manager.

"Phyllis, why don't you grab a quick lunch now that business has died down? Once you get back, I'll take mine."

Phyllis nodded. "All right, hon. See you in a while."

After Phyllis left, Gabrielle leaned over the front window display and repositioned some of the discounted Halloween merchandise. Elaine Leland entered the store.

"Hi, Elaine. What can I help you with?"

"Gabrielle, you know I don't mince words, right?"

Gabrielle nodded.

"What is going on with you and my son? You're both moping around and avoiding each other. We haven't seen you at a family gathering since you left for France. I can't get any answers out of Andrew, so I'm coming to you."

Help. Gabrielle searched for Phyllis, but she'd already left the store. Great. She had to deal with Andrew's mother on her own.

Gabrielle shrugged her shoulders in a defensive gesture and steered Elaine to the back of the store.

"Drew pushed me too hard. He wanted a commitment I wasn't ready to make."

"You broke up with him." Elaine nodded in resignation.

"No, I didn't break up with him. He told me to find him when I was ready to commit. So in a way, Drew broke it off."

Gabrielle chewed her bottom lip, then inhaled a steadying breath. "Drew said he and Jack might not be around by the time I made up my mind."

Elaine frowned.

"Sorry. I'm not trying to complain about your son. You asked what happened."

"Well, I'll tell you what I told Drew. You've both made a mess of my wedding plans. I was hoping to plan one for next spring," she teased.

Elaine patted her hand. "It looks like you need to iron some things out between you. Just remember, you can't work things out if you don't talk to each other. I've got to be on my way. I still need more candy from the store for trick-or-treaters. We always run out. Are you coming to our house to see the kids in their costumes?"

Gabrielle hung her head. "I don't think so, Elaine. I can't come over, yet. I'm not ready to give Drew the answer he wants."

"I understand. Don't stay away too long, okay?" Elaine squeezed Gabrielle's hand.

A week later, the November wind followed Drew as he finished his Saturday errands. A quick check of his watch showed he had an hour to kill until Jack's playdate ended. He parked his truck in front of the Saltwater Café and sat down at a booth inside. Andrew ordered a hamburger from the waitress, then settled back to wait.

He was taking the first bite of his burger when a dark shadow settled into the seat across from him. What the hell? He looked up and almost choked.

With muscular arms crossed in front of his chest, Thomas Martin scowled. Drew had only talked to Thomas a few times since high school, but he did *not* have to guess why Thomas chose today to renew their acquaintance.

"Hello, Thomas." Andrew finished chewing. "What can I help you with?"

"What's up with you and my sister? Pop and Grand-Père tell me you don't bring Jack around anymore. They say Gabrielle shows up at family meals thinner and sad."

Why did everyone corner him in this café? He needed to stop coming here.

"Well?" Thomas raised an eyebrow.

"I gave her an ultimatum. One I'm beginning to regret," he answered quietly.

Thomas gave a low whistle. "Tactical error on your part, dude. Brie doesn't let anyone tell her what to do. How do you think she survived growing up with three New England men?"

Andrew groaned.

"Yeah. The last time any of us tried to influence her decisions, she married a Frenchman and moved to Europe."

At Thomas's revelation, a rock sank in Drew's gut. However, he dug in with natural stubbornness. "I need her to come to me this time, Thomas. I have to stand my ground and wait for her to realize she belongs with me."

"It's a calculated risk." Thomas stood and gave him a light punch on the shoulder. "Good luck. I hope it works out for you."

Having said his piece, Thomas wound his way across the room. Several ladies in the café shot admiring glances at Thomas's wavy hair and muscular frame. There was a collective sigh after Thomas slipped out the door.

It was Thanksgiving week. Gabrielle took time off from the store to visit Eden's loft for more of her sculptures. She had only been to Eden's loft one other time, but Gabrielle loved its eclectic furniture, bold colors, and creative accents. At the outside door, she pushed the buzzer on the intercom.

"Yes?"

"Hi, Eden. It's Gabrielle."

A minute later, the door popped open, and Gabrielle entered the building. At the top of the stairs, Gabrielle knocked on a dingy beige door. It was obvious Eden wasn't allowed to paint it; otherwise she was sure Eden's apartment door would reflect the occupant's personality. The door swung open, and Drew's flame-haired sister waved her inside.

"Gabrielle! Come in! It's so good to see you!"

"The store sold your last sculpture yesterday, so I thought I'd bring your commission check. Do you have any more pieces for me to look at?"

Gabrielle handed Eden an envelope, which the artist tucked into her jeans pocket.

"Sure, come on in. I can't believe you've sold three of my pieces already. Before you came along, I only sold the occasional piece online."

The room was multifunctional. Half of it was living space with a small galley kitchen and a doorway off to the left. Gabrielle assumed it led to a bedroom and bath. To the right lay a cozy sitting area with an industrial-style coffee table.

Closest to the windows was Eden's studio. She worked in a variety of mediums, but her current project was made of wood. A partially finished sculpture stood on the workbench in the far corner.

"Oh! Eden, can I take a look?"

"Sure."

Gabrielle was already at the workbench. She examined the swirled grain of the wood. The base was one solid piece that separated into two branches and then grew into one piece again at the top. Eden had already carved the two separated parts into stylistic forms of a man and a woman. At the top, the man and woman entwined in an embrace. It was sensual in its simplicity.

Gabrielle sighed. It was perfect.

"I've still got to finish sanding it, adding a few basic details, and then varnishing it. What do you think?"

"I love it. It reminds me of—"

"You and Drew?" a voice interrupted behind her.

Gabrielle spun around to see Andrew's other sister leaning against the kitchen counter.

"Grace! I didn't know you were here! I shouldn't interrupt your *sister time*." She turned to Eden. "I can come back and look at your pieces another time. Don't sell that one, okay?"

Eden motioned to the sitting area. "Why don't you stay for a while? Grace just stopped by to show me something. Right, Grace?"

At her sister's not-too-subtle prompting, Grace held out a piece of paper. "Look, Gabrielle."

Gabrielle took the piece of paper and realized it was a photo. Actually, it was an ultrasound picture.

"Oh! You're pregnant."

Tears pooled in Gabrielle's eyes as she gathered Grace in an impulsive hug. "I'm so happy for you!"

Grace hugged her back.

"I'm due at the beginning of March. Why're you crying, Gabrielle?"

"I...don't...know," Gabrielle sobbed.

Grace patted her. "Sure, you do."

"I'm crying, because..." Gabrielle took a hiccup-style breath.

"Because why?" Eden prompted.

"Because I miss him."

Gabrielle sniffed and pulled a tissue from her pocket. "You two are the closest I can get to him right now."

Eden threw her arms around both Gabrielle and Grace. It was the ultimate group hug. Gabrielle began to weep all over again. They held on to each other in that little circle, lending support. In that moment, Gabrielle realized what it was to have sisters.

Once her tears subsided, Grace urged Gabrielle down on the couch. Eden shoved a cup of tea into Gabrielle's hand.

"I don't know if you like tea or not, but Mom always gives us a cup of tea when we're upset."

Grace slid onto the couch next to Gabrielle.

"We miss you at family gatherings. Drew sits around like a shadow. He either refuses to talk to us, or he bites everyone's head off. He has even been short a couple of times with Jack, which isn't like him. With Jack, he is always patient. We're worried about the two of you. From the looks of it, neither of you are happy apart."

Eden chimed in. "Mom says you told her Drew tried to push you into a commitment of some sort. Don't get me wrong, we're not gossiping about you—well, not too much anyway. We just want everyone to be happy."

Gabrielle sighed. "Drew wants the whole package. Marriage. Family. Babies. Everything. I'm not sure I can do that yet."

"Did he tell you he *loved* you?" Eden stressed the word like an elementary student.

"More like, he roared it. He screamed it at me before he stomped out of my house. How was I supposed to answer that?" Gabrielle sniffed with injury to her feminine sensibilities.

Grace tapped her chin in thought. "You know what Drew's problem is? He hasn't had to work too hard for anything. Any girl he wanted fell in line. He amassed a fortune on Wall Street and made it through vet school in record time. You're his first real challenge, I think."

Eden twisted a red curl around her finger. "Do you think it's your first husband? You know, the reason you're not ready to commit to Drew?"

"Eden," Grace reproached.

Gabrielle thought for a moment. "It could be part of it. I'm also terrified."

With mirrored looks of surprise, Eden and Grace listened as Gabrielle continued. "I lost my first husband in a car accident. It almost destroyed me. The sheer pain was crippling. I barely ate. Or slept. Or moved. Especially after I found out I wasn't pregnant." She took a shaky breath. "If that were to happen again, I'm not sure I'd survive it."

Grace hugged a pillow to her tummy and leaned forward. "What was Jean-Luc Levesque like? Maybe if you talk about him, you know, the happy memories, it'll help."

Gabrielle hesitated.

Eden took up the line of conversation.

"All the papers said he was compelling. Was that what attracted you to him?"

Gabrielle thought of Jean-Luc and the way it felt to be with him: the absolute exhilaration of having his complete attention focused on you. How could she describe it to someone who had never met him?

"Have either of you ever ridden a roller coaster?" Gabrielle asked after a moment.

When they both nodded, she continued, "You know that feeling at the top of the loop, breath held, anticipation in your belly, adrenaline racing through your veins?"

Red and blond heads bobbed again in agreement.

"Well, that was Jean-Luc. Life with him was like that. All keyed up and alive."

Silence reigned in the room while each woman thought about the analogy.

Grace reached over and took Gabrielle's hand. "How would you describe your relationship with Drew?"

Gabrielle chewed her lip. "If we're sticking with the roller-coaster analogy?"

Eden and Grace nodded their encouragement.

"Drew's the ground."

Their eyes shot up in surprise.

"I know that sounds unflattering, but hear me out. I am *terrified* of roller coasters. My brother used to make me ride them when we were younger. When you're at the top of the loop, you're always anticipating the fall. It's exhilarating, but it's also nerve racking because you know that the drop is inevitable. The ground is safe. On the ground, I know where I stand. The ground is where you always want to return."

"Drew's the ground." Eden sighed.

Grace sat back and patted her pillow-covered tummy.

"Drew's the ground." A slight smile touched the corners of her mouth.

All three women mulled over that revelation for a few moments.

"I know!" Eden jumped to her feet and pointed at Gabrielle.

"You need a symbolic gesture. The experts say it's necessary when they talk about grief. A way to find closure. For some people, it's taking a trip they were supposed to take with their loved one. For others, it's donating the loved one's clothes. On TV, one person said she planted a tree—"

"Really, Eden," Grace interrupted.

"No. Seriously. Gabrielle, maybe you can't commit to Drew because you haven't said the final goodbye."

"*The final goodbye?* Eden, you've been watching too much daytime television." Grace accused.

Gabrielle stared into her teacup and ran her finger back and forth around its rim. After a moment, she set her cup down on the coffee table. She stood up with new purpose.

"You might be right, Eden. I just have to figure out what my *symbolic gesture* is." Gabrielle glanced at her watch. "Oh, I've got to get back to the store soon. Phyllis wanted to leave a little early. She has a date with my dad."

"*Your* dad and Phyllis?" Grace asked.

"Yeah, it was quite a surprise. But I'm happy for them. They've both been alone a long time. Before I go, Eden, do you have those consignment pieces for me? I'd like to have some of your art on display when Small Business Saturday hits this weekend."

Gabrielle left a few minutes later with three sculptures wrapped in bubble wrap. As she drove back to the store, she pondered the idea of a symbolic gesture. Was there a way she could say goodbye to Jean-Luc? Was she ready?

It was Saturday. Gabrielle stared out her bedroom window where December snow flurries drifted down to the windowsill. It was a peaceful sort of snow. A snow that promised sled riding, cross-country skiing, and all those fun winter sports that made the season exciting.

Gabrielle shook her head and turned back to the open suitcase on her bed. It was time to travel to Paris. Again. Discouragement weighed down her limbs. She pulled items out of drawers and clothes from her closet. When she lifted up the black bustier and garter belt, she frowned at them.

"You guys have caused enough trouble," she said, reproaching the items in question and stuffing them back into her lingerie drawer.

Because she had a six o'clock flight the next morning, she had dropped Rocky off at her father's house earlier in the afternoon. The house felt empty. Just like her heart.

The peal of her cell phone broke the silence. Gabrielle grabbed it off the nightstand.

"Hello?"

"Gabrielle?" Andrew's deep voice on the other end sent a tremor of pleasure down her spine.

Refocusing, Gabrielle realized there was a sense of urgency in his voice.

"Drew? Yeah, it's me..." she couldn't quite hide the surprise and hope in her voice.

"I'm sorry to call, but Mom and Dad are out of town. Grace and her family have the flu, and I can't get a hold of Eden."

"Okay."

She waited.

"I've been called into work for an emergency surgery. I hate to ask this. I know it's not your responsibility, but could you watch Jack?"

Gabrielle deflated. But the thought of Jack buoyed her again.

"Sure. No problem. I can be over there in five minutes."

"Thanks! You're a lifesaver. Literally. If I don't do this surgery, the dog won't make it."

"Let me grab my keys, and I'll be on my way."

Five minutes later, Gabrielle pulled into the driveway next to Drew's truck. The front door opened as soon as she got out. Jack jumped up and down.

"Brie! Come see our Christmas tree!"

"Okay, Jack."

She laughed; her heart full of love for the little boy waiting inside the door.

"Give me a minute to talk to your dad, and I'll be right there."

Drew waited, blue winter parka zipped, gloves in hand. Hazel eyes watched her approach. His hand came halfway up like he wanted to touch her cheek.

Drew lowered his hand back to his side. "I'm not sure how long this will take."

"No problem. As long as I'm home before four tomorrow morning, I'll be fine."

He raised an eyebrow.

"It's the new quarter. I'm headed to Paris tomorrow. My flight leaves at six," she explained.

"Well, I hope it won't take that long."

"Just go. Jack and I will be fine here. Won't we, Jack?"

They waved goodbye to Drew as he backed out of the driveway. Gus followed as Jack tugged Gabrielle over to the Christmas tree. He pointed out his favorites, then handed her a photo ornament that resembled a gilt picture frame.

"These are my first parents. That's Paul, and that's Julie. Dad said they loved me so much that when they died, they wanted him to adopt me. We've been a family ever since. I don't remember them, but they seem nice, don't you think?"

Gabrielle gazed at the family photo in her hand. Dark-haired Paul and blonde Julie smiled up at her, baby Jack held between them.

"They look very nice, Jack. And I know they loved you a lot. How could they not?"

He nodded like young children do, then showed her several decorations he had made in school. After a while Jack got bored, so Gabrielle suggested they go outside and make a snowman.

An hour later, Gabrielle's clothes dripped melting snow onto the floor since she hadn't brought anything but a coat and gloves with her. After helping him out of his snow gear, she sent Jack up to change. Gabrielle trudged into Drew's laundry room. She pulled the wet clothing away from her body and tried to wring it out as she walked.

On a drying rack, she hung up Jack's wet snow pants, gloves, and hat. Gabrielle noticed a pile of clean T-shirts and sweatpants folded on top of the dryer. Without hesitation, Gabrielle stripped out of her wet clothes and pulled on one of Drew's T-shirts. It hit just above the knees. Next came the sweatpants. She cinched them around her waist as tight as they would go, then grabbed a pair of Drew's athletic socks. Gabrielle tucked the drooping ends of the pants into the tops of the socks. Not exactly high fashion but she was warm and dry.

She threw her clothes into the dryer and went into the kitchen to make dinner.

Jack caught sight of her and laughed. "You look funny wearing dad's stuff."

"I know, but my clothes were wet. I didn't have snow pants like you did. Now, what do you want for dinner?"

They ate spaghetti. After dinner, they played Jack's favorite board game until Gabrielle noticed Jack's eyes begin to droop.

"Hey, bud. Why don't you get pajamas on, and I'll read you a story before bed?"

While Jack changed, Gabrielle let Gus out one more time and checked all the downstairs doors to make sure they were locked. She left a light burning over the kitchen sink, then went upstairs. Gabrielle snuggled next to Jack on the bed and picked up a book about superheroes. The little boy snuggled against her.

"This is nice. I wish you could read me a story every night."

"I know, Jack. I like this too."

Gus settled on the floor next to the bed.

Gabrielle read about a team of superheroes who defeated an evil scientist. After the story was over, Gabrielle set the book on a nightstand and started to get out of bed. Jack stopped her with a hand on her arm.

"Can you lay by me for a while?"

How could she resist the sweetness of a sleepy little boy?

"Okay."

Gabrielle stretched out next to Jack. He rested his head on her arm. Within minutes, they were both asleep.

At eleven o'clock, Drew stood transfixed in the doorway of Jack's bedroom. Gabrielle lay on Jack's bed, a protective arm curled around the little boy sleeping next to her. She wore his sweatpants. And his T-shirt. The oversize clothing swallowed her slight frame and made her appear fragile.

Gus raised his head when Drew stepped into the room.

"Good dog. You were protecting them, weren't you?" he whispered and patted the dog's head.

Andrew gazed down at the two most important people in his life. Would he and Gabrielle ever make things work? He regretted his harsh words. He just wanted to be near her again. He reached out and smoothed a wavy strand of hair away from her face.

Her blue eyes met his. Their eyes held. Breaking contact, Gabrielle slipped her arm out from under Jack and slid off the bed. She followed Drew downstairs.

"How was the surgery?" she asked when they stood in the kitchen.

"I think he's going to make it. Annabelle will stay overnight and check on him every few hours."

Starved for each other's company, their eyes devoured each other. Neither spoke.

Gabrielle cleared her throat. "I left your dinner in the fridge. All you need to do is pop the plate in the microwave."

"Thanks. I'll probably take it for lunch tomorrow. I'm too tired to eat."

Another pause.

Gabrielle skimmed the back of his hand with her finger. "I miss my friend. I miss you, Drew."

"We've always been friends, Gabrielle. But we've also been something more."

"I know. Maybe we can talk after I get back from France?"

Drew stepped closer and cupped his hand against her cheek.

"Yeah," he murmured. "I'd like that."

Gabrielle stepped even closer to Andrew. He urged her against his chest. They clung together. God, it felt good to hold her again.

"I should go." Her voice was muffled against chest. "I've got a few more things to pack. The car will be at my house at four thirty."

"Yeah, okay."

Gabrielle stooped to put on her boots. She paused in the process of zipping her coat.

"Your clothes. Jack and I made a snowman, and mine were wet," she offered in explanation.

"Just wear them home. You can give them back the next time I see you."

Gabrielle nodded her thanks and grabbed her purse. She paused, then took a step toward him. Drew met her halfway. He waited. It was her move.

Gabrielle stood on tiptoes and urged his head down. She placed a tender kiss on his lips, then scooped up her partially dried clothes and trudged out to her SUV.

Andrew watched her pull out of his driveway. Maybe there was hope for them. On his way upstairs, his step was lighter than it had been in weeks.

# CHAPTER TWELVE

At Michel and Sophie's penthouse in Paris, Gabrielle sipped wine and reclined against the divan. They had celebrated Christmas together, and then the various family members had trickled away to their own pursuits. Gabrielle and Michel were the only two left in the room.

"I brought the information and paperwork you requested, Gabrielle," Michel told her from an adjacent armchair.

He pulled his briefcase onto his lap and rummaged inside. After a moment, Michel drew out a stack of papers held together by a black clip. Gabrielle's brother-in-law placed reading glasses on his Gaul nose, then summarized the contents for her.

"Just as stated at the time of Jean-Luc's death, you received all of Jean-Luc's company shares and dividends.

You are the trustee of his trust until Luc turns twenty-one. Then the trust transfers to Luc since he was Jean-Luc's namesake. You also maintain the right to reside in one of the company's penthouses. Lastly, you remain chairperson of the company's charitable donations..." his voice trailed off for a moment as Michel skimmed through the document.

Finding the information he needed, Michel continued, "However, in the event you should remarry, the shares are split evenly between Vivienne and Luc since you and Jean-Luc had no children. You lose the right to be on the board of trustees and the penthouse is no longer at your disposal."

Michel eyed her over the top of his glasses. "Are you sure you want to do this Gabrielle? If you remarry, you will give up almost everything."

"You know me, Michel. I weigh my options before I make a final decision. To sum up, I rescind all claims to the company, right?"

Michel paused and scanned the document again.

"No. In the event you remarry, you still receive a percentage of all company profits for the rest of your life or the duration of the company."

Michel glanced at Gabrielle and threw his hands in the air. "It is miniscule compared to what you make now."

Gabrielle laughed.

"That miniscule percentage of company profits is more than a neighborhood of people make back in Maine."

Michel sat back and regarded her with solemn dark eyes.

"Is he worth it? Maybe he will not marry you once he finds out you lose your holdings in the company. I think Jean-Luc designed this to protect you from fortune hunters."

Gabrielle shot him a look of disbelief. "Come on, Michel. You checked out Andrew Leland when we started dating. I'm sure you know his net worth, so you know he isn't interested in me for my money. Besides, he hasn't asked me to marry him. I just want to know my options, that's all."

"He'll ask. Soon."

Michel put the papers in a manila envelope, then set it on the coffee table in front of her. He took her hand.

"If you marry him, you will still be welcome here. You will still be *ma belle-soeur*, and I will continue to look out for you. Jean-Luc would wish it."

Gabrielle squeezed his hand and smiled with tears in her eyes. "Thank you, Michel. I love you, Sophie, and the kids. You'll always be family."

It was the week of Christmas. There was a lull in patients, so Andrew decided to catch up on an article about pet allergies. He was sitting at his desk, magazine in hand, when one of his assistants knocked on his office door.

"There's a package here for you, Dr. Leland."

"Okay, Hope. Just bring it in," he responded, his eyes fixed on the page in front of him.

"Sorry. You have to sign for it up front. The guy won't let me do it for you."

Curious, Andrew trudged to the front desk. The Man in Brown stood near the reception desk and shifted impatiently. Andrew knew this was the busiest time of year for those who worked package delivery. He scribbled his signature. The man surprised him by handing Andrew a cardboard envelope.

With a nod of thanks, he headed back to his office, envelope in hand. Drew paused in the hallway when he saw the return address was Paris, France. His breath caught. Three quick strides took him inside his office. He closed the door and tore open the package.

A single sheet of the finest vellum met his fingertips. He withdrew the folded note and flipped it open.

Embossed at the top were overlapping initials *G* and *L*. Andrew's hands shook as he read Gabrielle's graceful handwriting.

*Dear Drew,*

*No one actually sits down to write letters anymore and sitting here, thinking about what to write to you, I find that sad. Physically writing a letter gives one perspective that emailing, texting, or calling can never do.*

*I've brought Jean-Luc's ring with me to Paris. Eden says I need a symbolic gesture to achieve closure, and I think she's right. Jean-Luc has wanted to come home for some time now; I believe that in my heart. I've arranged for his ring to be placed in the Levesque vault, where he is interred. As for my wedding band, it's been reset into a pendant, so I can wear it on a necklace when the mood strikes.*

*Why am I telling you all of this? I want to show you that I am moving forward, my*

*love. I'm ready to pick up the conversation
we started in my kitchen so long ago. If
you haven't given up on me yet, here's my
invitation:*

*Dinner for two at my house on New Year's
Eve. Seven o'clock. I'll cook for you, and if
you like the food, maybe next time Jack can
come too.*

*I won't be home until Christmas Eve, and
I'll spend that with my family. Let's take
this time to think about what we really want
and need out of life, no pressure from the
other person. If you're willing to continue
where we left off, just show up. If it's too
late, don't come. I'll get the message.*

*Love,
Gabrielle*

Hope surged in his chest. She had signed the letter
with the word *love*. Drew took a deep breath, ran a hand
through his hair, then grinned. She wanted to pick up
their conversation from the kitchen. Maybe Gabrielle
realized they belonged together!

Andrew tucked the note back into the cardboard envelope, then strode to the front desk. He asked Donna to pull up his schedule for the rest of this week. After they made some adjustments, Drew strode back into his office to make a few phone calls.

Two days later, Andrew pulled up in front of the Martin house with Jack tucked into his car seat in the back. He helped his son out of the truck. Together, they trudged through the snow to the front door and knocked.

Pierre opened the door and waved them in. "Hmph."

Drew and Jack followed him to the familiar kitchen at the back of the house. David sat at the plank table, working his usual crossword puzzle.

"Ah, Andrew and Jack. We haven't seen you in a while. We were beginning to wonder when you'd be back."

Their nonchalance threw Andrew off kilter. The two men acted as if he and Jack had only been there a week ago, rather than the three months that had passed.

Jack slid onto one of the bench seats and folded his hands. He gazed at Pierre, who had come around the table to stand next to David's chair.

"Grand-Père and Grand-Pop, we've come to ask you an important question," Jack began in his most adult tone.

Andrew rested a hand on Jack's shoulder. "They probably want to hear this from me."

As unmoving and stalwart as any native New Englander, both men eyed Andrew, their faces impassive. They would wait. It was his job to talk.

He cleared his throat. "Gabrielle has written to me from France. She's asked me to dinner on New Year's Eve so we can talk about the future. At least that's what I hope…"

Both men nodded. David gestured for Drew to continue.

Jack interrupted. "We want to ask Brie to marry us, but Dad says we have to come and ask you first. Not sure why we ask you, then her, but that's what Dad says."

"You bring a boy to do a man's business?" David asked.

"Not at all," Drew replied. "This decision involves Jack as well as me, so I thought he should be part of the process. Besides, when he heard I was coming to see both of you, he wouldn't quit nagging to come along."

"Hmph," Pierre commented from his standing position.

"Do you have a ring already?" David asked.

Andrew withdrew a light-blue box from his coat pocket.

"Mr. Martin, I would like to ask for your daughter's hand in marriage."

Andrew opened the box and showed the ring to Gabrielle's father.

David whistled.

"Is that box from the *real* Tiffany's?" Grand-Père peered over his son's shoulder.

"Yep. I flew to New York yesterday afternoon to pick out a special ring."

"They don't just let anyone in there, son," Grand-Père commented.

"I knew someone from my Wall Street days. They were happy to help me unload my hard-earned cash." Andrew grinned.

David shifted his stern gaze back and forth between Andrew and Jack. "Do you love my daughter?"

Andrew detected a glimmer in the older man's eyes but knew he wasn't in the clear yet. Jack and Andrew glanced at each other, then back at David. They answered in unison.

"We do."

"Well then, you have my blessing. If you can convince her to marry your sorry lot."

David grinned to soften the impact of his words.

"Now, we have some chili on the stove and too much for two old men to eat. Stay for dinner?"

Andrew slipped the ring box back into his coat pocket and breathed an internal sigh of relief. Her father and grandfather approved. Now all he needed to do was convince Gabrielle.

On Christmas Day, Gabrielle sat in her father's kitchen dressed in an outfit of winter white. Her Irish wool sweater hugged her curves and her cream-colored pants accented the length of her long legs. As she sipped hot cocoa at the counter, Gabrielle watched Phyllis package up Christmas leftovers. The gray-haired woman wore a gaudy holiday sweater and glasses decorated with holly and ivy. From time to time, Phyllis glanced at the couch where Gabrielle's father sat.

"Phyllis, are you *sure* you can bear living with those two old salts? Don't you want to push the wedding back so you have time to rethink things?" Gabrielle teased.

Amy, Phyllis's daughter, sat on a stool next to Gabrielle.

"Yeah, Mom. I married a New Englander. I know how stubborn they are," commented the strawberry blonde.

Amy shot an affectionate glance toward her husband, Ryan, who was sitting in the living room with the other men.

"Oh, you girls." Phyllis waved a dismissive hand. "We're neither of us getting any younger. Valentine's Day is as good a day to get married as any. We just want a small ceremony with family. There's only two months to plan, so I'll need your help."

Phyllis beamed.

As they hashed out wedding details, Gabrielle shook her head in disbelief. Her father had finally done it. Two days ago, he had asked Phyllis to marry him. At the age of twenty-nine, Gabrielle was about to acquire a new stepmother, stepsister, and brother-in-law. Life's little curveballs continued to amaze her.

The talk of weddings focused Gabrielle's attention on the topic she had tried to push to the back of her mind all day: her dinner with Drew.

That morning, she had made a pact with herself not to worry about it. However, all the wedding talk caused her fears to flood back. Would he show up? If he did, would she be brave enough to finally start living again? Could she take that final step and commit to him?

"Mom, you can't get married in some old dress." Amy's comment pulled Gabrielle from her reverie. "Gabrielle and I will take you to Bar Harbor or Bangor, and we'll find you something age appropriate and stylish enough to mark this special occasion."

"Sure, Phyllis." Gabrielle smiled. "We could even fly to Paris if you wanted to shop there."

Phyllis pointed her poinsettia-decorated fingernail at Gabrielle.

"No way, missy. I am not fussy nor froufrou. Paris is too posh. Besides, you wouldn't get me on a plane in the middle of winter anyway."

She shook her head. "I don't know how you do it all the time. I would be too nervous the plane would go down."

Phyllis sighed in acceptance. "Okay. Bangor will be fine, girls."

Gabrielle got out her cell phone to check dates for the shopping trip. They settled on a day, then moved to the guest list.

# CHAPTER THIRTEEN

It was New Year's Eve. The beef Wellingtons were in the fridge, chilling until time to bake them. Gabrielle had already finished the individual chocolate mousses, which were hanging out with the Wellingtons. In order to stay busy and avoid nerves, she washed down her kitchen countertops, then moved to mop the kitchen floor.

Would Drew show up? Had she blown her only chance with him?

Rocky lay in the doorway of the remodeled living room and eyed her industry with his head on his paws. He was content, like all dogs, to watch her do all the work. While Gabrielle was wringing out the mop, her cell phone signaled an incoming text. She wiped her hands on her old sweatpants, then checked the phone's screen. It was Drew!

"Should I bring Gus tonight? He's been missing you and Rocky."

She collapsed against the counter in relief. He was coming. There was hope for them. Gabrielle reread his text. She knew what he was asking. Should he bring Gus because he would be at her place all night?

She didn't want to give away all her secrets.

"Weather's supposed to be bad tonight. Better bring him just in case. See you at seven," she texted.

Gabrielle finished mopping the floor. A quick glance at the retro clock in her kitchen told her it was time to shower.

When Drew arrived at Gabrielle's house, he parked his truck behind her SUV in the driveway. It would be easier for the snow plows to clear the streets, plus he wouldn't have to move the truck later. Especially if the night went according to plan. The falling snow muffled Andrew's footsteps as he and Gus mounted the steps to Gabrielle's back door. Through the mudroom window, he caught his first sight of Gabrielle in weeks. She glided around the kitchen in a silky shirt and black pants that draped softly around her hips.

Tonight, she used the kitchen island for prep space. A large dining table took up another corner of the vast kitchen, but he noticed she had opted for the more intimate setting of the breakfast nook, which sported candles and a tablecloth. Muffled music played somewhere in the house, and Gabrielle mouthed words to a song as she moved between the island and the stainless steel range.

It was time for their future to begin. He shifted a bottle of wine to his left arm, then knocked on the window.

Gabrielle heard the tap at her back door. Drew peered through the window, his face unreadable. She had expected him to come to the front door. This was more intimate, familiar somehow. That was the goal of the whole evening, right? To become more intimate.

With a smile of greeting, Gabrielle opened the door for dog and man. An icy wind gusted inside. She shivered in her lightweight blouse.

"Hi. Come in and get warm. Hey, Gus. I missed you too."

She patted the Lab on the head as he nudged her leg.

Rocky came over. He gave the man and the other dog the *sniff down*. After they passed inspection, Rocky returned to his vantage point near the living room.

Gabrielle smiled when Drew handed her the bottle of wine. "Thanks."

She set it on the counter, then turned to watch him while he hung his coat on a hook near the back door. His masculine scent tantalized her senses, evoking bedroom fantasies. Gabrielle resisted the urge to throw herself into his arms. Instead, she found a corkscrew and went to work on the wine bottle. Andrew circled the kitchen while she uncorked the wine and poured them each a glass.

"Wow, I remember what this kitchen looked like the first time I was here. The renovations look great."

He leaned against the doorframe into the living room. "I can't believe this room is done too. You've done so much to the house."

Gabrielle came up next to him and handed him his wine glass. "Yeah. It looks so much bigger now since we got rid of the formal dining room and combined it with the kitchen."

Being so close to him, she felt like she'd come home. Gabrielle inched closer and rested her head against his arm.

"I've missed you," she said quietly.

Drew touched a finger to her cheek, his eyes boring into hers. "I missed you too."

He was leaning in to kiss her when an upbeat song roared to life on a nearby speaker. Startled, they jumped apart.

"Sorry." Gabrielle pulled away and turned back to the kitchen. "I can turn that down. Or turn it off completely. Whatever you prefer."

"Where's it coming from?" Drew asked, curiosity lighting his hazel eyes.

"Where? Oh, everywhere."

At his questioning glance, Gabrielle clarified, "This is one of my bigger splurges for the house. I had it wired for intercom and sound throughout all the main rooms. There are control panels on every floor, and I can decide which rooms play music. The system streams live music, plays off an electronic device, or taps into radio stations."

"Awesome!" Drew grinned. "Show me how it works."

After a brief explanation at one of the control panels, the oven timer chimed. Gabrielle left Andrew to play with options while she retrieved dinner. She smiled to herself as every few seconds Drew switched between different songs and genres of music. He was a kid with a new toy.

"Drew," she called. "You can play with the technology after dinner. Let's eat."

They carried dishes to the table. Gabrielle slid onto the booth-like bench next to Andrew and rested her thigh against his. He gave her knee a gentle squeeze, then left his hand there. Gabrielle held her breath and hoped he would kiss her. He gazed at her for a few seconds. Doubt crept into his eyes. He removed his hand and turned to his plate.

"Everything looks great." His smile was a little forced.

Gabrielle returned his smile. "Let's eat."

An hour later, Drew sighed and slumped next to Gabrielle. "That was one of the best meals I've ever had. And you made that from scratch?" Andrew patted his stomach.

Gabrielle nodded. "Beef Wellington was one of the first dishes I fell in love with when I started eating at high-end restaurants. I paid a chef to teach me how to make it. I've never regretted it."

Eventually, they cleared dishes and stacked them in the dishwasher. Gabrielle enjoyed the companionable mood because the after-dinner conversation was bound to be more serious. She finished putting containers of leftover food into the refrigerator as Andrew moved out of the kitchen.

Drew wandered into the living room, wine glass in hand. He sat down on one of the oversize couches and reclined on the broad seat. The couch accommodated his large frame perfectly. Being six feet five inches, it was rare that he found comfortable furniture. He hoped Gabrielle had picked out the couches with his height in mind.

On the coffee table, Andrew noticed a stack of papers with a fountain pen resting on top. He glanced at them. They were in French.

During his years in the corporate world, Drew had seen enough contracts to recognize one in almost any language. What was Gabrielle up to? Did she leave those papers out for him to see?

A minute later, she floated into the room; her wine glass dangled at her fingertips. Gabrielle settled next to him on the couch and tucked her feet underneath her. She nodded and pointed her glass toward the papers on the table.

"I see you noticed the papers. Any idea what they are?"

Andrew shook his head. "They look like contracts, but no, I don't know enough French to even guess what they say."

Gabrielle set her glass on the table and turned to him. Her eyes searched his face. They begged him to understand.

"There were many reasons why I couldn't commit to you before, including those papers, which outline the conditions of Jean-Luc's will. I had to be sure with you and be sure of myself before I made life-altering decisions. Decisions that don't affect just my life but the lives of many other people."

Drew sensed her change in mood. He set his glass on the coffee table and skimmed his fingers along her arm.

"It's all right, love. We've got all night to talk this through. No interruptions this time."

For a moment, her blue eyes bored into his. Then she took a deep breath. "Before we talk about anything else, I need to tell you something."

"Okay." He held his breath.

"I know you've been waiting on me for a long time. And I'm finally ready to tell you. I love you, Drew."

"Gabrielle!" He crushed her to him, then pulled back. "I've waited so long to hear you say it! God, I love you!"

She feathered kisses over his lips, then his face and his neck. When she made her way back to his lips, she paused and murmured, "I love you as desperately as you love me."

Andrew took control. He pressed her back against the couch, then devoured her mouth. When his temperature started to rise, along with certain body parts, he pulled back and cleared his throat.

"Was that the promise, or the commitment, you wanted to discuss tonight?"

Gabrielle grinned. "That was just fact."

She gestured to the papers on the coffee table. "Before we talk about promises and commitment, I need to tell you about the stipulations in those papers."

Gabrielle explained how her status with the textile company would change if she remarried.

"You're telling me you won't have any involvement in the company except to receive a miniscule share of the profits?" Andrew clarified.

Gabrielle nodded.

Andrew ran his hand through his hair. He grinned. "I won't lie. I'm ecstatic about this. I have enough money to support us and our children's children's children without ever having to work again. I love that you wouldn't be tied to the company. You wouldn't have to commute every quarter; you could just go to Paris when you wanted. But I also understand why you were so hesitant to make this decision."

He gazed at her, unable to resist touching her cheek, her ear, and her mouth with his fingertips. "How do you feel about this, honey?"

She sighed. "I've been part of Jean-Luc's company for most of my adult life. Eight years. In fact, when you and I first started dating," she said, lacing her fingers through his, "I couldn't ever imagine giving up that piece of my life."

Andrew frowned.

"But the last two trips to France have been an eye-opening experience. I dreaded those trips. It was agony being so far away from both you and Jack. That day, when Jack was hurt at school, I was miserable because I couldn't be there to comfort either of you. I realized my priorities had shifted. The company in Paris is my old life. You and Jack are my future."

She smiled at him. "I'm ready to make you and Jack my family. If you'll have me."

Her declaration was almost a proposal. It was the cue he had been waiting for. Drew slid off the couch and left her sitting alone. He noted the stunned expression on her face as he moved away from her, but it couldn't be helped. With a specific purpose in mind, Drew passed through the kitchen and found his coat in the mudroom. He rummaged in his coat pocket. Once he found the item he was looking for, he returned to the living room.

Drew took a deep breath, his heart pounding in his ears as he approached Gabrielle. With wariness, she watched him cross the room. He stopped in front of her, then dropped to one knee.

He held up the blue box and took her hand in his large one. "Gabrielle, I love you so much. I can't even think of any comparisons right now because I'm so nervous."

He gripped her fingers harder.

"Just know that I love you and I want you to be my wife." He looked down at their joined hands and then back up into her eyes. "Will you marry me?"

"Yes!" she cried, throwing herself into his arms.

He held her to him, his hands shaking with relief. She'd said yes!

He pulled back and wiped her tears away. "Say it again, love. I think I need to hear it at least ten times tonight."

She smiled. "I love you, Andrew Leland. I will be your wife."

Gabrielle devoured his mouth.

After a moment, he pulled back and smiled. "You haven't even opened the box. Maybe you'd better let me put this ring on your finger; otherwise it won't seem real."

Andrew slid onto the couch next to her as Gabrielle slipped off the top of the Tiffany's box. She pulled out the ring box inside and cracked it open.

She gasped. A large baguette diamond rested in the center of the ring, with two medium-size diamonds resting on either side. The gems accented a plain platinum band. The setting was elegant and deceptively plain. Andrew knew Gabrielle's trained eye registered the simple beauty of quality diamonds. They needed no additional decoration. Their quality was superb.

"It's beautiful, Drew. How did you have time to buy this, let alone go to Tiffany's?"

He took the ring from the box, kissed it, and slid it onto her ring finger.

"I took a half day and flew down there last week."

At her surprised look, he shrugged. "I know a guy. He took me in his private jet."

Drew grinned and planted a quick kiss on her lips. He pulled his cell phone from his pocket.

"All of our family is waiting to hear your answer. Can I snap a picture of the ring on your finger? Then we can move on to celebrating?"

"Wait. All of our family? Like Pop and Grand-Père?"

He nodded.

"How do Pop and Grand-Père know?"

Drew smiled. "Jack and I asked their permission to marry you, before you got back from France."

"You *and Jack* asked my father's permission?"

He nodded again.

"How very traditional. And romantic. No wonder they approve of you! You know exactly how to include them in our lives. I love you even more for asking him."

She kissed him lightly. "Okay, take the picture. But get both of our hands in it."

She pulled Drew's arms around her from behind. Gabrielle rested her left hand on top of his, then steadied his other hand while he snapped the picture on his phone.

"She said yes!"

Drew typed the message under the picture, then hit send. He threw his phone onto the coffee table, turned her around in his arms, and proceeded to kiss her thoroughly.

They ignored the responding text messages as the kissing heated up. Hands ran along smooth, hot skin and buttons opened causing fabric to fall away. As they lay together on the couch, Gabrielle and Drew took time to touch and explore.

Two dog whines from the doorway caused them to pause. Both Rocky and Gus waited near the kitchen, tails wagging with expectation.

Andrew groaned. "I'll take them out. It's bound to be cold out there. It might help me cool down a little."

He offered a self-deprecating grin.

"Don't cool down too much."

Gabrielle winked, then pulled the edges of her blouse together in her hands. "I'll blow out these candles and make sure the rest of the house is shut down for the night."

Drew made his way into the mudroom and shrugged into his winter parka. He braced himself for the cold as he hooked on Gus's leash. Rocky waited by the door, familiar enough with the yard that he had free roam.

Gabrielle checked the oven to make sure it was off, then glanced over her shoulder. Drew stood in his winter parka, shirt still hanging open to show his six-pack abs and broad chest. God, he was sexy. If she continued to watch him, she would probably melt into a pool at his feet.

"Do you mind locking up after you're done?" she called.

"Nope."

He grinned over his shoulder. "Soon this'll be routine for us."

She smiled back. "I'll be upstairs. Can you find your way up?"

Drew swallowed. "I think I'll manage."

She made her way up the back stairs. When he was out of sight, Gabrielle slumped against the wall. She could do this. They loved each other. They were going to be married. It was time. She straightened her spine and entered the master bedroom.

Gabrielle switched on the lamp next to the bed and made a quick trip to the bathroom. When she came out a few minutes later, Drew stood at the vanity and gazed at the small pile of his clothes on the seat.

"I washed the clothes I borrowed from your house that night I watched Jack. I left them there in case you needed them."

Drew took in the sight of her silky robe and his nostrils flared. An instant later he stood before her. He reached a hand out to touch her, but he paused. His hand trembled.

"God." He sighed. "You're so beautiful. With the light shining behind you, you look like an angel. You're almost too perfect to touch."

Her hand also shook as she rested it on his chest and looked up into his burning eyes.

"Drew, I've only ever been with one person. It's been a long time. I'm nervous." She shrugged and smiled with chagrin.

"I'm nervous too. Look at my hands shaking. It's been a long time for me too. And then I have to live up to Jean-Luc's precedent…"

She hoped he was gentler than Jean-Luc had been their first time. Granted, she had been a virgin then, but Jean-Luc had been anxious to make sure she was his. In typical Jean-Luc fashion, he had taken what he wanted, then waited for her to catch up. Surprised at the thought, Gabrielle pushed it to the back of her mind. Right now, she wanted her whole attention focused on the six-foot-five golden god of a man before her.

Gabrielle wrapped her arms around Drew's neck and pressed herself against him. "You don't have to live up to Jean-Luc. Just be Andrew. That's who I want in my bed. In my life."

He picked Gabrielle up and carried her to the bed. Drew set her down with care and sat next to her. He reached for the tie of her robe.

"Can I see?"

She nodded, and he opened the belt to reveal the white lacy bra that resembled flower petals cupping her breasts. Matching white panties completed the ensemble.

He swallowed once. Then twice.

"No black bustier?" he murmured.

"You kidding? That thing has caused us nothing but problems."

At his pained expression, Gabrielle reassured Drew. "Don't worry, honey. I'll wear it another time. I just wanted something pure and untouched for tonight. Are you too disappointed?"

He took her hand and guided it to his erection.

"Do I seem disappointed?" he groaned.

"No…" she said, breathlessly.

Drew stood abruptly, then shed his clothes. His nakedness dazzled Gabrielle as he slid onto the bed next to her. Her breath caught. He was magnificent. Powerful. All man.

With studied care, he nuzzled her neck, then pulled back. "I was such a brute when we were in the kitchen."

Kiss.

"Last fall," he amended.

Kiss.

"I won't put you through that tonight, love. I'll be gentle even if it kills me."

She pulled his lips down to hers. The petal bra and panties soon followed his clothes onto the floor. As their lovemaking progressed, his tenderness overwhelmed her. Gabrielle had never felt more cherished or loved. He took his time learning her preferences, and he let her explore him. Drew allowed her to set the pace and never pressured Gabrielle to move faster than she was comfortable.

"Now Drew," she urged as he paused suspended above her.

Andrew knelt between her legs and held himself immobile. He gazed at her with passion-darkened eyes.

"Drew?" Gabrielle panted.

"Just making sure I remember this moment for the rest of my life," he ground out.

"Please, Drew. I love you. Make love to me," Gabrielle responded.

He tore open a foil package and filled her a moment later. They matched each other's passion, stroke for stroke, and found fulfillment together.

Later, as they lay entwined on her bed. Drew ran his finger along her cheek. He caught a tear and held it up between them.

"Ah, shit. I mean shoot. I made you cry after all. I'm sorry, love," he whispered and kissed her cheek.

Gabrielle swiped at her tears and smiled at him. "I'm not sad. These are happy, overwhelmed, and completely satisfied tears. I've never felt so cherished."

She kissed his lips, tasting her own salty tears.

Drew pulled back. "Completely satisfied, huh?"

She nodded.

A smug look creeped over his face. Drew placed a peck on her mouth and slid out of bed.

"I'll be right back."

He headed to the bathroom.

Gabrielle must have dozed off. When she opened her eyes, Drew sat next to her on the edge of the bed. His face was half in shadow, the only light in the room coming from the bathroom door, which was slightly ajar. He was so still.

"Drew? Is something wrong?" She propped herself up on her elbow.

"Wrong? No. Not wrong."

"You're not having second thoughts, are you?" she grabbed his arm.

"Never, love," Drew soothed and climbed back into bed.

He pulled her into his arms.

"You see, I'm thirty-one years old."

"Yes, I know. And?" Gabrielle prompted.

"I was just imagining my baby growing inside of you. I want children. Or at least a child. Soon, Gabrielle. I love Jack as if he were my own flesh and blood. But the idea of a child with you, a child we made together, I don't want to wait too long."

Gabrielle sighed. "I'm worried that I won't be able to give you children. Maybe I'm infertile or something." She bit her lip. "I've told you that Jean-Luc and I were trying for a baby when he died. But what I didn't tell you is that we had been trying for years. I just never conceived."

Drew tucked her against his chest. "Maybe you weren't the one with the problem. Jean-Luc was a lot older than you. Maybe it was him. Anyway, I would love for us to have a child together, but we have Jack. If we can't have our own children, I'll be happy as long as you're my wife."

They snuggled for a while in the cocoon of her bedroom. After a few minutes, Drew pulled back. His eyes were serious.

"Did you know I was engaged once?"

Gabrielle shook her head. "Your mom said something once about a no-good fiancée. But that's all I know."

"I've never mentioned it before because it seems like a different person's life. I don't want secrets between us, so I should tell you about it."

Gabrielle nodded her encouragement.

"Her name was Serena. We met in college and dated off and on until we graduated. Then I moved to New York to work on Wall Street. We got back together after the disastrous relationship I had with Chantal, the woman I was with when you and I ran into each other at that party in New York."

Gabrielle nodded again. "I remember."

"I was sure I was in love with Serena. So I proposed, and she accepted. We had just begun wedding plans when Paul and Julie were killed. I should have known something was wrong when she refused to come with me to the funeral. After Jack came to live with me, she broke our engagement. She told me she didn't want to raise someone else's child."

"Her loss," Gabrielle whispered.

"Yeah, her loss. She missed out on an amazing kid. I thought I would miss her more, but I was relieved when she didn't come back. Ever since Serena, I've been careful about who I dated or introduced to Jack. That's why it astounded me when he ran up to you that first day at the dog park and asked if you were his mom. I guess he knew you should be his mom even before we did."

Gabrielle snuggled closer to Drew and wrapped her arms around his neck. "After we're married, I'd like to adopt Jack, if he'll have me. Then I'll truly be his mom."

Andrew took a shuddering breath, and Gabrielle saw him swipe moisture from the corner of his eye. "That's sounds like the best idea I've heard in a long time. He'll have you, Gabrielle. He's already claimed you."

His kiss was insistent, wiping conscious thought away. It was a long time before they slept.

# CHAPTER FOURTEEN

On New Year's Day, Drew stood outside Gabrielle's back door in a T-shirt, sweatpants, and a winter parka. Gus and Rocky ran into the snow to do their morning business, the snow up to their chests. Drew glanced at the road. There was at least two feet of unplowed snow.

Snowed in today. He grinned at the thought of Gabrielle still asleep upstairs, her love-tousled hair spread over the pillow. Drew turned his attention back to the dogs.

Neither dog lingered. As soon as they finished, Rocky and Gus ran into the house. In the kitchen, Gus and Rocky shook the snow off their fur and licked their paws. Drew locked the back door and refilled the dog bowls. He washed his hands at Gabrielle's new kitchen sink, then found a decorative tray in a nearby cabinet.

After Drew added some fruit, muffins, and juice to the tray, he headed up to the master bedroom.

The bed was empty, but the shower beckoned from the adjoining bathroom. Drew set the food on the vanity and entered the steamy bathroom. He stripped off his clothes and tossed them on top of the counter.

Gabrielle was standing with her back to him when Drew pulled back the shower curtain. She glanced at him over her shoulder. Surprise registered as her gaze took in his arousal.

His eyes ate up her naked body. "I let the dogs out and gave them some food and water." He trailed a hand at the edge of one breast. "We're snowed in today. I'll have to call Mom later and make sure Jack is okay there for another day." His other hand cupped Gabrielle's cheek. "There's two feet of snow on the road and not a plow in sight."

Drew kissed a trail from her face to her neck. He hovered at her breast. Gabrielle gasped and pressed herself against him. Drew groaned at the feel of her slick body against his. The water ran cold before they left the shower and moved to the bed.

Andrew and Gabrielle spent the day snuggled on Gabrielle's couches. They napped and talked and made love. Andrew placed a video call to his mother just before lunch.

"Are you sure Jack is okay there, Mom?" he asked.

"He's fine, honey. No one is going to make it on these roads today. You just stay snuggled up there with Gabrielle. By the way, you look much more relaxed and rested than the last time I saw you. It's amazing what lack of sleep will do, right?" She wiggled her eyebrows at him.

"There are some conversations I will never have with you, Mom. This is one of them." He grinned.

Elaine smirked in return. "Here, talk to Jack. He wants to say hi."

Andrew waited while she passed the phone to his son.

"Hey, Dad," Jack said. "Is it true?"

"Is what true, Jack?"

"Did you do it? Did you ask Gabrielle to marry us? Did she say yes?"

Out of the corner of his eye, Andrew saw Gabrielle step into the living room. She smiled when she heard Jack's question.

"Yep, Jack. I asked her, and she said yes. Here, I'll have Gabrielle show you the ring."

Drew tilted the phone screen toward her. She stepped closer and held up her glittering diamond.

"Brie! Is it true? Are you going to be my real mom?"

Gabrielle smiled. "It's true, Jack. I heard you went with your dad to ask Grand-Pop and Grand-Père's permission."

"I did." He grinned, then asked, "When are you coming to get me?"

Gabrielle glanced at Drew, and he turned the phone back.

"It'll probably be tomorrow, bud. The roads are covered with snow, and the plows haven't gotten them cleared yet. How're you doing at Grandma and Grandpa's?"

"They're spoiling me," Jack bragged. "I got to eat as many pancakes as I wanted. We're going to watch one of my favorite movies after lunch. Here's Grandma."

Drew chuckled at the boy's quick change in subject. He was done talking, ready to move on to the next activity.

Elaine's face reappeared on the screen. "Okay, son. Before we go, I'm *dying* to know, when's the wedding?"

Gabrielle avoided his gaze.

"We haven't had a lot of time to talk, Mom. I'll let you know when we've made some plans, okay?"

He hung up a few minutes later and found Gabrielle in the kitchen. As she made sandwiches, Gabrielle continued to avoid eye contact. They took their plates to the breakfast nook and slid onto the padded bench.

After taking a couple of bites, Drew turned to her. "Okay, spill it."

"What?" she asked midchew.

"You closed up when Mom asked about the date of the wedding. Are you having second thoughts?"

"No. I just don't want you to be angry with me." Gabrielle took a sip of lemonade.

"Angry about what? We haven't talked about anything yet."

She sighed. "I don't want to get into major wedding plans until after my dad's wedding next month. You know he and Phyllis are getting married on Valentine's Day, right?"

"They are?" Drew asked in surprise.

"Yeah. I found out when I got home on Christmas Eve. Phyllis's daughter, Amy, and I are the matrons of honor, so we're knee deep in wedding plans. It's just over a month until the big day. They didn't give us much notice."

Andrew held up his hand to pause their conversation. "Let me get this straight. *Your* dad and *Phyllis*, your store manager?"

Gabrielle giggled. "Yep. Back in October, I went into work early and discovered my father leaving Phyllis's personal entrance. Phyllis was wearing a fuzzy robe. It was the first time I've ever seen Pop embarrassed."

Andrew shook his head and grinned. "I still can't imagine your stoic father and flamboyant Phyllis. So how does this affect our own wedding plans?"

Gabrielle snuggled closer to him, sandwich forgotten for the moment.

"I don't want to overshadow their big day. Can we wait until after their wedding to start our planning?"

Drew draped his arm across her shoulders.

"I'm going to need a general time frame to satisfy my mom. Plus, you could always bribe me."

He grinned and rubbed her thigh suggestively.

Gabrielle snuggled even closer. "Well, I've always had a picture of my dream wedding in my mind."

"Wait a minute." Drew gazed at Gabrielle in confusion. "You mean, your first wedding wasn't your dream wedding?"

She waved her hand in a dismissive gesture. "My first wedding was Jean-Luc's dream wedding with a few of my touches whenever the wedding planner allowed it."

She smiled shyly. "I would love to get married on Pop's back lawn. Right on the shore, near the water.

I don't want a huge gala event. Just a relaxed New England wedding with close friends and family. What do you think?"

Drew mentally shook himself. He was still bowled over by the fact that her wedding to Jean-Luc Levesque had not been the wedding of her dreams. It gave him confidence. Gabrielle *did* love him just for himself.

Drew tilted his head against Gabrielle's. "I can see it. Us. Relaxed wedding by the lake. All of it. Throw in Jack as the ring bearer, and I think we're good. When?"

"Summer? I've got to ask Pop and Grand-Père's permission to have the wedding at the house. There might not be a good time before the Valentine's Day wedding."

"Summer." He groaned. "We have to live apart that long? I mean, I don't think it would set a good example for Jack. You know, living together before we're married."

"I agree." Gabrielle nodded. "I also hope that'll give us time to renovate the upstairs. That is, if you and Jack are willing to move here."

"Here?" Drew glanced around him. "I hadn't really thought about it. I guess it does make sense. It *is* the larger home. How many bedrooms are in this place anyway?"

"Nine. Including those on the third floor."

"*Nine?*" He was incredulous. "After we finish eating, you better give me a tour of this place. I've never actually seen the whole house yet. How many bathrooms?"

She sent him an impish look. "Six. Plus the powder room down here next to the kitchen."

Drew shook his head at the enormity of the house. "Are we planning to have a large family?"

Gabrielle laughed. "A big family. Or maybe lots of houseguests. We'll have to see. After all, we already have one child."

Drew's pulse increased when she referred to Jack as their child. If the size of his heart could grow with love for her, he suspected it might burst knowing that she loved Jack as much as he did.

After lunch, Gabrielle dragged Drew through the Victorian house. They started in the basement, which had a bathroom, including a shower, but was mostly unfinished. The first floor held the renovated kitchen, living room, and the powder room. Then she showed him the library.

When Gabrielle led him to a door just under the main staircase, Drew thought it was a closet. She opened the door and he saw the massive room ran along the back of the house. On the left side of the room sat an antique grouping of couches in front of a massive fireplace. To the right, Andrew saw a grand piano on a raised dais. Original bookcases filled in the gaps around the room. All of them were filled with books.

He whistled in amazement.

Gabrielle nodded. "I know. I haven't even begun to explore this room yet. All the furnishings in here are original to the home, including most of the books. I've been itching to spend some quality time in here, looking at everything. But a functioning HVAC system and kitchen were priorities."

Next, Gabrielle led Andrew to the second floor where she showed him four more bedrooms and two bathrooms. All of them were decorated in styles that denoted the decade in which they had last been renovated.

A look of disgust crossed Gabrielle's face as she showed Andrew the avocado green fixtures in one of the second-floor bathrooms.

"As you can see, none of the rooms on this floor have been renovated yet. This house still needs a lot of work."

Drew took her hand and nibbled her fingers. He pulled Gabrielle to him.

"But if you marry me, you might not have the money to make the renovations, especially since you'll lose your company shares. Is that one reason you want to push the wedding back until summer?"

Gabrielle raised her eyebrows in surprise.

Drew continued, "If you're worried, Gabrielle. I have the money. Once this house is ours, we'll be able to continue with whatever you have planned."

Gabrielle chuckled. The chuckle became a laugh. And then she laughed so hard, she had to lean against the wall for support.

Andrew smiled at her laughter but was confused by the source of it.

When she could breathe, Gabrielle patted his arm. "I'm sorry. You were trying to reassure me, and then I laughed in your face."

She moved closer and wrapped her arms about his neck. Her hands urged his head down to eye level. "My darling, between the two of us, we'll never have to worry about money."

"How do you know—"

She pressed a finger to his lips. "I might as well tell you. Michel, Jean-Luc's brother, hired a private investigator to check you out when we started dating."

Andrew frowned, but she continued, "I didn't know about it until my last trip to France. When I asked, Michel confirmed my suspicions."

She gave him a peck. "I know how much money you have, so you might as well know my net worth as well."

She whispered a figure in his ear.

"Holy—"

Gabrielle interrupted him again. "When we marry, my miniscule percentage will still yield more than enough income to refurbish or renovate any number of houses I might invest in."

She whispered another number into his ear.

Drew's eyebrows flew up. "That's miniscule?"

She nodded and chuckled again.

Drew shifted his weight from foot to foot. "So. You don't *now*, and won't *ever*, need me financially?"

"Not financially. But I need you in my life because I love you, Drew. My life's empty without you and Jack in it."

She kissed him and skimmed her hands under the hem of his T-shirt. He sucked in a breath, then picked her up. A wicked gleam appeared in his eyes as he entered the master bedroom, Gabrielle in his arms. Drew kicked the door shut. They finished the tour much later.

# CHAPTER FIFTEEN

The first Saturday after the new year, business was slow at The Treasure Trove. Most people had spent their money on the holiday season, so there was little left for anything but necessities. The sun shone outside, but the winter wind was brisk and bitter. Few people moved around on the streets.

Gabrielle waited on the occasional customer and worked on inventory. Because business was slow, she gave Phyllis the day off to manage wedding plans. Hailey was scheduled to come in at lunchtime so Gabrielle could eat. The two of them would work on inventory for the rest of the day.

Just before noon, the doorbell chimed. Gabrielle watched the bundled teen enter the store.

"Hey," Gabrielle called as Hailey approached the back room, "you're right on time."

Hailey waved a mittened hand, then worked on unwinding her long scarf. "It's bitter today. I'll punch in and be right out to help you."

A few minutes later, Hailey came out wearing a bulky pink sweater and jeans. Her blond hair was swept back into a ponytail.

"What do you need me to do?"

Gabrielle couldn't help but notice the girl's pale face.

"You feeling okay today? If you're sick, we're slow enough that you could go home."

Hailey shot Gabrielle a startled look. "What? Oh, no. I'm fine. I'm just a little tired today."

They worked for a while, before Gabrielle broke the companionable silence.

"Hailey, I'm really going to miss you when you go off to college next fall. You're such a hard worker. I'm not sure I'll find anyone as reliable as you."

Gabrielle checked off a number of sculptures in the locked display case. She smiled to herself when she saw all of Eden's pieces had sold again. A muffled sob from the counter caught Gabrielle's attention. Hailey was hunched over, her shoulders shaking.

"Hailey? What's wrong? Maybe I should call your parents."

With a sob, Hailey threw herself into Gabrielle's surprised arms. Helpless, Gabrielle patted her back. As the girl's sobs began to subside, she led Hailey into the back room and left the connecting door open in case a customer entered the store.

Once they took their seats in the break room, Gabrielle faced her employee.

"Now tell me what's the problem."

"I'm pregnant." Hailey sniffed and wiped at the corners of her blue eyes. "My parents say that I can stay with them until the baby is born. But since I'm eighteen, I need to start looking for my own place. They'll help out some, but if I'm old enough to be a parent. I'm old enough to support myself and the baby. Oh, Gabrielle. What am I going to do?"

Hailey sniffled again.

Gabrielle squeezed the girl's hand. "What about the baby's father? Is he still around?"

"He's in the Marines. I haven't heard from him since he left for basic training. I've tried to contact him, but he doesn't respond. I'm on my own, I guess."

Gabrielle fumed at the inconsiderate young man who fulfilled his pre-enlistment urges, then abandoned Hailey. Gabrielle peered out into the store to make sure it was still empty.

She glanced back at Hailey. "When's the baby due?"

"The end of May."

Gabrielle bit her lip. "Well, the first thing you must do is take care of yourself. You also need to finish your senior year of high school."

Hailey gazed at her in surprise.

"If you're going to have any hope of supporting yourself and the baby, you need your high school diploma."

Hailey nodded. "You're right."

"Okay. You take this one step at a time. Stay with your parents for now, save the money that you make here, and finish your high school career."

Hailey took a shaky breath. "Okay. One step at a time. I can do this."

A thought occurred to Gabrielle.

"Do you want to give the baby up for adoption? You could still go to college in the fall like you planned."

"No." Hailey shook her head. "I want to keep my baby. I still love the baby's father, even though he seems to've forgotten me. And I think I love the baby too. Most of the time, I'm too scared to think, but I've been feeling the baby move around. Every time I do, I know I'll never give it up."

Gabrielle smiled wistfully. What might it feel like to have Drew's baby move inside her? Would she ever be able to conceive? Maybe she was infertile. Gabrielle snapped her attention back to the distraught girl in front of her.

"Phyllis and I have been talking about hiring more help. I need to spend more time recruiting suppliers. Maybe you can work extra hours after school."

Hailey nodded and smiled.

"As you know, Phyllis is marrying my father in a month. The upstairs apartment will be vacant. Think about this for now; after graduation, you could rent the apartment and work here full time."

"Really, Gabrielle?"

Gabrielle nodded.

"I love working here. Maybe by working full time, I can support the baby and still take some online classes."

"That sounds like a great goal! Now let's see if we can make a dent in this inventory," Gabrielle replied.

Three weeks later, Gabrielle moved around the store eyeing the displays. She tried to visualize a new arrangement in order to showcase the jewelry made by her friend, Abigail Moon. Abigail was a member of the Penobscot people under the Wabanaki Confederacy. She incorporated elements from her culture into her jewelry designs, melding modern style with traditional Wabanaki elements. Repeated nature motifs dominated

Abigail's jewelry and were popular with the general population.

They needed to move the mahogany display case to the front of the store. Customers would notice the jewelry as soon as they entered. She was eyeing the furniture in question when the doorbell chimed.

Just inside the door, Drew stomped the snow off his boots. Unable to stop herself, Gabrielle beamed at the man she loved. Lately, they had barely seen each other. It was only two weeks until Phyllis and David's wedding and Gabrielle was busy as the default wedding planner.

"Hey, handsome." Gabrielle wrapped her arms around Andrew's neck for a kiss.

In order to let her know how much he missed her, Drew took his time kissing Gabrielle. With a sigh, Drew pulled back and rested his forehead against hers.

"What brings you into my store on a snowy Wednesday just before lunchtime?" she asked, a huskiness to her voice.

White teeth flashed. "I was hoping we could go to lunch. We've hardly seen each other this week, with Jack having a cold and you busy with Phyllis's wedding."

"What do you mean *my* wedding?" Phyllis called from the back of the store. "I'm not getting married by myself you know."

"C'mon, Phyllis, we all know David would be happy with a quick ceremony at city hall. This little party is for you, not that you don't deserve it."

Phyllis chuckled and adjusted her turquoise-blue glasses.

"I do deserve it, future son-in-law. David's not over-ly romantic, so we need to celebrate this marriage with a little pomp."

Gabrielle enjoyed the exchange between Phyllis and Drew. By a convoluted series of events, the two of them would soon be related by marriage. Life was full of surprises.

Drew answered Phyllis's chuckle. "You don't have to convince me. Do you mind if I kidnap Gabrielle for lunch? We won't be gone long; I have patients at one."

"'You two go ahead. I'll watch the store." Phyllis waved them off.

Ten minutes later, Gabrielle sat across from Drew in a booth at the Saltwater Café. When the waitress appeared, Drew ordered a hamburger.

The waitress smacked her gum at Gabrielle. "And what can I get you? Do you wanna a burger too?"

The thought of eating greasy meat turned Gabrielle's stomach. "Uh, no. I'll just have a cup of chicken noodle soup and water please."

"That's all you're having?" Drew asked after the waitress left.

"Yeah, I'm not very hungry." She smiled. "Is Jack feeling better? When can I see you guys again?"

"Well, you could see us every day, if we were married." Drew teased.

"I know. But we did agree to wait until after Pop's big day to get into full wedding plans. By the way, the contractor's started work on the master suite, and they've torn out the green bathroom upstairs. Can you guys come over this weekend so Jack can pick out colors for his new room?"

"He's a six-year-old boy, Gabrielle. He's not going to care about colors."

"Nonsense, Drew. He's got ideas. Jack's already told me he wants a superhero bedroom."

Gabrielle clasped her hands together with enthusiasm. "On second thought, why don't we take him shopping this weekend? We could see what toys and furniture he likes. That'll show me the direction to head with the decor."

Drew played absently with her engagement ring.

"Yeah, okay." He lowered his voice. "When can I see just you again? I miss you. And it's been a while."

Gabrielle blushed. His sultry tone caused desire to pool in her belly. An image of their naked bodies, in his big four-poster bed, flashed before her eyes. She wished they were alone.

"I know. I miss you too." She breathed through her nose. "How do you do *this* to me with just one little sentence?"

Drew raised an innocent eyebrow. "Do *what* to you?"

The waitress saved her from responding by setting their food in front of them. Gabrielle shot Drew a glance across the table.

*You know.*

With a flash of white teeth, he sat back and popped a french fry into his mouth.

"You're supposed to eat food, not consume each other with your eyes," a voice commented.

They looked up to find Drew's mother at the end of their table. Elaine bestowed a Cheshire cat grin and then winked.

"So much for a private lunch," Drew muttered.

"I heard that Andrew," she chided. "I wanted to stop and say hi since I saw you both together. By the way, any more progress on wedding plans? You know I love to plan a good wedding." Elaine rubbed her hands together.

Before Gabrielle could respond, Andrew turned to his mother.

"How about this, Mom? You watch Jack on Friday night so Gabrielle and I can have time to work out some of those wedding details you're craving."

"Your father and I would watch Jack anytime, honey. Why don't you have him spend the night at our house? It must be difficult for you and Gabrielle to find alone time, especially with a little boy around."

Elaine's blue eyes sparkled.

Gabrielle blushed. Drew patted her hand and gave her a mocking smile.

"How does that sound, *darling*? Does Friday work for you?"

Gabrielle smiled back with sugary sweetness.

"On one condition, *sugar buns*. We take Jack shopping in Bangor on Sunday."

Not fazed by her comment, Drew grinned. "Deal."

He turned back to his mother. "I'll drop Jack at your house around five thirty, if that's okay?"

"Sounds good." Elaine patted his shoulder. "Enjoy your lunch."

Drew shook his head at his mother's retreating figure. "You know, I've never eaten a single meal in this place without being interrupted."

Gabrielle took a sip of water and nodded. "It's a small-town café. Everyone comes here to see and be seen. Admit it. That's why you wanted to come today. To make a statement. To reinforce our status as a couple."

"I wanted to have lunch with my fiancée. Reinforcing our status was just a side benefit."

He stroked her hand. "You said your master bedroom is gutted?"

She blinked at his change in topic. "Yep."

"Where are you sleeping?"

"I'm sleeping on my mattress. On the floor in the office."

Drew raised an eyebrow. "Must be pretty uncomfortable. Why don't you come to my house on Friday? We can make dinner together. And you *know* my bed is really comfortable."

She smiled. "Okay. You win."

"I like the sound of that. Make sure you file that phrase away for future use."

He squeezed her hand. They finished eating a few minutes later. Drew paid the bill. Outside the café, Drew kissed her goodbye. They split up and headed back to their respective jobs.

For the rest of the week, Gabrielle was conscious of something being off. She couldn't place the cause of her restlessness; she just felt different. When she was at work, she was conscious of time ticking away. At home, she sensed she was missing something.

A glance at her kitchen calendar told her she didn't have any appointments because she had cleared time to work on the wedding. What was she forgetting?

Thursday night, she sat at her kitchen counter and reviewed her list for Pop's wedding. She still had so much to accomplish, but the items left on the list were last-minute details that she couldn't complete now. It was probably those prewedding details that made her feel like time was slipping away.

Gabrielle shook her head. A week from Tuesday, her father and Phyllis would marry. Their honeymoon in the Caribbean left Gabrielle running the store through Sunday, although she did have Hailey coming in to help after school.

It wouldn't be a problem. Before Phyllis came to work for her, Gabrielle had run the store by herself. She could do it again.

Gabrielle sighed. She was probably just tired. After Rocky went outside, Gabrielle closed up the house. With heavy feet, she climbed the stairs to the uninviting mattress on her office floor.

# CHAPTER SIXTEEN

On Friday night, Gabrielle let herself and Rocky into Andrew's condo. Gus woofed, and the two dogs greeted each other with a token butt sniff. She switched on lights as she moved over to the sliding door and let both dogs out into the fenced backyard. Gabrielle figured Drew was probably still at his parents' house, dropping off Jack.

She switched the oven to preheat, then pulled out chicken breasts and spices from the grocery bag she had set on the counter. Ten minutes later, the dogs circled around her legs as she moved to the oven.

"No way, guys. You're not getting this. Go in the living room," she ordered and pushed them out of the way with her knee.

As she bent over to slide the pan onto the oven rack, she heard a deep voice behind her.

"Nice view."

She closed the oven door and stood up to see Andrew lounging in the door way.

"Hi." She smiled as he took off his gloves.

"Hi, yourself." He grinned back and stashed his coat in the hall closet.

Gabrielle cleaned the counter with disinfectant, then moved to wash her hands at the sink. While she washed her hands, strong arms came around her from behind. Drew kissed down her neck as she dried her hands, then spun her around to face him.

"How long 'til the chicken's done?" he asked.

"About twenty minutes."

"I can do twenty minutes, how 'bout you?"

She nipped Drew's chin.

He captured her mouth and worked at the buttons of her shirt. When the shirt hung open, Drew led her over to the couch. He moved to the sliding door. With a quick twist of the wrist, he shut the blinds. A moment later, he was beside her on the couch.

"God, I feel like it's been forever. Gabrielle, you make me crazy. I never get enough of you."

They shed the rest of their clothes, and she welcomed him into her arms. Their lovemaking was quick and urgent, both of them starved for the other.

Later, Gabrielle and Drew ate the chicken dinner half-clothed. They cleaned up the kitchen in record time. After shutting off the lights, Drew lead Gabrielle up the stairs to his bedroom. His king-size, four-poster bed welcomed them with its clean lines and dark wood.

"I'll only be a minute." She picked up her bag and moved into the adjoining bathroom.

Drew pulled down the comforter and turned on his bedside lamp. The rest of the lights went off. Inside his walk-in closet, he shed his clothes and threw on a pair of silk boxers. Returning to the bedroom, he froze.

Gabrielle leaned against a bed post in the notorious black bustier and garter belt. Her dark hair cascaded down her back. Her smile was self-assured and seductive.

Drew didn't remember walking over to her. But suddenly he stood before Gabrielle and ran a finger from her collar bone to the tip of her breast. He took a shaky breath.

"Ah, love, now I can die a happy man. You've fulfilled my fantasy. I have to warn you, I'm not quite civilized when that bustier is around."

Gabrielle smiled in anticipation. "That's what I'm counting on."

Drew picked her up and half tossed her on the bed. In seconds, he covered her and skimmed kisses down her body. He nipped between her legs, and her back arched in pleasure. Drew broke off abruptly and fell back onto the bed, pulling her with him. Gabrielle took over the position of dominance. She straddled him and drove them both to a frenzied end. They fell asleep in each other's arms.

Gabrielle's eyes flickered open. It took her a moment to realize she was in Drew's comfortable bed. A quick glance at her phone told Gabrielle it was five in the morning. She tried not to wake Drew as she slid out of bed and went to the bathroom. Half-awake on the toilet seat, Gabrielle realized her breasts were sore.

They must be sore from the enthusiastic lovemaking of the night before, right? Or maybe she was getting close to her period. Sometimes her breasts got sore the week she was supposed to get it. Wait. When was her last period?

Gabrielle sifted through the early morning fog in her brain. Oh God! It was before Christmas! She was at least two weeks late!

Don't panic. It's probably just the stress of Pop's wedding. Gabrielle had been late before when she was stressed. Just for peace of mind, Gabrielle decided she would stop at a pharmacy in Bar Harbor later. No way she would buy a pregnancy test in Jacobs Landing. There were no secrets in this town.

Satisfied with her plan, Gabrielle crept back into the bedroom. She kept an eye out for dark shadows on the floor that signaled Gus or Rocky. When she slid back under the covers, Drew rolled over and spooned her.

"Everything okay?" he murmured into her neck.

"I had to go the bathroom," she whispered.

He nodded against her neck, splayed his hand across her abdomen, and pulled her against him. She felt the warmth of his hand seep through the nightgown she had donned during the night.

What if he was unknowingly guarding their baby? Gabrielle waited to see if she felt panic over the situation. Instead, she was exhilarated. She smiled to herself and rested her hand over his. They could protect the baby together.

Saturday night, Gabrielle sat at her kitchen island. She tried to concentrate on the color chips for Jack's bedroom, but the pregnancy test stared at her from the opposite counter. It didn't matter that it was inside a brown bag and she couldn't really see it. The possibility of a baby hung in the air. Gabrielle tried to ignore the little brown bag and refocus on the color swatches in front of her.

Tomorrow, she and Drew would take Jack shopping for his room. Before they left, Gabrielle wanted to show Jack a couple of choices. She suspected Jack would pick primary colors, probably blue and red, since his favorite superheroes usually wore those colors.

It was no use. The bag spoke to her.

*You've been wondering all day, why don't you come find out?*

Gabrielle sighed. She needed to use the bathroom anyway. She might as well do the test. Earlier she had read the directions, so she strode over to the bag and picked it up. With feigned nonchalance, Gabrielle swung the bag back and forth and walked into the bathroom. The little bag wasn't a big deal. It didn't hold the power to change her life, right?

After she was done, Gabrielle set the timer. She returned to the counter and paged through the other sample books on the island. It wasn't like her mind was counting the seconds until the buzzer went off.

When the timer beeped on the stove, Gabrielle ran a shaky hand over her face. She shut it off and found the stick right where she had left it, on the edge of the sink. Like an automaton, Gabrielle picked up the pregnancy test. After a deep breath, she read the message in the little window.

Not pregnant.

Tears ran down her cheeks as she threw the offensive item into the garbage. Once again, she was not pregnant. How many times had she seen those same results when she and Jean-Luc had been trying for a baby? It didn't matter that she and Drew had always used protection; Gabrielle was so sure she was pregnant this time.

Her sniffles turned into sobs. Having a baby with Drew would have complicated things, but Gabrielle ached for the possibility that no longer existed. She slid to the floor in the cramped bathroom and crossed her arms over her flat belly. Giving in to her disappointment, Gabrielle allowed herself to mourn.

A while later, Rocky whined from the doorway. He inched over to Gabrielle and rested his head on her lap. What would she do without this dog? He offered comfort when she was sad, and he guarded her when she was vulnerable. Gabrielle relaxed against the wall and allowed the soft feel of Rocky's fur beneath her fingers to sooth her ragged emotions.

Eventually, Gabrielle pulled her aching body up by the edge of the sink. She washed her hands and examined her tear-streaked face in the mirror. No more decisions tonight, disappointment had worn her out.

Gabrielle dragged herself up to the second floor and climbed onto the mattress in her office. Rocky flopped down on the floor, and Gabrielle reached out a hand to stroke his fur. His warm body comforted her. Finally, she slept.

Sunday morning Gabrielle was in better spirits. It was her shopping day with Drew and Jack. She tried to push away her disappointment over the would-be baby and climbed into the passenger seat of the truck. She felt emotionally battle worn, but the sun shone into the truck and cheered her a little.

Drew shut her door and started the truck. As if he sensed her mood, Drew searched Gabrielle's face.

"You okay, honey? You seem quiet today."

"I didn't sleep well last night," she murmured.

"I can imagine. Sleeping on a mattress for one night is fine, but you've been camping out in your office for weeks now. I'm sure that gets old."

She nodded and turned to Jack in the back seat.

"Brie, I can't believe I'm getting a brand-new room at your house. Dad says we get to move in when we marry you this summer. Is that true?"

"It's true, Jack. We need a little time to plan the wedding. Then we'll be a family, all of us living together," Gabrielle reassured him.

"After Dad and I marry you, do I still have to call you *Gabrielle*?"

Andrew laughed as he exited onto the highway.

Gabrielle smiled. "You don't call me *Gabrielle* now. Why would you start after the wedding?"

"Well, everyone's always telling me to call you Gabrielle because that's your real name. I just wondered if it would be the same after we become a family."

Gabrielle squeezed the boy's hand. "Jack, I hoped you would call me mama, or mom, when you're ready."

"Cool! I'll finally have a dad *and* a mom."

Jack took her hand, raised it to his mouth, and kissed it.

"I saw that in a movie once." He grinned at her, a look that was reminiscent of his adoptive father.

When they arrived in Bangor, Jack picked blue-and-red items to go in his new bedroom. He picked out superhero toys and bedding to match. Andrew followed Gabrielle and Jack from store to store. He enjoyed the time out with his family. Each time they ordered or purchased items, Drew whipped out his credit card before Gabrielle could find her wallet.

When she raised an eyebrow at him, he replied, "You're providing the house, so I'm getting the furnishings."

Gabrielle nodded.

Later that night, the three of them ended up back at Gabrielle's house. They sat at the kitchen island and ate pizza. Drew noticed Gabrielle just picked at her slice, but he figured she would tell him what was wrong when she was ready.

Mentally, Drew scratched his head. Sometimes, he had no idea how to read his fiancée. Unlike his sisters, Gabrielle remained closemouthed about her emotions. He figured it was a by-product of growing up in the Martin household with a bunch of men. Maybe she was preoccupied with the last-minute wedding details for David and Phyllis's ceremony. He'd give her a little more time.

They played a board game until Jack's eyelids started to droop.

"Come on, bud. It's time to head home." Drew held up Jack's coat.

"Why do we have to leave, Dad?"

"Because you have school tomorrow, and there isn't anywhere to sleep in this house right now. Remember when Gabrielle showed you your room upstairs? There aren't any walls, let alone a bed."

"Okaaaay." Jack flopped into his coat and headed to the back door.

Andrew leaned toward her. "When will we see you this week?"

Gabrielle glanced at the calendar on her phone.

"Hmm. This last full week before the wedding is pretty crazy. Do you think we could meet for lunch Tuesday? Otherwise I can probably do dinner Thursday night."

Drew pulled her into his arms and pressed a quick kiss to Gabrielle's lips.

"Let's do lunch here, Tuesday." He wiggled his eyebrows at her. "Say noon? And then we can do Thursday night dinner at my place. We'll order takeout. How does that sound?"

"Sounds like a plan."

Drew gave Gabrielle a more thorough kiss while Jack made fake gagging sounds in the background. Gabrielle laughed, then went over to Jack and hugged him.

"Have a good week at school, bud. I'll see you Thursday."

On Tuesday, Gabrielle let Drew in the back door of her house for their lunch date. The sounds of electric saws and hammers pounded above their heads and accompanied their extended kiss.

"I don't know how you live with this," he called to her over the noise.

Gabrielle carried their lunch plates over to the table.

"Lately, I've been hiding out at work. I try not to come home until they're almost done for the day."

For a few minutes, they munched on fresh veggies and grilled cheese sandwiches.

Drew raised his voice to comment, "And here I thought we were going to have a romantic lunch."

Gabrielle smiled and shrugged.

Seconds later, the saws and hammers quit. Work boots tromped down the back stairs. Three men in jeans and flannel shirts waved as they donned their winter coats and left through the back door.

A dark-haired man in jeans and a T-shirt called to Gabrielle from the top of the stairs.

"Hey, Gabs! I need you and Romeo to come up to the master and tell me how you want the custom cabinets in the walk-in."

Gabrielle eyed Andrew as he registered the hunk of a man with curly black hair and solid muscular arms. Olive skin, dark eyes, and a dimple completed the package.

"Johnny Caprese?" Drew exclaimed. "Your lead contractor is the *Italian Stallion* of Jacobs Landing?"

Gabrielle shrugged and took a bite of her sandwich. "He's the best contractor around."

"How did I *not* know this before?" Drew's face was appalled.

"Johnny and my brother are friends. Too late to be jealous, Drew. If we'd wanted to hook up, we'd have done it long before you and I started dating. He's been my contractor the whole time."

"Hellllooo?" Johnny called. "I'm still here. You have a problem with the only Italian family in Jacobs Landing, Leland?"

Andrew turned on him. "Your family's heritage is *not* the reason your nickname was the Italian Stallion in high school."

Johnny grinned without remorse. "Yeah, I know. So, Gabs, I'd like to get to lunch soon. You guys wanna come up and tell me your thoughts on the closet? I'm six two, but Leland's got inches on me. We might need to make some adjustments."

"*Gabs?*" Andrew threw his hands up in the air. "Who calls you *Gabs?*"

Gabrielle wiped her mouth and tossed her napkin on the table. "Only idiots who want to get kicked in the tool belt. Come on, Drew. He'll just keep nagging until we do what he wants."

As Drew followed Gabrielle up the stairs, she heard him mutter behind her. "Johnny Caprese."

All right, Drew admitted a few minutes later. Johnny was a complete professional when he talked shop. Johnny's work was legendary in Jacobs Landing. As the contractor outlined the steps for finishing the master suite, he gave them options for their custom closet and showed them the completed plumbing overhaul in the master bathroom. Once they made choices for bathroom tiles and flooring, Johnny took off for lunch.

Drew turned to Gabrielle. He rubbed her arms and stepped closer. "I'll admit it. Johnny knows what he's talking about." Drew surveyed the bedroom and turned back to her. "It's starting to feel real. Up to this point, I've only thought of this house as *your* house. Now that I've had input on the master suite, it's starting to feel like *our* house."

Gabrielle wrapped her arms around his neck and pulled him closer. "I was hoping we could use your bedroom furniture, plus my antique vanity in here. Your bed's so much more comfortable than mine. We've already made some great memories there."

Drew inhaled as the memory of the black bustier shifted his libido into overdrive. He pulled Gabrielle to him. He kissed her lips. Her cheek bones. Her neck. Mentally reigning himself in, Drew sighed and rested his chin on top of her head.

"I'm trying to be patient, but I'm anxious to be married and start our lives together. I'm tired of meeting up for stolen moments or having to get a babysitter for Jack. I just want us married so I can see you every day and go to bed with you every night."

"I know, honey." Gabrielle soothed him with a kiss. "Only another week until Pop's wedding, then we start our own plans. By the way, I talked to Pop and Grand-Père yesterday. You know, about having the wedding on their back lawn."

"And?" Drew prompted.

"And they said yes! Well, Pop said 'That would be fine,' and Grand-Père just said 'Hmph,' but he said it with a smile this time, so I think he's pleased."

Drew smiled, then looked around the room. "Oh, crap. What time is it?"

Gabrielle glanced at her watch and sighed. "It's a quarter to one. I guess we both have to get back to work."

"Okay." Drew nuzzled her. "But just a minute."

He pulled her to him and devoured her mouth. Their faces were flushed and their breaths came in little gasps by the time they pulled apart.

Drew caressed her cheek. "I love you, Gabrielle. Sometimes it's physically painful to be apart from you. I know I sound like a lovesick teenager, but I don't ever want you to doubt how I feel."

Gabrielle looked up at him with tears in her eyes. "Drew, it kills me that I sometimes see doubt in your eyes. It's like you can't believe it's possible for me to love you because I loved Jean-Luc."

She placed his hand over her heart. "How do I make you understand that my love is not a competition between you and Jean-Luc? I loved Jean-Luc, and I think I'll always love his memory. But you are my present and my future. You are the man my heart sings for."

She grimaced and looked down. "God, that sounds like a bad greeting card."

He touched her cheek, and she looked back up at him.

"Gabrielle, I *do* know you love me, but I need to be reminded. I'll be jealous every time another man looks at you."

He smiled. "It's funny, but years ago, when I saw you and Jean-Luc in New York, Jean-Luc was possessive, jealous, and completely in love with you. I thought I understood how he felt back then. I was envious of him. I knew if I had you for a wife, I would never let you go. That's still true. Only now, with us about to be married, do I really understand how Jean-Luc felt that night."

Gabrielle smiled. "And how did he feel?"

"Like he wanted to punch every man in the face. Because that's how I felt when I found out the Italian Stallion was your lead contractor."

She laughed and kissed him.

"You know what I love most about you?"

"What?" He grinned in delight.

"I love that you make me laugh. You make sure I only take the serious stuff seriously."

He chuckled and led Gabrielle to the back door. "Come on, love. We're going to be late for work."

On Thursday night, Andrew wiped down the counters of his kitchen. Fifteen minutes ago, Gabrielle and Jack had gone upstairs to read a bedtime story. While he waited for Gabrielle to come back downstairs, he shut off all the lights except the one over the kitchen sink. He let Rocky and Gus outside for a bathroom break and wandered toward the stairs.

Maybe Jack was stalling, and that's why Gabrielle was still upstairs. He decided to check on them. At Jack's door, Andrew hesitated. He eyed the scene before him. Gabrielle lay next to Jack, both of them sound asleep. He was used to finding them like this; it seemed to be a habit now. When he moved into the room, Andrew noticed dark crescents under Gabrielle's eyes and the paleness of her skin.

The mattress in her office was not the best sleeping arrangement. He could see Gabrielle was exhausted from not having a normal bed. He picked her up in his arms, and she barely stirred. Drew carried Gabrielle down the hall to his room. Once he slid her into his bed, her eyes fluttered open.

"I'm sorry." She yawned. "I must be tired tonight. What time is it?"

Drew knelt next to her and smoothed some hair away from her face. "It's only eight thirty, but you're exhausted. Stay here tonight. Get a good night's sleep."

"What about Jack?"

"He's asleep. I'll wake you up early. Maybe five thirty?"

Gabrielle nodded.

"You can head home in the morning and shower."

When it looked like she would protest, he held up his hand to stop her. "Seriously, Gabrielle. You look done in. Just stay. Sleep. That's all."

She sighed and burrowed under the covers. "Okay. Your bed is much more comfortable than what I've been sleeping on."

Drew waited for her to continue. After a minute, he realized she had fallen asleep. Tenderness overwhelmed him when he looked at her fatigue-ridden face. He kissed her forehead and left the room. Downstairs, he flipped the television to a game and settled on the couch.

# CHAPTER SEVENTEEN

Valentine's Day. Phyllis and Pop's wedding day. Gabrielle closed the store at noon and drove to the church where her father and Phyllis would marry. When she entered the church, Amy; her husband, Ryan; and Thomas were already there.

"Thomas!" Gabrielle exclaimed and threw herself into her brother's arms. "I haven't seen you since before Christmas!"

"Hey, Brie. I hear Leland finally convinced you to marry him. Let me see the rock."

Thomas grinned and pulled her left hand into view. He held his other hand up to shade his blue eyes. "You're blinding me with the size of that thing! When's the big day? I need to know so I can request leave."

Gabrielle shrugged. "Summer sometime. I've been pretty overwhelmed with Pop's big day, so we've put off planning our own wedding. I'll let you know soon."

She glanced at Amy and Ryan who stood at the front of the church.

"Can you believe that after today we'll have a step-sister and a brother-in-law?"

"Ah, no. It took me completely by surprise. I mean, I like Phyllis, but I just never thought Pop would marry again."

They ambled over to Amy and Ryan.

"What can we do to help?" Gabrielle asked.

"Well, we need to get all these pews decorated. Do you two want to take that side? Ryan and I will take the other."

"Sure," they agreed.

An hour later, the group finished the church decorations, then drove their respective cars over to city hall. Phyllis and David had rented the same conference room used for Art Fest. After the wedding, they would host an open house from six until eight. Then the happy couple would fly to the Caribbean for their honeymoon.

Amy, Ryan, Gabrielle, and Thomas attacked the tables in the conference room. They added tablecloths and centerpieces in Valentine's Day colors. It was three thirty by the time they finished.

"Well, it's time to go change. See you guys at the church in an hour or so?" Amy asked.

"Sure," Gabrielle responded, then turned to Thomas. "Are you changing out at Pop's?"

"No. I've got my tux out in the car. I was hoping I could change at your house."

"No problem."

They took separate cars back to the Victorian.

At five o'clock, Gabrielle waited at the back of the church for the music to start. Amy stood behind her. Lastly, Ryan waited with Phyllis on his arm, ready to escort his mother-in-law down the aisle. Phyllis wore a classy tea-length gown in muted lavender with a lace overlay. In contrast, Gabrielle and Amy wore silver gowns of their own style preference. Gabrielle's dress was a toga-inspired chiffon that draped over one shoulder. Amy wore an empire waist strapless gown with rhinestone detailing at the bust line.

The music began and Gabrielle stood poised to advance down the aisle. She eyed her father, who waited in a black tuxedo at the front of the church. His gray beard was trimmed, and his hair was brushed neatly.

Suddenly, Gabrielle was overwhelmed with love for him. He had always been her rock. When her mother died, David tried to fill in the best he could. When Jean-Luc died, it had been her father who flew to Paris and stayed with her. It was her father who had urged her to find a new purpose in life. He supported Gabrielle through every important moment in her life. She was glad she could make this day special for him and Phyllis.

With tears in her eyes, Gabrielle walked toward the front of the church. Halfway down the aisle, she spotted Drew and Jack on the left where they sat to make Phyllis's side look more balanced in numbers. Gabrielle smiled when Jack waved, then shot Drew a look of promise.

*Soon*, she told him with her eyes.

She took her place at the front of the church. When the wedding march began, Gabrielle saw her father's face light up. He smiled a real smile, and Gabrielle realized it had been years since she had seen her father truly happy. Grand-Père, who stood behind him, rested a hand on her father's shoulder for a minute. Thomas stood behind Grand-Père, and as the short ceremony progressed, he gave Gabrielle a nod.

*Pop is happy. Life is good.*

Gabrielle nodded back in agreement.

Later at the open house, Drew and Jack found Gabrielle standing at the side of the room. She watched as her father and Phyllis chatted with their guests. Both of them beamed with happiness.

"Hey, *Mom*!" Jack threw himself at her legs and gazed up at Gabrielle. "I'm trying out your new name. You look really pretty."

"Thanks, Jack," Gabrielle hugged him back. "My, don't you and Dad look handsome. I'm not sure I've seen you in a tie before."

"Dad said we had to wear one 'cause it's a special 'ccasion. But," he pulled on her arm until she bent down to his level, "I feel like it's choking me."

Gabrielle laughed. She patted Jack's arm and looked up into Drew's intense gaze. Her breath caught. He was so handsome, and dangerous looking, in a black-on-black suit. With his sandy blond hair, golden skin, and hazel eyes, the contrast against his black shirt and tie was lethal.

"I see Grandma! And Robbie! I'm gonna go talk to them. Okay, Dad?" Jack asked.

Drew nodded, and the little boy ran over to the other side of the room.

A smile flitted around the corners of Gabrielle's mouth as she stepped closer to her fiancé. Drew wrapped an arm around her waist and pulled her to him.

She murmured in his ear, "Are you auditioning for the next James Bond movie?"

"What do you mean by that, ma'am?" he drawled. He blew on his knuckles and rubbed them against his lapel.

"Because that suit is so sharp, it's deadly. God, Drew. You make me weak in the knees."

Gabrielle sighed.

Drew grinned at her, then leaned in to nibble her ear. A wave of dizziness hit Gabrielle. She stumbled and grabbed Drew's arm to steady herself. Drew's reflexes were quick as he cupped her elbow.

"Gabrielle, honey? Are you okay? You're not joking right now, are you?"

Gabrielle leaned her weight against him. "I'm just a little lightheaded. It'll pass in a moment."

Drew's arm took the brunt of her weight as he guided Gabrielle out into the hallway. He motioned to the red upholstered office chair standard for most waiting rooms.

"Here, love. Sit down for a minute."

She sat heavily on the chair and leaned her head back against the wall.

Drew crouched before her. "Are you sick to your stomach?"

Gabrielle nodded and closed her eyes. "A little. And lightheaded. I'll be okay in a minute."

"When was the last time you ate anything?" Drew ran his hand across her forehead and down her cheek. "At least you don't have a fever."

"I think I had some cereal this morning..."

"Well, no wonder. It's almost seven o'clock. I bet it's been at least twelve hours since you've eaten. Stay right here. I'll be back."

Within minutes, Andrew returned with some flat soda and a small plate from the hors d'oeuvres table. He pushed the cup into her hand.

"Sip this first. Maybe in a minute or two you can try some crackers and fruit."

Gabrielle offered him a weak smile, then took the cup. "Thanks."

Ten minutes later, half the plate of food was gone, and Gabrielle's stomach had returned to its normal equilibrium.

"Thanks for taking care of me." She gave Drew a peck on the lips. "It was so busy today, I guess I forgot to eat."

Andrew smiled at her and ran his finger down her cheek. "I'm just relieved to see you feeling better. You had me worried for a minute."

Gabrielle sighed. "I should probably head back inside and fulfill my wedding party duties."

"In a minute." Drew took her hand. "I haven't had a chance to tell you how beautiful you look." He kissed her hand in a chivalrous way, then gazed into her eyes. A smile played at his lips. "I learned that from Jack."

Gabrielle returned his smile, then pulled his face to hers. She kissed Drew fully on the mouth.

"We should have known you two would be out here, playing kissy-face."

Gabrielle and Drew pulled apart to see Eden, and a very pregnant Grace, gliding up to them. Both sisters smirked.

Grace turned to Eden. "I think visions of their own wedding are dancing in their heads."

"More like their honeymoon." Eden chuckled.

Both sisters pulled up chairs and settled in for a chat. Andrew shot Gabrielle a look.

*Sorry.*

She smiled and shrugged in response.

"Grace, how are you feeling?" Gabrielle eyed her future sister-in-law's extended abdomen with a twinge of envy.

"I feel like a whale encased in Grandma's old tablecloth."

Gabrielle eyed Grace's cute maternity dress and thought it flattered her blossoming figure.

Grace continued, "You know, what seemed like a great idea eight-and-a-half months ago isn't so great now. But I wouldn't change this for anything. In just a few weeks, I'll hold my precious son or daughter. And it'll be worth it."

Grace beamed, and her eyes glittered with unshed tears. "Oh, don't mind me. It's just pregnancy tears."

Gabrielle turned to Drew's other sister. "Eden, I've sold all your pieces. Do you have anything else for me?"

"Sure, Gabrielle. I'll bring some by the store next week. I know you won't be able to get out much with Phyllis gone on her honeymoon."

Thomas signaled Gabrielle from the doorway.

She rose. "Excuse me, all of you, Thomas is beckoning. I need to check in on the bride and groom."

Andrew scanned her with an assessing look. She smiled.

*I'm okay.*

He nodded his acceptance.

The reception wound down after that because many people had stopped by on their way to or from Valentine's dinner. At eight o'clock, only Gabrielle's immediate family and Drew's family remained to clean up. The three new siblings walked the newlyweds to their waiting limo.

Gabrielle hugged her father. "Be happy, Pop. You deserve it!"

She turned to Phyllis and hugged her. "Congratulations, Phyllis. I'll miss you at the store, but you guys have a great time in the Caribbean! If you need a couple extra days, just let me know."

She kissed Phyllis on the cheek.

Thomas and Amy took turns saying their goodbyes. They stood shivering in the cold and waved their parents off.

Thomas linked one arm through Gabrielle's and the other one through Amy's.

"Well, looks like the three of us are stuck with each other. Anyone up for shots at Gabrielle's place after this is all cleaned up?"

Amy laughed. "Only if they're shots of milk. Ryan and I are expecting a baby in June, so I'm off alcohol for a while. I guess that makes both of you a soon-to-be aunt and uncle. You're the only siblings I have."

Internally, Gabrielle flinched. She couldn't believe her luck. She was surrounded by pregnant women.

"Sorry, Thomas. I've got to run the store by myself for the rest of the week, so I can't be hungover. I hate to put pressure on you, but don't you think Grand-Père might be lonely without Pop at the house?"

"Ayuh. You're right Gabrielle." Thomas tapped his temple. "I'd forgotten. I promised Pop I would keep Grand-Père company until my leave is up on Friday. Come on ladies, let's get out of this wind."

When they returned indoors, Drew approached Gabrielle with a sleeping Jack draped over his shoulder.

"I'd love to stay and help…"

"No, you've got to get him home to bed. He has school tomorrow."

Gabrielle kissed Jack on the forehead and ran her hand over his curly hair.

Drew touched her elbow. "You going to be okay? Still feeling dizzy?"

"I'm all better now." Gabrielle smiled. "Thanks to my personal doctor."

She gave him a thorough kiss, then pulled back. "I love you, Drew. I can't wait for our own wedding."

"I love you too, honey. Now we can start our own plans. Make sure you're eating better. You've been pale lately. I'm worried about you."

"I will, Drew." He raised an eyebrow. "I promise. I'll make sure I'm eating at least three meals a day from now on. And I'll get more rest."

"Okay. Text me when you get home, so I know you're safe. Love you."

"Love you too."

Twenty minutes later, fatigue weighed down Gabrielle's limbs as she locked up her house. She texted Andrew and then went upstairs to her mattress. Gabrielle shed her wedding finery, then crawled under the covers. With her hand on Rocky's warm body, she slept.

A week later, Gabrielle rested her head on the break room table and tried to quell the nausea that threatened another dash to the bathroom.

"Phyllis, I'm dying," she moaned.

Phyllis laughed. "You're not dying, you're pregnant."

"But I'm not." Gabrielle half raised her head. "That's the thing. I've done two pregnancy tests now. Both times they said *not pregnant*. How can I refute the test? I mean, I am *surrounded* by pregnant people."

She threw her arm out in a circular gesture. "Grace is due any day now. Hailey has two months left. And Amy just hit her third trimester. Not me. Maybe I'm having sympathy symptoms."

Phyllis shook her head, and light reflected off her newest pair of glasses. They were beach blue with palm trees at the corners.

"Why don't you just make a doctor's appointment and get it checked, hon? My cousin's daughter had a pregnancy that didn't show up until they did a blood test. Have you said anything to Drew?"

"No." Gabrielle sat up and grabbed Phyllis's hand. "You can't say anything to anyone. Not even Pop, okay? You're my stepmom now; this has to stay between us until I actually have news."

Gabrielle groaned again, then rested her head back on the table.

Phyllis patted her hand. "I won't say anything, on one condition."

"What?"

Phyllis got up from her seat. She rummaged through Gabrielle's purse and brought her cell phone to the table.

"Call the doctor. Make an appointment. That way you can put your mind, and mine, at ease."

Gabrielle glanced at the cell phone. "Okay, Phyllis."

She levered herself off the table, then paused when another wave of nausea hit. Gabrielle heard the distinctive click of a soda can opening. Phyllis pushed it into her hand.

"Here. The carbonation from clear pop helps settle your stomach."

Gabrielle sipped the beverage, then nodded after a minute. "You're right. It *is* a little better. I'm going upstairs to the empty apartment. I'll call the doctor from there. Drew has been stopping in at random times to check on me. He thinks I haven't been eating well and that's why I'm so pale. Last week, while you and Pop were gone, he brought me lunch three times. He wanted to make sure I didn't skip meals." She swallowed down some bile. "Can you watch the store?"

"Go ahead, hon."

After placing the call, Gabrielle waited while Phyllis finished with a customer. When the store was empty, she leaned against the counter.

"All right, you'll be happy to know that I have an appointment tomorrow afternoon. It's out of my hands now. I've been so miserable; I haven't even asked about the honeymoon. How was it?"

Gabrielle grinned, some of her old sense of humor returning. "Make sure to leave out anything I wouldn't want to know about my father."

At closing time, Drew ambled into the store, Jack in tow. Gabrielle finished ringing up a late arrival, then followed the customer to the door. As she passed Drew, he winked at Gabrielle. An air of excitement and anticipation emanated from both of them.

"What are you two up to?" she asked when the customer was gone and the closed sign placed in the window. "You look like the cats that ate the canary."

"Are you almost done?" Drew took her hand in his and smiled with an air of mystery.

Jack grabbed her other hand. "Finish up quickly, Brie. We've got to take you somewhere."

"Where are we going?" Gabrielle asked in confusion.

Andrew and Jack shared a smile. "We're going to see a baby. We thought you might want to come," Drew answered.

"A baby?" Gabrielle questioned.

"Aunt Grace had her baby today. Dad said we should wait until you got off work so you could come with us to see it." Jack jumped up and down.

"Grace had the baby?" Gabrielle exclaimed. "Let me run the end-of-day report and lock the till in the safe. I won't be a minute."

Fifteen minutes later, Andrew and Jack met Gabrielle at her house, where she dropped off Rocky. In Andrew's truck, they grabbed a fast-food dinner, which they ate on the way to the hospital in Bar Harbor.

Outside his sister's room, Andrew knocked on the door. A rumpled-looking Adam, his dark hair sticking up, opened the door and grinned at them.

"Come in," he spoke quietly. "Grace has been waiting for you guys."

They entered the dimly lit room, where even Jack was in awe. A little bundle with a pink knitted hat slept in Grace's arms.

"What's her name, Grace?" Drew eased the baby into his own arms.

"Her name's Elizabeth. We're going to call her *Elizabeth*—no shortened versions. Everyone's been asking."

Grace smiled the serene smile of a new mother.

"Let me see her, Dad!" Jack jumped up and down.

Gabrielle lifted Jack up, so he could look at the tiny baby in Drew's arms.

"You just missed Robbie and Sara," Adam spoke from behind them. "They were here most of the afternoon, but Elaine and Bob took them home for the night. Let me move these blankets and you can sit down on this minicouch where I'll sleep tonight. Trust me, Drew, these things were not made for guys taller than the average fourteen-year-old. You'll find out someday."

Andrew eyed Gabrielle across the baby. He hoped they would soon have their own hospital experience.

Jack squirmed to get down. "Can I hold the baby?"

Andrew looked at his sister for permission.

Grace nodded. "As long as you sit down, Jack. That's fine."

A few minutes later, Gabrielle smiled as Drew sat next to Jack on the small couch. He supported the baby from underneath while Jack held Elizabeth and grinned.

"This is definitely a photo op." Gabrielle grabbed her phone and snapped a picture.

"Send me a copy, Gabrielle. I'll use it for Elizabeth's baby book," Grace urged from behind her.

"I will." Gabrielle smiled over her shoulder.

When she turned back, Gabrielle found Andrew studying her.

"Do you want to hold Elizabeth?"

"Oh. I don't know, Drew. I can't remember the last time I held a baby. What if I do it wrong?"

"Come on," he urged with a smile. "I bet you're a natural."

Drew took the baby back from Jack and stood up from the couch.

"Go on. Sit down." He nodded to his vacated spot.

Reluctantly, Gabrielle followed his directions.

Andrew bent toward her and murmured in a low voice, "You know about supporting the head, right?"

She nodded and then the baby was in her arms. Gabrielle marveled at how light the infant was. She touched Elizabeth's sweet little fingers, and the baby made a silent sucking motion while she slept. Gabrielle was in baby love.

She might be holding her own baby soon. No. She couldn't afford to hope. Not yet. Gabrielle had been disappointed too many times before.

"Isn't she amazing?" Gabrielle looked into Andrew's fathomless eyes.

Drew swallowed. He rested his hand against her face for a moment. They both looked back at the baby. The unspoken future lay between them.

Gabrielle wiped a tear from the corner of her eye. "She's perfect. Grace. Adam. I can't believe you guys created this little person. What a miracle! I don't think I've ever seen a newborn before. Thanks for letting me be a part of this moment."

Grace smiled. "Well, you'll soon be her auntie, so of course you should be here to greet her."

"When is the wedding by the way? I need to know how quickly I should lose this baby weight. You did say I'd be a bridesmaid, right?"

Gabrielle chuckled. "Of course you're in the wedding. You and Eden."

Drew raised an eyebrow in expectation.

"I need to call the minister this week so we can set a date. The wedding is going to be at Pop's, so at least we already have the venue."

A look of relief passed over Andrew's face. He nodded with approval. They were moving forward with their wedding plans. After a few minutes, the baby started to fuss.

"She's probably hungry. Sorry, Gabrielle. I think she wants me."

Gabrielle gave the baby a light kiss and passed Elizabeth into her mother's arms. Andrew shook Adam's hand and Gabrielle gave him a hug. They kissed Grace's cheek and offered their congratulations.

Gabrielle squeezed Grace's hand. "We'll bring dinner after you're home."

Grace nodded. "That would be nice."

Andrew took Jack's hand, and the three of them walked out to the snow-covered truck. Drew drove with caution on the snowy roads. Halfway back to town, Gabrielle glanced at Jack. He was asleep in his seat; his dark curls bobbed whenever the truck hit a bump.

"Drew, he's sleeping. He looks so cute!" Gabrielle exclaimed.

"Yeah. It's past his bedtime, but I thought seeing his new cousin was more important than having him in bed on time."

Gabrielle leaned her head against Drew's shoulder and sighed. "I agree. She was a beautiful baby, wasn't she?"

Andrew chuckled.

"Yes, she was." He sighed. "I can't wait for us to start a family. To see you, belly round with our child, it would be a dream come true. I know you couldn't conceive with Jean-Luc, but I don't think it was your problem. He was a lot older than you."

Now would be a great time to tell him. But Gabrielle didn't know anything yet. She didn't want to get his hopes up. Guilt gnawed at her, so she withdrew into herself and stared out the passenger window.

After a minute, she glanced back at Drew. Except for his hands on the wheel, he was still; he had sensed her withdrawal.

"I want a family too. And soon, Drew. Let's just plan the wedding first, okay?"

He shook his head. "What's going on with you? You've been withdrawn since your father's wedding. You don't want to plan our own wedding. Jack and I've barely seen you this week. Spill it, Gabrielle. What's going on?"

"Drew, don't be mad at me," Gabrielle urged.

"I'm not mad at you. I just want to know what the problem is. We can't work anything out if you don't talk to me."

Gabrielle debated whether to tell him about the suspected pregnancy. No. There was no indication she was pregnant. Both pregnancy tests had been negative. She should go to the doctor's appointment first. Gabrielle opted for part of the truth.

"I haven't felt very well for the last couple of weeks. I don't know if I'm fighting a bug, but I've just been off. It's hard to plan something that should be exciting when you don't feel well."

Andrew's shoulders relaxed at her explanation. He squeezed her hand.

"Yeah. I've noticed you've been pale lately. You haven't felt well since they tore out the master suite. Maybe there's something in the house you've been breathing. You should see a doctor, just to make sure there wasn't mold in the walls or something."

Gabrielle curled back against Drew's shoulder.

"Actually, I made a doctor's appointment for tomorrow afternoon in Bar Harbor. Just to get things checked out. It's probably a virus, but I wanted to be sure."

"Good." He patted her knee. "You'll sleep at my house tonight. No protesting. Until we can make sure the house isn't making you sick, you and Rocky will come to my house. "

"What about Jack?"

"Gabrielle, this is about your health. We'll stop at your house. You can pack a few things and pick up Rocky. End of story."

"Okay, on one condition."

Drew's mouth thinned, but he waited for her to continue.

"You drop me off and take Jack home to bed. I don't want him sleeping in the car while I'm packing."

Drew sighed. "All right, honey. I won't fight you on that one."

Twenty minutes later, Gabrielle showed up at his condo with an overnight bag and Rocky in hand.

Without commenting, Andrew took her bag and carried it up to his bedroom. Gabrielle followed Drew upstairs but paused in Jack's room to give him a good-night kiss.

When she entered the master bedroom, Gabrielle turned to Andrew. "I feel so gross after opening boxes in the stockroom today. I'd love a shower. Do you mind if I take one before bed?"

Desire darkened his eyes. He skimmed his finger across one shoulder. "Can I come too?"

She answered him with a kiss.

# CHAPTER EIGHTEEN

Dazed, Gabrielle sat on the exam table in the doctor's office. She held the visit summary slip in her hands. It was time to get dressed. She just needed a minute to absorb the information from the paper. *Due date: September 23.* She was pregnant.

Gabrielle gave a half laugh and swiped at the tears easing from the corners of her eyes. A weight lifted from her shoulders, and even though the trademark nausea lurked in the pit of her stomach, it was easier to bear now that she knew the cause. A baby. Drew's baby. Their baby.

After she was dressed, Gabrielle made a follow up appointment. She paused at the building exit and eyed the gray sky. In the parking lot, wet rain fell in sheets, freezing on any exposed surface. A nasty ice storm was about to hit. Gabrielle took out her phone and sent a quick text to Phyllis.

"You were right. Sept. 23 due date. Will be back there soon to pick up Rocky. Thanks for keeping him at the store while I went to my appt."

With her phone stashed in her purse, Gabrielle scraped at her ice-covered windshield. Once the windshield was clear, Gabrielle switched the defrost on high and eased into traffic. On the way back to Jacobs Landing, Gabrielle dropped her SUV down to a creep. The freezing rain continued to fall.

Halfway back to town she neared a crossroad. Out of the corner of her eye, Gabrielle noticed a truck sliding into the intersection from the left. She tapped her brakes and tried to slow down even more, but it was no use. Both vehicles continued to slide. The last sounds she heard were the grind of her antilock brakes and the resounding crunch of metal against metal. With a painful jolt, the world went black.

Andrew took a minute to check his phone in between patients. He hoped Gabrielle would text after her doctor's appointment. Even though they had dinner plans tonight, Drew was worried about her illness.

Were the renovations the cause? He didn't want to wait to find out.

Drew was in the middle of texting Gabrielle when sirens caught his attention. He paused. The roads were icy. It was probably an accident. When a second set of sirens passed the building, Drew wandered up to the front desk and stood next to his receptionist.

Andrew slipped his phone back onto the belt clip. "Any idea what the sirens are about, Donna?"

"It looked like a couple of volunteer firemen heading out of town. I've checked the scanner; you know that's my thing. All I know is there's a two-car accident half-way to Bar Harbor."

"Keep me posted, Donna. What's next on my schedule?"

"You've got a dalmatian in room four."

"Thanks."

Andrew strode down the hall to his next patient, his unfinished text message forgotten.

Gabrielle struggled to open her eyes. Pain radiated through her left arm. Her chest was on fire. Every time she inhaled, it was like breathing through a straw. She finally got her eyes to stay open. At first, she couldn't see anything. Something warm and sticky dripped in her eyes. Gabrielle raised her right hand and wiped it away. She eyed her fingers. Blood.

Where was she?

Gabrielle inched her head to the left and urged her eyes to focus. Her head rested against glass cracked like a spider web. In front of her, more glass and a larger web radiated across the windshield. The annoying sound of a car horn blared somewhere outside.

The truck. The intersection. The boom of impact. The grind of metal. She remembered. Baby. Gabrielle moved her good hand down to cup her abdomen. She blacked out.

The next time she came around, someone was calling her name.

"Gabrielle!"

"Drew?" she murmured.

"No, Gabrielle. It's Cole Marsden. We graduated high school together."

A blurry face came into view. Brown hair. The man looked familiar.

"Cole?" she wheezed.

"We were in Mr. Lake's geometry class, remember? You've been in a car accident, Gabrielle. I'm a paramedic. I'll get you out okay?"

Gabrielle tried to nod, but the pounding in her head threatened to split it in two.

"Cole?" she wheezed again.

"Yep, I'm right here. Gonna put a neck brace on now."

"Can't breathe."

"I know, Gabrielle. I think you've got a collapsed lung. The ambulance is here. We'll get you fixed up."

Gabrielle felt the seat belt across her chest slacken. That's when the real pain hit. Blackness.

She came around again in the ambulance. The muffled wail of the siren barely registered through the pressure in her chest. Spikes of pain radiated each time she took more than a shallow breath. There was something, something she needed to tell someone.

"Cole?" she breathed.

A hand touched her forehead. "Right here, Gabrielle. We're almost there. Have to take you to Bangor."

"Pregnant," she rasped.

"Gabrielle, you're pregnant?" he confirmed.

She nodded once. It was too hard to speak.

"How far along?"

She moved her right hand until four fingers showed.

Cole glanced at her flat abdomen. "Four weeks?"

She shook her head. With the last of her strength, Gabrielle held the four fingers up not once, but twice.

"Eight weeks?"

A single nod.

"I'll let the doctor know when we get to Bangor. You hang in there, okay? You've got to stick around for that baby."

Gabrielle didn't hear him; she had passed out again.

Andrew forgot about the sirens. He saw three patients, one of them was a feisty cat who bit his hand. After Annabelle applied a bandage, Drew stepped into the hallway to see his next patient. When his cell phone buzzed, he pulled it off his belt clip with an impatient gesture. His hand hurt like hell.

Drew glanced at the screen and almost dropped the phone. David Martin, Gabrielle's father. He never called Andrew. A knot of anxiety formed in his gut.

"Hello?" he answered.

"Andrew? This is David."

Drew noted an edge of panic in David's voice.

"David? What's wrong? What is it?"

Drew thought he heard a swallowed sob.

"David! Is it Gabrielle?"

The sirens from earlier flashed to the forefront of his mind. And then he knew.

"Is she alive? What hospital?"

"On her way to Bangor for surgery. My father and I are on our way now. She was in a car accident. They said she was in and out of consciousness in the ambulance. It's all I know."

"I'm on my way."

Drew disconnected. "Annabelle!"

Dr. Pete Standish stepped out of an exam room and raised a questioning eyebrow at Andrew's shout. Thank God it was Tuesday and Pete was there to cover.

"Pete! Gabrielle's been in a car accident. I need to go."

"No problem." Pete nodded in his unruffled way. "I've got your patients covered. Keep us informed."

The next few hours passed in a blur of anxiety. Andrew, David, and Pierre took turns pacing the waiting room. Bob Leland showed up around dinner time.

"Any news?" he asked Drew.

"A nurse came out a while ago to give us an update. She's still in surgery, Dad. They say broken ribs punctured her left lung. She was lucky it missed her heart." Drew scrubbed his hand through his hair. "She's got internal bleeding. They're trying to stop it."

Andrew slumped into a chair and held his head in hands. "I can't lose her, Dad. I can't."

Bob rested his arm around Andrew's shoulders. He pulled Drew against his chest like he had done when Drew was a little boy.

A few minutes later, Drew pulled back. "I was so critical of her not being able to let go of her grief. Now I know what she might have felt when she lost Jean-Luc. The fear and pain, it's a sort of madness."

Andrew shook his head and roused himself to ask, "Is Jack okay? What about the dogs?"

"Jack's worried about Gabrielle, but he's fine with your mom. The whole family is praying for her, Drew. Grace is beside herself since she's still in the hospital in Bar Harbor. Mom had to promise to update her as soon as we knew anything; otherwise Grace was going to insist on an early discharge." Bob took a breath. "The dogs are with Phyllis at the Martin house. Is Thomas here?"

"No. David's been trying to get in touch with him, but he's on duty. The only thing he could do was leave a message. The Coast Guard said they would contact his supervising officer and see if he could be granted immediate leave."

"I better go call your mother with an update. Otherwise, she'll be over here with the whole family."

Andrew nodded and resumed pacing.

At eight o'clock, Drew sat in a semistupor between his father and David Martin. Pierre Martin was slumped next to his son. Both Gabrielle's father and grandfather had aged ten years.

In Coast Guard blue, Thomas rushed into the waiting room. His curly dark hair was disheveled, and his blue eyes were dark with shock. He looked so much like Gabrielle that Drew's heart ached anew.

"Pop? Pop! How is she?"

David updated Thomas about the surgery's progress. Thomas slumped into a chair next to Pierre. All five New England men continued their vigil.

It was almost midnight when Andrew caught sight of the man in scrubs walking toward them. Drew tapped David's shoulder. Gabrielle's father had been dozing next to him, but all the men sat at high alert when the doctor introduced himself.

"Are you the family of Gabrielle Levesque?" At everyone's nod, he continued, "I'm Dr. Harris. I'm happy to say that Gabrielle is stable."

The men let out a collective sigh of relief.

"She has three broken ribs on the left, one of which punctured her left lung. Her left ulna and radius were both broken, one of them with a compound fracture. I had to insert pins for now to keep the bones together.

After the bones heal, I'll take the pins out. She also had some internal bruising and bleeding in her upper abdomen, but we took care of that. We're continuing to monitor Gabrielle because she also has a concussion."

"She's okay? My daughter is okay?" David asked.

"Physically, the surgery was successful. For the next few hours, we'll have to keep her under observation. The main concern is..." The doctor paused to look at the anxious men. "She hasn't woken up from surgery yet. We're not sure if this is a complication from the concussion or if she is in a trauma-induced coma. Until she wakes up, we'll keep her in intensive care."

"I need to see my daughter."

"Once they move her from recovery into a room, I'll send a nurse to get you. I'm limiting it to two people in the room at a time, so you'll need to take turns visiting."

The doctor walked out of the waiting room. Broadsided with the news of a possible coma, the men slumped back in their chairs.

After a few moments, Bob pushed himself into a standing position. "I'd better call Elaine with an update. Sounds like it's going to be a long night."

He turned to David. "Do you need Elaine to contact Phyllis?"

David shook his head. "No, I better call my wife. She has been frantic all day, something about Gabrielle and a doctor's appointment."

Both men walked out of the room together.

A few minutes later, a nurse approached. "I can take two of you back at a time. Which of you would like to go first?"

Andrew glanced at Pierre and Thomas. He was frantic to get back to Gabrielle, but in truth, he needed to see her alone. Not sure if he would completely break down when he saw her, Drew needed privacy for the first glimpse of the woman he loved.

"Go ahead," he urged Gabrielle's brother and grandfather. "Don't take too long, okay? I've got to see her soon."

Thomas and Pierre followed the nurse. Ten minutes later, Bob and David returned from their phone calls. Their faces were ashen. Drew was sure he looked just as bad. Minutes later, Pierre and Thomas returned.

Andrew nodded to David. "You go. She's your daughter."

When David raised an eyebrow, Andrew replied, "I'd like to see her alone, if that's okay. I'll go when you come out."

Thomas helped Pierre sit down. "It's funny. If you look past the bandages and cast, she looks like she's sleeping. I want to scream at her to wake up."

Stooped from the impact of seeing his injured daughter, David limped out a few moments later. He approached Drew.

"You'll stay with her tonight."

It was not a question.

Acknowledging the honor and responsibility David passed to him, Andrew gave a curt nod.

"You will call me if there's any change. No matter what time of day or night."

"Yes, sir," Andrew replied.

"Okay. Thomas, you'll drive me and Grand-Père home."

David turned to Bob. "Thank you for coming to support us and your son."

Bob shook David's hand. "We're family. That's what family does."

With a nod, Thomas helped Grand-Père to his feet. The three Martin men shuffled out a few minutes later.

"Do you want me to go in with you?" Bob asked Andrew.

"No. Give me a few minutes on my own. Okay, Dad?"

Bob nodded and watched his son move down the hallway.

Andrew stood in the doorway and looked at the woman who was his world. Thomas was right. It looked like she was sleeping. Gabrielle breathed on her own, although there was an oxygen tube in her nose to make it easier. He approached her cautiously because her left side had taken the brunt of the accident and he didn't want to risk bumping her.

Medical tape attached a bandage to her forehead. A bulky wrap encased her left arm from above her elbow all the way down to her hand. Where the doctor had used pins to hold the bones together, a large metal bracket stuck out of the bandage. Her fingers and hand were so swollen, they looked like an eggplant with purple sausages attached.

Andrew leaned over her and pressed a light kiss to her lips. "Gabrielle, it's Drew. I'm here, honey. I'll be here all night."

Gabrielle didn't move. Drew kept waiting for her to open her eyes, but she was immobile except for the reassuring rise and fall of her chest.

"Are you the fiancé?" asked a middle-aged nurse bustling into the room.

"Yeah. Andrew Leland."

"My name is Kay, and I'll be Gabrielle's nurse tonight. Here, I have something you'll want to hold on to. Well, two things actually."

Kay scrounged around on her cart and pulled out a small envelope. She handed it to Drew. Andrew opened the envelope and poured Gabrielle's engagement ring onto his palm.

The nurse rested her hand on his shoulder. "Don't get the wrong idea. I think she'll pull through. You don't want to leave a rock like that on her finger though. There are people around here that might see that as an opportunity. Besides, the fingers on her left hand are too swollen to get it back on."

Kay smiled and rustled around on the cart again.

"You're lucky she added you to the papers at her doctor's appointment earlier today. Otherwise, I wouldn't be able to give you this."

Andrew slid the ring back into the envelope and tucked it in the pocket of his shirt, near his heart. He promised himself he would slide the ring back on her finger. They would get married.

"Ah, here's the other thing you'll want."

The nurse handed Andrew a square slip of paper; there was a black-and-white image imprinted on it.

"What's this?" Andrew asked.

"Not, what. Who. That's your baby's first ultrasound photo. One to go in the scrapbook."

"Baby?" Andrew repeated without comprehension.

"Yep." Kay smiled. "The paramedic said Gabrielle was conscious enough in the ambulance to mention she was eight weeks pregnant."

At Andrew's stunned expression, the nurse continued, "Yeah, she was really brave. It must have hurt like crazy to talk, considering she had a collapsed lung at the time. The doctors were able to monitor the baby during surgery. He or she is fine. I'll be back to check on Gabrielle again in a while. If you need anything, just flip on the call light over there."

The nurse indicated a switch on the bed, then swept out of the room.

Stunned, Andrew looked at the ultrasound photo in his hand. This was his child. It all made sense: her nausea, additional fatigue, and unwillingness to commit to wedding plans. He slumped down in the chair next to her bed, trying to reconcile the happiness of a baby with the uncertainty of Gabrielle's condition.

After a moment, Andrew stretched out his hand and rested it gently over Gabrielle's abdomen. Their baby. Right there. Underneath his hand.

*Dear God*, he prayed, *please bring her back to me. Let her live to see our child born. And for many years to come.*

He rested his head on the bed next to her and sobbed with the pent-up emotions of the day.

A few minutes later, Andrew's father entered the room. "Hey, son. Drew, what can I do to help?"

Andrew pushed himself into a sitting position and handed his father the ultrasound photo.

"What's this?" Bob asked as he examined the image.

"That's your newest grandchild, Dad. Gabrielle's pregnant. I didn't know. I shouldn't be angry with her. For God's sake, she's lying there in a coma, but all I can think is, *Why didn't you tell me?*"

Andrew scrubbed his hands over his eyes and wiped away the last remnants of tears.

Bob grinned. "Well, we needed some good news. It's been a rough day, Drew. Cut her a little slack. From what I gather, Phyllis has been concerned about a doctor's appointment Gabrielle had today. Maybe she just found out about the baby. Maybe Gabrielle didn't have a chance to tell you because of the accident."

Drew took a shaky breath. "You're probably right. There's just been so much that's happened. Finding out

I'm going to be a father—you know, a child of my own blood. I'm overwhelmed."

"Do you want me to stay with you tonight?"

Drew thought for a minute, then shook his head. "No. Thanks, Dad. I think Gabrielle and I need this time together. I need to be here for her with no distractions."

Bob stayed with Andrew for half an hour, then took his leave. Andrew settled into the uncomfortable chair next to Gabrielle's bed for a long night. Unlike his sister's hospital room, this one didn't have a couch for family to sleep on.

# CHAPTER NINETEEN

Gabrielle drifted through blackness, but it wasn't oppressive. There was a cool quiet that soothed her as she floated along. A tiny sparkle of light appeared in front of her. It wasn't much larger than a grain of rice.

"Baby?" she asked into the darkness.

The light grew to the size of her thumbnail, then intensified for a minute.

"Hello, Baby," she greeted the light as it bounced around in front of her.

A swooping sensation gripped her. Gabrielle tumbled through the blackness until she came to a stop. As she regained her equilibrium, Gabrielle realized she stood on unseen ground below her. No more floating.

To the left, a doorway opened, and a warm yellowish glow beckoned. Just as Gabrielle stepped toward it, another door opened to her right. Light spilled out from this doorway as well, but the light had a bluish tinge and a slight chill seeped toward her. Muted sounds came from that doorway.

Gabrielle realized she was in some sort of hallway. Which door should she choose? The little light bobbed near her and caught her attention again.

"What do you think, Baby?"

The light flickered near Gabrielle as if it awaited her decision. Gabrielle eyed the warm, cheerful light on her left. It beckoned to her. With stilted movements, she took two halting steps toward that door. It felt like someone had tied weights to her feet. Baby bobbed in front of her face, but Gabrielle could barely see it. The glare from the yellow door overshadowed the small beam of light.

Was Baby smaller? Gabrielle held up her hand and compared its shadowy form. Yes. Baby had shrunk back to its initial size.

With a deep breath, she turned back to the blue door. Muffled sounds teased her ears. Gabrielle strained to hear. Was that chanting?

Curious, Gabrielle slid a foot to the right. Her foot was so heavy, she couldn't even lift it off the ground. Wow! Her feet got heavier when she moved toward the blue door. An additional pressure also weighed down her left arm. When she stepped away from the yellow door, it felt like someone was holding on to that arm.

Maybe she should move back to the yellow door. It was easier to move in that direction. Gabrielle glanced at Baby.

Now that she stood closer to the blue door, Baby had grown in size again. Gabrielle's maternal instinct kicked in. If she went toward the yellow door, Baby shrank. If Gabrielle turned toward the blue door, Baby grew. She would get to the blue door, no matter the effort it took her. She would protect Baby.

Her left foot was so heavy now she could only move it an inch at a time. Gabrielle lost count of how many times she moved her right foot toward the blue door, then dragged her left foot over to meet it. Eventually, fatigue weighed her down. She bent at the waist and paused to catch her breath. As she tried to slow her heart rate, she eyed the blue door again. The chanting was a little clearer now. The voices seemed deep and familiar.

Was it Pop and Grand-Père? Wait! Thomas's voice blended with the two older men. She recognized the familiar cadence now. The men were reciting the Our Father prayer in French:

*Notre Père qui est aux cieux:*
*que ton nom soit sanctifié;*

*que ton règne vienne;*
*que ta volonté soit faite*
*sur la terre comme au ciel.*
*Donne-nous aujourd'hui notre pain quotidien;*
*et pardonne-nous nos offenses,*
*comme nous pardonnons à ceux qui nous ont offensés;*
*et ne nous induis point en tentation,*
*mais délivre-nous du mal.*
*Amen!*

The powerful prayer gave Gabrielle the strength to take another step toward the blue door. Baby effervesced, then returned to thumbnail size. Blackness surrounded her again.

Gabrielle's next return to consciousness was sudden. No swooshing sensation. One moment Gabrielle was outside of consciousness, the next moment she stood again in the dark hallway. The yellow door was still on the left, and it beckoned with a warm, cheery glow. On the right, the blue door waited; its cool air seeped into the dark hallway. The murmur of voices caught Gabrielle's attention.

Gabrielle slid her right foot toward the blue door. Once again, she dragged the heavier left foot over to meet it. An unseen force tugged on her left arm and urged her back toward the yellow door. Doubt crossed her mind. Was she making the right choice?

Baby appeared before her again. The little light pulsated and floated in the direction of the blue door. She would follow Baby.

Gabrielle continued her labored steps. She inched her left foot over to meet her right foot, then repeated the process until she was out of breath. Right foot, step. Left foot, inch by inch, to meet the right foot. Repeat.

After some time, Gabrielle paused to catch her breath. Moving in this dark limbo was like swimming through Jell-O, slow and exhausting.

Grace's voice beckoned from the blue door. "Hi, Gabrielle. It's Grace. Elizabeth and I just got out of the hospital, and we had to come see you. Gosh, I feel stupid talking to you like this."

"No! Keep talking," Gabrielle called out, but Grace couldn't hear her.

However, as she listened to Grace, energy began to pulsate in Gabrielle's legs.

"Anyway," Grace continued, "it's my turn to keep you company. We sent Drew home for a little while.

Hopefully he'll sleep. He looks like death; I've never seen him so haggard. He's worried about you."

"I'm coming," Gabrielle answered, frustrated by her inability to get to the blue door.

Determined, she slid her right foot out and paused. Did she have enough energy to move that left foot again?

"Elizabeth wants to see her auntie. Adam and I hope you and Drew will be godparents, so you need to get better. We can't have the baptism without you."

Gabrielle inched her left foot a little closer to her right. The distinctive scent of a new baby tickled her nose.

"Here. I've tucked Elizabeth against you. Don't worry, I'll make sure she's supported. I hope since she just came from the Beyond and you're hovering there that maybe she'll be able to help you."

Gabrielle felt energy course through her. She took three steps toward the blue door before blackness swallowed her again.

The cycle repeated itself over and over. Gabrielle would suddenly become conscious in the black limbo. She suspected she was pulled there by one of her loved ones on the other side of the blue door. And as she got closer to that door, Baby grew in size and luminosity.

Her goal was closer now, but Gabrielle tired more quickly. The continued weight on her left side made movement increasingly difficult.

Voices drifted to her again. "Dad, what's a coma?"

"Well, Jack. It's like a really deep sleep. We're hoping Gabrielle just needs to heal some more, then she'll wake up."

Gabrielle paused. She heard the rough edge of fatigue and despair in Andrew's voice. She wanted to reach out. To comfort him. She had to get to Drew and Jack. Gabrielle channeled all her willpower into her legs. She lifted her right foot off the ground and stepped as far as her legs would go. Her legs trembled from the strain. There was no energy left to inch the heavier foot over. Baby bobbed around and moved in the direction of the blue door.

"You sense your father, don't you?" Gabrielle asked the light.

Baby grew into a globe of light and rotated back and forth before it returned to its original two-dimensional state.

Gabrielle flinched when something touched her cheek; it was like the wings of an insect brushing her face. Was there a bug in here? She waved her hand around. Nothing.

Jack's voice grabbed her attention. "Brie, you've got to wake up soon. Dad and I are waiting for you. I love you, Mom."

That tickle on her cheek was back. By some miracle, Gabrielle could feel Jack's kiss. Jack needed her. She had to get back to the little boy who had already lost one set of parents. He didn't need to lose another mother. Gabrielle grunted as she used both hands to lift her left foot off the ground. Her whole body shook from the effort. She placed the foot next to her right one. Blackness.

Gabrielle grew frustrated with the blackouts. They slowed her down. She needed to reach the blue door. How long had she been in the black limbo? Although there was no way to measure time, she felt like she had been stuck in the dark hallway for days.

As Gabrielle drew closer to the blue door, sensations in her body seemed to revive. Her left arm began to throb. A weight pressed down on her chest, which made breathing harder. Her head ached. She wasn't sure if these were side effects from the energy it took to move or if they were sensations from the other side.

Many times, Gabrielle questioned why she was moving toward the pain and cold that the blue door promised. The yellow door was warm and inviting at the other end of the hall. Whenever doubt assailed her, Gabrielle would glance at Baby. Throughout the whole process, Baby floated right beside her. Baby moved toward the blue door. She followed Baby.

"Do you want to help me wash her hair?" Gabrielle heard Phyllis ask. "Gabrielle is fastidious about her appearance. I think she'd like to be clean. The nurse said we could do it."

"Sure. Why don't we give her a sponge bath too? After all, it's been two days. She wouldn't want to smell. She's still got blood caked in her hair and under her fingernails, for Pete's sake."

Elaine. That was the other voice, Gabrielle decided. Her two mothers: stepmother and future mother-in-law. Like any mother would, Elaine and Phyllis bathed her broken body and gently massaged her head as they washed her hair. Gabrielle could only feel the lightest of sensations, but the love pouring from these two women gave her enough strength to take another step. Gabrielle reached out her hand and realized she was close to the door now. The blue light was just a few steps beyond her reach. Baby was now the size of a softball. Blackness.

Andrew spent Wednesday and Thursday at the hospital, with only a few hours at home during the day to shower and catch a couple of hours of sleep. Dr. Standish promised to fill in at the clinic, so Andrew didn't need to reschedule patients.

While he was at home, Gabrielle and Drew's family members took turns at the hospital. They reassured Drew that they would phone if Gabrielle's condition changed.

He took Jack to see Gabrielle on Thursday. He wasn't sure if that was the best parenting decision he could make. But after Jack's third nightmare, Andrew decided reality might be less scary than what the imagination could create. After Jack saw for himself that Gabrielle was alive, his nightmares subsided.

While Drew kept his vigil over Gabrielle, occasionally he glimpsed a dark shadow out of the corner of his eye. Whenever he turned his head, nothing out of the ordinary was in the room. Drew wasn't sure if it was his imagination or fatigue, but it happened enough over the course of those two days that Drew became sure of a presence in the room.

Thursday night, Andrew returned from getting dinner in the cafeteria to find Eden in Gabrielle's room.

"Hi, Drew. I told Mom and Phyllis I would stay with her until you got back. They were both tired after giving Gabrielle a bath and washing her hair. She looks much better now, don't you think?"

Andrew looked at the still form of his fiancée. She would only look better if she were awake and smiling again. However, her skin gleamed with a new freshness and the dried blood in her hair was finally gone.

He nodded at Eden, then caught sight of Gabrielle's toenails.

"Eden?"

"I decided to paint her toenails. I wanted to do her fingernails too, but the nurse said they needed to monitor the blood flow in her left hand. It's hard to feel pretty when you have pins in your arm, a chest tube, and broken ribs. I want her to feel pretty when she wakes up. Oh, and I put some lip balm on her lips. They looked chapped."

Neon-pink nail polish decorated Gabrielle's toes. Andrew didn't think it would have been Gabrielle's first choice, but he nodded at his sister.

"I'm sure she'll appreciate it, Eden. Thanks."

Drew realized his family felt as helpless as he did. Everyone wanted to do something for Gabrielle. Drew grew frustrated with his inability to heal her. There was nothing he could do, but wait. It was his duty to remain on guard and protect his wife and unborn child. Even though they weren't officially married, in his heart, Gabrielle *was* his wife. The accident had solidified that for him.

A few minutes later, Eden picked up her purse. She leaned over and kissed Gabrielle's cheek. "Bye, Gabrielle. I'll be back tomorrow to check on you."

Eden turned to Drew and gave him a squeezing hug. "Take care, big brother."

An hour later, Andrew sat in the hospital room's chair. He kept an eye on the dark shadow in the room. If he looked directly at it, it disappeared. But if he pretended to look forward, he could watch it for an extended length of time out of the corner of his eye. Mostly, the shadow was a black blob. But from time to time, it solidified into the shape of a person.

Drew shook his head. He was probably going crazy from lack of sleep and worry.

"You must be Andrew Leland," a heavy French accent observed from the doorway.

Drew turned to see a man of medium height with a gray goatee and graying brown hair. His long coat and masculine scarf indicated wealth, along with the man's air of assurance. Piercing dark eyes gazed at him. Andrew knew who he was: Michel Levesque, Jean-Luc's brother.

Andrew offered his hand to the older man. "You must be Michel. Gabrielle has mentioned you often. I'm sorry we have to meet like this."

Michel shook Drew's hand, then wandered over to Gabrielle's bedside. A hint of expensive cologne trailed in his wake.

"She looks, ah, smaller like this," Michel commented, brushing a curl from her forehead.

Andrew sat down and watched as Michel leaned over and murmured something in French to Gabrielle. He kissed both cheeks in the French custom, then sunk down in a chair next to Drew.

Palms up in the typical French manner, he shrugged his shoulders. "What can we do? She lies there like a rag doll. There is life in her still, but it's…" Michel searched for the right word, "muted."

"I'm beginning to wonder if she'll come out of it." Andrew avoided Michel's gaze. "But I can't give up on her. I love her too much."

Michel nodded. "Gabrielle inspires great love in others because she loves everyone. The love and compassion we are *supposed* to feel for other human beings, Gabrielle feels that. That love gives people dignity."

He tapped Drew's arm once. "I hear congratulations are in order. You and Gabrielle are going to be parents."

Andrew couldn't suppress his grin. Maybe it was wrong to brag to Gabrielle's brother-in-law, but he pulled the ultrasound picture out of his shirt pocket and handed it to Michel.

Michel took the picture and smiled his rare smile. "I remember when my wife, Sophie, and I were expecting each of our children. This is a special time. Cherish it."

Michel handed the picture back to Andrew and stood up.

"I will be staying at the hotel tonight, and I will come again tomorrow. Let me give you my cell number in case there is a change."

Drew entered Michel into his contact list. A few minutes later, Michel was gone in a whirl of cologne and expensive tailoring.

Back in the dark hallway, Gabrielle bent over to catch her breath. One more step and she would cross the blue door's threshold. Her whole body ached now. She tried to draw in a deep breath but winced as fingers of fire radiated up her left side. Drew was just a step away. She'd heard him talking to Michel.

She also heard Michel whisper in her ear, "Sois brave." *Be brave*, he said, as if he knew she was fighting a battle.

Baby radiated like a star in front of her. *I'm waiting*, the little light seemed to say.

Gabrielle straightened to a standing position. She gathered her strength to make that final step, but an insistent tug on her left shoulder drew her attention. The light from the blue door shone onto the object weighing her down. Except, it wasn't an object at all. It was her dead husband, Jean-Luc.

"It's the final choice, chérie." He gripped her arm. "You can still come away with me. Away from pain and into the place of ultimate joy."

Andrew sat up, roused out of his doze by...something. Had Gabrielle said something? Made a noise?

The room was dim. Only a crack of light filtered out from the bathroom door, where Andrew had left it open earlier. His phone told him that it was early on Friday morning.

Andrew glanced at the head of the bed and saw the dark shadow was back. Drew shook his head to clear his vision, but the shadow shifted near Gabrielle. Suddenly, he knew who occupied the room with them; Jean-Luc was here for Gabrielle.

Drew grabbed Gabrielle's good hand.

"No!" he told the shadow. "She's mine now. You can't have her. You will *not* take her from me!"

Andrew rested his other hand over Gabrielle's abdomen. "This is my baby, and she is my wife. You will not take them. Your time is over, Jean-Luc. Move on."

In the darkness of the hallway, Gabrielle turned to Andrew's voice. Through the connecting link of their hands, she felt his strength course through her. Baby twirled frantically.

"If I go with you," Gabrielle responded to Jean-Luc, "Baby's light goes out."

He shrugged in typical Jean-Luc fashion. "The light will pass to someone else."

"But you're dead, Jean-Luc. If I go with you, I die too."

"Dying's not so bad, chérie. I can't tell you what to do. I can only give you the options. Choose wisely. If you go back to the world, it will be a long time before you see the *light* again."

"Gabrielle," Drew sobbed from the other side of the blue door. "Don't go with him. I love you. We have a life waiting for us. Come back to me. Dear God, please help us!"

Gabrielle squeezed Jean-Luc's spectral hand. "I loved you as a girl. When I remember being a girl, I will remember our love."

Gabrielle glanced to the blue door. "But I am a woman now. I've grown up. I've changed. I'm not the same person I was when you knew me."

She turned back to Jean-Luc. He gave her a spectral kiss on the cheek and pointed at the threshold.

"Everything you've always wanted is right there. You just have to step through. But before you do, tell him he better take care of you. Tell him to cherish this miracle."

He chuckled. Before Gabrielle realized his intention, Jean-Luc shoved her through the blue door.

# CHAPTER TWENTY

Pain. That was the first thing Gabrielle noticed when she opened her eyes. She took mental stock. Sore abdomen. Pinpricks burning through her ribs. Throbbing head. Her left side was one aching mass of misery.

The sound of sobbing arrested her attention. To her right, Drew gripped her good hand. His head was turned away from her on the bed. Gabrielle tried to call his name, but nothing came out. She swallowed and tried again.

"Drew," she rasped.

His head shot up, and he searched her face.

"Gabrielle? Did you say something?"

"Drink," she wheezed.

Drew grabbed a foam cup from a side table. His hands shook as he brought the straw to her lips. "Here, love. A little sip for now."

Gabrielle drank from the straw and waited for the moisture to work its way down. Her throat felt like it had been scraped with a rough utensil.

Andrew set the cup down and ran his hand along the side of her face. Tears streamed unchecked down his cheeks. "You're awake. Thank God! I thought I was going to lose you."

He kissed her on the lips, careful not to bump anything sore.

"You almost did," she whispered. "The baby?"

He chuckled through his tears. "Yeah, that was quite a surprise for me. But don't worry, the baby's fine. Here, look."

Drew switched on a dim light in the corner, then pulled a piece of paper out of his shirt pocket.

"See…"

Gabrielle lifted her shaking right hand and took the picture of her baby. Her child was only a small white orb with vague shapes that would develop into arms and legs. Baby didn't look much different than he or she had in the dark hallway.

Tears rolled down her cheeks. "It finally seems real," she rasped. "Only found out today at the doctor's office. Now, look at him. Or her."

Andrew shifted. "About that, honey…"

She glanced from the picture to Drew.

"You've been in a coma for almost three days. It's early Friday morning."

"That's right," she said, sighing and handing him the picture. "I think I heard your mother say it had been two days."

"You heard that?" Drew asked. "You heard us while you were sleeping?"

"Wasn't sleeping, Drew," Gabrielle wheezed. "Was fighting. Fighting the whole time. To come back to you. So tired."

Gabrielle could see Andrew was bursting with questions. However, he noted her exhaustion and kissed her cheek.

"Rest, love. I need to let the nurse know you're awake. Then the whole family needs to know. Don't fade out on me again, okay?"

"Can't go back," Gabrielle whispered. "I made my choice."

Andrew flipped on the call button. When he turned back, Gabrielle was asleep.

Gabrielle stayed in the hospital through the following Wednesday. Nurses and doctors rotated in and out of her room. They checked her breathing tube and took her for X-rays and a CAT scan of her brain. Andrew worked on Monday and Tuesday while various family members, including Michel before he returned to France, sat with her. Drew returned every evening and spent the night in her hospital room.

During those quiet nighttime hours, Gabrielle explained her experiences in what she had dubbed; the Dark Hallway. They told their families she had heard their voices while she was in the coma but kept the details of her struggle between them.

Andrew told her how Jean-Luc's spirit hovered in the room and about his constant urge to protect her. Through this near-death experience, they shared an intimacy most couples never achieved. It bonded them more permanently than any ceremony could.

Wednesday morning was monumental. The breathing tube came out. Andrew, ever patient, helped Gabrielle into comfortable yoga pants and one of his T-shirts since it was easier to get over her cast and head. Inwardly, Drew cringed at the sight of Gabrielle's bruised torso, her body covered in shades of purple, green, and yellow.

Gabrielle must have read something in his eyes. "I know. My whole body looks so ugly."

Drew sat on her right side and circled his arm gently around her back. "It's not ugly, honey. I just hate to see your body so abused. I hate to see you in pain."

He kissed the side of her neck.

"However," he smiled against her shoulder. "Your toenails look awfully pretty. Eden picked out a nice color, didn't she?"

Gabrielle chuckled, then wrapped her good hand around her ribs, and chuckled a little more.

"Don't make me laugh. It hurts."

After a second, her eyes turned serious.

"Drew. It was your love that kept me rooted. You kept drawing me to you from the darkness. Saying, *I love you* doesn't seem an adequate way to tell you how I feel about you. Thank you for not giving up on me, for leading me home."

"Gabrielle, you're my wife in every way but the ceremony. I was not, and am not, ever going to give you up."

He placed his hand on her abdomen. "We're a family now. Me, you, Jack, and this little one. I love you. Now, hurry and heal, so we can get married."

She gasped and looked at her left hand. "My ring! I must have lost it in the car accident."

Andrew took the small enveloped out of his shirt pocket, flipped it open, and shook the engagement ring out into his left hand.

"I've been keeping it safe for you. The nurse gave it to me that first night. I've had it next to my heart ever since."

"Can I wear it?" Gabrielle held up her right hand. "On this hand for now? I know my left fingers are too swollen, but I want to recommit to you right now. I want to wear your ring."

Just as he had done the night he proposed, Andrew kissed the ring. He slid it onto her ring finger and claimed her mouth.

A nurse interrupted by clearing her throat. "I've got your paperwork right here. As soon as we go over it, you're ready to go home. "

A week later, Gabrielle was restless. Andrew was at work. Jack was at school. She had napped and read, and now she had nothing to do. Living at Andrew and Jack's condo was more comfortable than the construction zone at her house, but Gabrielle didn't have any of her projects here. She was a businesswoman, used to juggling many projects at once. Her brain was bored. How could she keep her brain busy while her body healed?

The car accident had destroyed Gabrielle's old cell phone. Drew had bought her a replacement and downloaded all her contacts. Gabrielle picked up the new phone from the table next to her, searched her contacts, and dialed.

Twenty minutes later, there was a knock on the condo door. Gabrielle opened it to a wall of six-foot-two muscle. Dark hair and biceps the size of milk jugs completed the package of testosterone in front of her. She could appreciate his sex appeal with an artist's detached eye, but she was not attracted to him.

"Jesus, Mary, and Joseph! Gabs, you look like hell! You shouldn't be up moving around yet," Johnny Caprese exclaimed and took her gently by her good arm. "Here, let's get you back to the couch or wherever's comfortable."

Gabrielle indicated Drew's recliner, where she spent most of her time due to its ease of exit and entry. By the time Johnny had helped her back into the chair, Gabrielle's legs were shaking. Okay, maybe she had overdone it.

Gabrielle rested her head against the back of the chair and closed her eyes for a moment. She opened them again when Johnny shoved a glass into her good hand.

"Here. Drink some soda. The sugar will perk you up."

Gabrielle took a few sips, then set her glass on a coaster next to her. She was less shaky now.

"Okay, Johnny." She leaned forward. "Each day, you'll bring an update on the house, along with samples and materials we need to continue the renovations."

She held up her good hand when he started to speak. "Things need to move forward, and I'm bored. I won't overdo it, but I need something to keep my mind busy."

Johnny sighed. "All right, Gabs. You've always been stubborn, so it's no use fighting you on this." He shook his head. "Leland's going to skewer me when he finds out."

Gabrielle ignored that comment and smiled. "I'm especially interested to hear about the master suite. What's the progress?"

He outlined the changes to the bedroom and bathroom. Despite her protests, Johnny only stayed half an hour.

"No. You're not ready for more work," Johnny told her as he rose to leave.

He tucked a blanket around her.

"I'll lock the door on my way out. You rest."

Gabrielle was asleep before the door shut.

On Friday, Johnny perched on the couch. He jotted notes on his large notepad while Gabrielle sat in the recliner. The seating arrangement had become their routine as the week progressed. Today, he had brought flooring samples and paint chips for the upstairs hall bathroom.

"How's the master bath coming along?" Gabrielle asked as she compared two shades of blue.

"The tiling and flooring are almost done. Thank God we ordered all the supplies before the accident. It's given us stuff to work on while you were in the hospital."

"You ordered the supplies for the master bedroom, right?"

Johnny gave a curt nod.

"I need to decide on colors, flooring, and tiles for Jack's bathroom…" Gabrielle trailed off as the door to the garage flew open.

Andrew stomped into the house, all six feet five inches of him. Jaw clenched, face flushed, he looked like a bull ready to charge. Johnny Caprese was the red cape.

"Goddammit, Caprese. What the hell are you doing here?"

Johnny stood up just before Drew grabbed him by his shirt. The contractor shot a helpless glance at Gabrielle, then turned back to Drew who looked as if he was moments away from throttling him. Gabrielle was taken aback. She had never seen this side of Andrew before.

Drew jabbed a finger in Gabrielle's direction. "Can't you see she's injured? She's supposed to be resting, and you're harassing her with renovation details."

"Drew—" Gabrielle began.

"What?" he snapped. A vein in his jaw throbbed with barely controlled anger.

"Drew, I called him. I'm bored out of my mind. I need to make sure the house gets done. So we can move in, all of us."

Gabrielle watched him slowly deflate. First the ticking in his jaw slowed. Then his shoulders relaxed. Finally, his arms slackened enough to let go of Johnny's shirt.

"If it was anyone else, Leland, I would've laid you out. I don't care if you have three inches on me. But it's Gabs. I understand. You've got to protect your woman."

Johnny poked Andrew once in the chest. "Now get out of my way. I've got a schedule to keep."

At a loss for words, Drew stepped back.

Johnny turned back to Gabrielle. "Look over those samples this weekend. I'll stop by on Monday."

Johnny edged around Andrew and left the house. Silence followed. Rocky and Gus, who were outside, scratched at the sliding door.

Drew let the dogs in. His normal countenance returned as he came over and knelt by her chair.

"Are you sure you're up to this?" He cupped her belly.

Gabrielle chuckled. "I thought pregnant *women* were supposed to be protective. But you just catapulted *protective* into a whole new category."

Drew had the grace to look sheepish. "You're not just pregnant. I almost lost you in a car accident two weeks ago."

"I know, honey," She cupped his face and urged him closer. "Come here." Gabrielle kissed him thoroughly.

A few minutes later, she pulled back.

"You know what would really help?" She gazed up at him through her eyelashes.

"What?" Drew traced the fading bruises around her forehead and jawline.

"I could use my laptop from the house. Would you stop by after work and pick it up? If I had it, I could start wedding plans."

"Wedding plans?"

"Yep. But I think we should move up the timeline, don't you?" Gabrielle rested her hand on her belly. "This little one isn't going to get any smaller."

Drew bent down and pressed a kiss to her lips. "Just tell me when and where."

# CHAPTER TWENTY-ONE

It was the end of May. Gabrielle sat in a silky robe in front of her vanity. She was in her old room at Pop's house. The muted sounds of wedding preparations drifted up through the open bedroom window, but for now she was blessedly alone. Gabrielle gazed at her reflection.

What did she feel today on her wedding day? Excitement. Love. Passion. They were all there. Jean-Luc's specter was gone, and Gabrielle had no regrets. The promise of Andrew teased her like the late afternoon sunshine.

What was he feeling right now? Was he as eager as she to finally say their vows?

In silent agreement, Gabrielle and Drew had not slept together since the accident. This hiatus of intimacy allowed her body to heal and stoked the anticipation for their wedding night. Gabrielle glanced at the antique clock on the vanity and counted the hours until she could make love with the man she loved. Would her body still excite him now that it had been through so many changes?

Gabrielle eyed her left arm. A few light scars dotted her flesh where the pins had been, but otherwise it looked normal. Breathing was no longer a strain. Her bruises were healed. Gabrielle's body had returned to normal.

Kick.

Well, almost normal. Baby. A life grew inside her. This was a new experience, one Gabrielle had waited years to feel. She grinned and rested her hand over the small mound of her belly. Now, at the end of her fifth month, Gabrielle frequently enjoyed Baby's kicks. They were proof of life.

Earlier this month, she and Drew had gone to the ultrasound appointment. They marveled at the little person moving around on the screen. Because everything about Baby had been a surprise, they decided not to find out the gender of their child. Boy or girl, they would be happy to welcome this new member to their family.

A knock on her door drew Gabrielle's attention.

"Come in," she called.

Thomas stepped into her room. His eyes roamed over Gabrielle's wavy hair, twisted away from her face and gathered in a loose knot at the nape of her neck. Her flawless makeup accentuated her sparkling blue eyes.

Thomas cleared his throat.

"Wow, Brie. You are more beautiful than any of the models you worked with in Paris." He gave her a bittersweet smile. "You look like Mom."

Gabrielle smiled and picked up a framed snapshot from the vanity. It was a photo of their mother, Isabelle Martin. She was snuggling toddler Thomas and holding baby Gabrielle on her lap. Gabrielle studied the photograph of the dark-haired woman who had died too young.

"Yeah. I guess I do look a little like her. It's on days like today, the special occasions, that I miss her. Even though she's been gone for a long time."

Thomas gave her shoulders a squeeze. "Drew's eyes are going to pop out of his head when he sees you."

Gabrielle swung around to face her brother. "Speaking of Drew. Aren't you supposed to be with him since you're one of his groomsmen?"

Thomas dropped an envelope onto her lap.

"Here. Drew sent me over as message boy. He knew I'd want to see you before the ceremony anyway."

Gabrielle eyed the envelope, her name scrawled across the front in Andrew's strong script.

"Drew hasn't changed his mind, has he?"

Gabrielle bit her lip.

Thomas chuckled. "You kidding? He's chomping at the bit to get this ceremony over with. I get the impression he's looking forward to the wedding night, as much as that disgusts me to say about my future brother-in-law."

Gabrielle grabbed Thomas's hand and pulled him to a crouch in front of her. She searched her brother's blue eyes, so much like her own.

"I thought I made the right choice the first time, but you opened my eyes to things about Jean-Luc. Is there anything you sense about Andrew that I should know, Thomas?"

Thomas patted her hand. "No, Brie. There's no surprises with Andrew Leland. He's the real deal. I see a healthy love between you. You're going to be that old couple on the porch swing, still holding hands, then dashing upstairs to the bedroom when your grandkids aren't looking."

Sadness came and went in her brother's eyes. Thomas caught her watching him, so he smiled and kissed her cheek. Not for the first time, Gabrielle wondered if her brother had loved and lost someone.

"Thomas? Has there never been anyone special in your life?" Gabrielle ignored the dark look Thomas shot her and continued, "You know almost everything about the men in my life. What about you?"

Thomas cleared his throat and Gabrielle inhaled at the desolation in his eyes.

"Yeah, Brie. There was someone. I met her in Vegas of all places. I know it sounds corny…"

"What happened?" Gabrielle prompted when he trailed off.

"I lost track of her. I've never been able to find her again."

After a moment, Thomas shook his head and cleared his throat. He forced a smile. "Hey, I've got to get back to your pacing groom. Be happy and be well, Brie." Thomas patted her shoulder and pointed to the envelope in her lap. "Don't forget to read his letter."

After Thomas swept out of the room, Gabrielle reached for the envelope, light glinting off her engagement ring, which sat in its rightful place on her left hand. She traced her name for a moment, then slid a finger under the partial seal and opened it.

*Dear Gabrielle,*

*You're right. Sitting down to write a letter gives one a certain degree of perspective. What do I want to say to my bride on our wedding day? "I love you" seems so inadequate to describe all my emotions.*

*First, I need to tell you how blessed I am to have a woman who loves Jack as much as I do. What chances are there that I would find someone who loves him because he is Jack, not because he is my son? I can't believe this is chance at all. I believe God sent you Rocky so we would meet again as adults. That was miracle number one.*

*Next, I just need to say thank you for taking a chance on me. Thank you for putting your faith and trust in me and for saying yes when I asked you on a date when we were 5,000 miles apart. Thank you for choosing me in the Dark Hallway. That was miracle number two.*

*Love is a term all-encompassing and inadequate at the same time. Dr. Seuss said, "You know you're in love when you can't fall asleep because reality is finally better than your dreams."*

*Today, my dreams become reality. Today you become my wife. That is miracle number three.*

*I hope we continue to appreciate the small miracles as well as the big ones and the perfect miracles that come about under less-than-perfect circumstances. They remind us of our love. I promise to love you, honor you, and cherish you as long as I'm alive.*

*Love,*
*Drew*

A tear threatened to ruin her makeup. Gabrielle dabbed at it with a tissue and read the letter again. How had she been blessed to find two men in her lifetime that loved her completely? Jean-Luc loved the girl she had been, and Andrew loved Gabrielle for the woman she had become. Gabrielle pressed Drew's letter to her heart and hung her head. She was humbled.

"Thank you, God," she whispered.

There was a rap on the bedroom door. Then the door flew open, and three women bustled inside. Grace and Eden wore elegant gowns, of their chosen style, in a muted blue green. Phyllis wore her lavender dress from the Valentine's Day wedding. She refused to buy a new gown and assured everyone she was happy to get another use out of it.

"Time to get you into that gown, hon," Phyllis announced.

She moved to the closet door where the wedding dress draped from a hanger.

"What do you have there?" Eden pointed to the envelope in Gabrielle's hand.

"It's from Drew." Gabrielle smiled and clutched it tighter against her chest.

With blond hair pulled into a chic twist, Grace peered over her shoulder. "Wow. Never knew my brother was a romantic. I guess if he was going to write a love note, his wedding day would be the day to do it."

Grace grinned. "Well, let's not keep him waiting. The wedding starts in an hour. Oh, Gabrielle, you look so beautiful! No wonder Adam is texting me that Drew's driving the groomsmen nuts!"

"Gabrielle has always been beautiful." Eden's comment was matter of fact as she helped Gabrielle to stand. "But the glow of love and motherhood has made her even more so."

Phyllis patted Gabrielle's arm. "Babies are such a blessing, no matter when they come. I bet you can't wait to hold your little one."

Gabrielle smiled and ran a hand along her rounded tummy. Her baby would come just four months after the ceremony.

Eden held an odd-shaped package out to Gabrielle. "I know it's selfish, but I want to see you open my gift."

"Shouldn't I wait for Drew?" Gabrielle asked.

"No. You'll understand why I wanted *you* to open it. Now go ahead, sister." Eden's green eyes sparkled with anticipation and love.

Gabrielle flashed a smile of appreciation. The term *sister* promised the acceptance of Drew's family and a larger group of people who loved her. Gabrielle unwound layers of white tissue paper. A wooden form emerged from underneath.

"Oh, Eden. It's the sculpture from your studio, isn't it? The one where the two branches entwined."

Eden glowed from Gabrielle's enthusiasm.

"I loved this when I saw it in progress, but now that you finished it, it's breathtaking!"

Gabrielle threw her arms around Eden and clung to her for a minute.

"It was always meant to be yours. Grace was right. It's you and Drew; two separate branches joined into one."

Again, tears threatened to spill from the corners of Gabrielle's eyes.

"Here," Grace shoved a tissue into Gabrielle's hand. "You don't want to mess up your makeup."

"Nice job showing the rest of us up, Eden," Grace teased. "I got her something off their registry."

"Oh, I'm sure I'll love it too…"

"It's okay, Gabrielle. I understand my limitations," Grace reassured her. "I may not be an artist like Eden, but I'm not jealous. I'm proud of her."

Eden preened at her older sister's praise. The youngest child never got over the need to impress her older siblings.

"All right, ladies," Phyllis gave a mock scold. "Let's get this bride ready. I've heard the groom is impatient enough to break down the door."

The women fussed about Gabrielle. They helped her into her gown and made sure her hairstyle was not disturbed. When her veil was in place, they circled Gabrielle in a group hug—a bond of sisterhood and support.

Andrew stood at the end of the white runner and waited for his bride. He tried not to shift with impatience since he was facing the crowd and all eyes were on him. His heart pounded at the thought that Gabrielle might change her mind, that she might never come out of the house.

"Don't worry. She'll be here," Adam murmured behind him. "The waiting's a bitch though, isn't it?"

Drew swallowed a laugh and schooled his face into a bland expression. Thank God for Adam. At least his humor helped distract Drew for a moment.

While he waited, Drew glanced at the crowd. Did Gabrielle get his letter? Was it too sappy? What if she was having second thoughts?

Adam cleared his throat, and Drew swung his head up in time to see Eden start down the aisle. Grace followed a few paces behind her.

When had the music started? He wasn't sure, but he craned his neck for a glimpse of Gabrielle.

Jack and Sara came down the aisle next. They made a cute ring bearer and flower girl: Jack in a little tuxedo and Sara wearing a pink flower girl dress. Andrew could tell Jack disliked holding his cousin's arm because his mouth was pursed around the corners. Arriving at the end of the runner, Jack rolled his eyes at Drew, then sat down next to Elaine and Bob.

Suddenly, Gabrielle was there. She floated out of the house, her arm linked with her father's. The gentle breeze stirred layers of champagne-colored lace. Evening sunshine glinted off the beading of the dress as if Gabrielle were adorned with diamonds. Her hair was twisted gracefully away from her face, and her luminous blue eyes never wavered from his.

One coherent thought popped into Drew's head: *Thank you, God!*

Then she stood before him. Gabrielle paused and kissed her father on the cheek. David placed Gabrielle's hand in Andrew's. He sat beside Phyllis and Grand-Père in the front row.

Gabrielle smiled up at Drew and whispered, "This *is* a dream. You're so handsome. I can't believe you're marrying me."

Andrew took the hand he held and kissed it with tenderness. "I thought you'd never get here. Marry me quickly before you change your mind."

The minister cleared his throat. "Shall we get started?"

The seated guests marveled at the physical beauty of the couple as they said their vows. Andrew's golden hair and white teeth contrasted against the traditional black tuxedo, which accented his broad shoulders and narrow waist. Gabrielle's champagne-colored gown, with cap sleeves, fell to a low vee in the back. An empire waist let material fall loosely over her small tummy. Unless a person specifically looked, her pregnancy was not obvious. Gabrielle's wavy hair shifted in the light breeze off the bay. The setting sun was the perfect backdrop as the photographer snapped pictures.

But all those details paled in comparison to the couple's smiles as the minister announced to the crowd, "Ladies and gentlemen, I'd like to introduce you to Dr. and Mrs. Andrew Leland."

When the minister introduced them as a married couple, elation soared in Drew's chest. He looked into his wife's radiant smile, then claimed Gabrielle's mouth.

"My turn! My turn!" Jack called amid the applause.

Gabrielle pulled back, smiled at Drew, and then crouched down to Jack's eye level.

"I love you, Mom!" Jack threw his arms around her neck and kissed Gabrielle's cheek.

"I love you too, Jack." Gabrielle held the boy against her.

Andrew crouched beside them and encircled his new family in his arms. The photographer snapped the image that would later sit in a place of prominence: on the living room mantle.

Hours later, the sun had set, and the dancing was well under way in the wedding tent. With his tie off, and the neck of his shirt unbuttoned, Drew searched the nearby guests for any sign of his wife. He spotted Emily Ross, the annoying woman who had hit on him the first day Gabrielle reentered his life. Emily twirled on the dance floor in a skimpy pink dress and stiletto heels. How did she get in here? She wasn't invited to the wedding.

Next to Emily, was Drew's friend Quentin Shaw. Quentin took Emily's drink out of her hand and pulled her into his arms. Drew shook his head. Emily was Quentin's date. He almost felt sorry for Quentin, but Drew was too happy.

Andrew scanned the crowd again and finally located Gabrielle. She stood near Hailey and Amy. Gabrielle's stepsister held Hailey's newborn son, Garrett, against her own distended abdomen. Baby love. Andrew saw the look of expectation in both Gabrielle and Amy's eyes as they thought about the imminent arrival of their own babies.

It was time.

Andrew found Jack with Bob and Elaine. He made sure Jack had everything he needed to stay with them while he and Gabrielle were on their honeymoon.

"We'll be fine," his mom reassured him. "Now go find your bride and disappear before everyone gets wind you're leaving."

Drew gave Jack a hug. "See you in a week, okay, bud? We'll call every day to talk to you. When we get back, you can move into your new room."

"Bye, Dad. Bring me back something cool, okay?"

"I will."

Drew couldn't resist. He ruffled his son's hair, then weaved through the crowd in the direction where he had last seen Gabrielle. A minute later, Johnny Caprese stopped Drew to congratulate him. He whacked Drew on the arm with a meaty hand. Drew tried not to let his impatience show. He chatted with Johnny for a few minutes, then politely excused himself.

When Drew looked up next, Gabrielle had disappeared. Great. Now where had she gone?

The next time Drew located his wife, she was back on the other side of the room. She stood in front of his parents with Jack wrapped around her waist. Drew smiled. She hadn't forgotten to say goodbye to Jack.

Before Drew could get to her, Michel Levesque and his family approached Gabrielle. She was speaking to the Levesques in French when he came up behind her and rested his hand at the small of her back. She smiled at Drew, then shifted her attention back to Michel.

"The wedding was very beautiful," Sophie Levesque said to him in heavily accented English. "Our Gabrielle is precious. Take care of her."

Drew's smile caressed Gabrielle. "I will take care of her. Always."

Sophie smiled at him and kissed his cheeks in the French fashion. "We leave now to return to Paris. Bring Jack and the baby when you come to visit. Maybe in the spring? You know what the old song says about *loving Paris in the springtime.*"

"We'll visit soon." Drew smiled and said his goodbyes to Michel's children, Vivienne and Luc.

Michel approached him. He shook Drew's hand and pulled him in so he could whisper in Andrew's ear. "I will kill you if you hurt her." He smiled amiably at Drew, but there was steel in his eyes. "Just so we understand each other."

"As her husband, it's my duty to protect and cherish her. You'll never have to worry," Drew reassured Michel.

Michel stepped back. His smile warmed as he included Gabrielle and Jack in it. "We will see you in Paris. You always have a place with us, no matter what."

They watched the Levesques leave, then Drew leaned over and whispered in Gabrielle's ear, "Are you ready, love?"

Gabrielle nodded and bent down to Jack. "I love you, bud. We'll all live in the big house together as soon as we get back from our trip."

"I love you too, Mom. It's all right to call you *Mom* now, isn't it?" Jack asked.

"It sure is. As soon as we get back, we'll file those papers to make it official, okay?"

She hugged Jack, stood, and turned to her new husband. "Ready, Dr. Leland?"

Drew grinned at her. "I'm ready, Mrs. Leland."

Elaine motioned to them. "There's a side exit over here. Hurry before you get stopped again."

Drew's mother slipped a small handbag into Gabrielle's hand as they passed through the exit.

"Here's your purse, dear. Everything else is taken care of."

Outside the tent, darkness had cooled the night air. Gabrielle shivered. Andrew slipped off his coat and wrapped it around her shoulders. He pulled the lapel toward him so she was pressed against his body. His kiss held the promise of passion and love.

"Let's go." He grabbed her hand.

They made it to the driveway before three dark shapes materialized.

"Everything's all set," Thomas spoke in the darkness.

"Your car is at the end of the driveway, so you can take off," David announced. "Don't worry about the dogs. We'll take care of them until you get back."

"Hmph. Here are the keys." Pierre held up a flash of silver, and Andrew grabbed them.

The three shapes huddled around them.

"Be happy."

"Be healthy."

"Be safe."

The Martin men engulfed Andrew and Gabrielle in a family hug, then urged them toward the end of the road.

The black sports car waited for them, half-hidden under an overhanging tree. Andrew helped Gabrielle inside the car, then went around to the driver's side.

When he turned the key, the engine purred to life, and they were soon out on the road.

Gabrielle rested her head back against the seat and sighed. "It was a wonderful wedding, but I'm so glad we're finally alone."

Drew rested his hand on her knee. "Tired, love?"

Gabrielle eyed him and smirked. "Not *that* tired. How long before we get there?"

"Get where?" Drew raised an eyebrow.

"I don't know. You're the one in charge of the honeymoon. Come on, Drew. You may look like a spy every time you wear a tux, but don't be so secretive. Where *are* we going?"

"Wouldn't you like to know?"

"All right, if you won't tell me, I'll have to…" She ran her hand over his lap and rested it on his arousal, "take matters into my own hands."

Gabrielle slid close to him and nuzzled his neck. The car swerved.

"Gabrielle," Drew ground out. "If you don't want to get in another car accident, you better give me some space. Otherwise I'll have to pull over right now and have my way with you."

"Would that be so bad?" she purred.

He groaned. "I'd like our wedding night to be spent in a comfortable bed, not in the back seat like a couple of teenagers. Please?"

"There's no back seat."

"A technicality."

Gabrielle relented and moved her hand back to his knee. She rested her head against his shoulder and asked again, "How long?"

Drew sighed. "Fifteen minutes. I have a friend who loaned us his cabin for the rest of the weekend. Then we head out Monday morning to somewhere tropical. That's all the information you get for now."

Fifteen minutes later, the *cabin* they pulled up to was really a lodge-style mansion set on a private wooded road. Andrew helped Gabrielle out of the car. He strode to the trunk and removed their luggage.

"Drew, this is no cabin. What kind of friends do you have?" Gabrielle asked.

"I know people." He shrugged and tromped up the steps.

Drew set their suitcases by the door, where a welcoming light shone out from flanking windows. Back down the steps, he came. He paused in front of Gabrielle and swept her into his arms. She squealed in delight, then wrapped her arms around his neck.

"I'm heavier than I used to be. Maybe I should walk," she urged.

"Not a chance. I've waited my whole life to carry my bride over the threshold. What do you think these muscles are for anyway?" He grinned and flexed his arms underneath her.

Inside, he refused to put her down. Drew moved through the lower level of the house where mellow lights welcomed them. At the back of the house, he opened a door to a massive master suite. With long strides, Drew reached the king-size platform bed and set her gently on it.

With a quick kiss, he returned to the door. "I'll be back with the luggage."

After Drew left the room, Gabrielle rose and found the adjoining bathroom. She made use of its posh facilities. She couldn't help but marvel at the giant bath tub, big enough for two.

When Gabrielle stepped back into the bedroom, Andrew stood at the large picture window. She admired her new husband as he closed the shades. At the sound of her footstep, he turned to her, hazel eyes dark and unreadable.

"All locked up?" she asked.

Drew nodded and stepped closer.

Gabrielle held her hand out in front of her and gazed at it for a moment. "I know it's silly, but I'm nervous. Look how my hand shakes. I know we've made love before, but it's been months. And it's our first time, married. It's more important this time, you know?"

Drew captured her hand and kissed its palm. He pulled her against him.

"It is important." He trailed kisses down her neck. "I'll try to go slow, honey, but I've been without you for so long."

He scooped Gabrielle up and set her on the bed. Coming down next to her, he held out his hand. "Look, my hands are shaking too. I want it to be perfect."

Gabrielle threaded her fingers through his and pulled him closer. "Forget about perfect, Drew. Just make me your wife." She pulled his head down for a kiss.

In a game of seduction, they helped each other out of their wedding clothes. When Gabrielle lay naked on the bed, Drew knelt between her knees. He paused and eyed the small mound of her belly. With a smile, he kissed it.

"I see Baby is growing nicely," Drew rumbled.

"I'm not thin like I used to be. Maybe my pregnancy is a turn off." Gabrielle worried her lip.

Drew entered Gabrielle in response and evoked a moan from both of them. He paused.

"Definitely not a turn off," he ground out. "I love you so much, Gabrielle."

"I love you, Drew," Gabrielle cupped his face and moved against him.

They drove each other to the peak of passion and groaned as completion washed over them.

Gabrielle and Drew spent their honeymoon on a private island in the Caribbean. Once again, the island was owned by a friend of Drew's from his Wall Street days. They returned to Maine a week later—tanned, relaxed, and eager to move in together as a family.

The first night in the Victorian, Gabrielle moved around the kitchen as she prepared dinner. Drew was upstairs with Jack. Gabrielle shivered and pulled her powder-blue sweater tighter around her body. It was colder here than it had been in the Caribbean.

Gabrielle grimaced as she glanced down at the cardigan that didn't meet over her belly anymore. Had her clothes shrunk in the week she'd been gone? Gabrielle rubbed the small of her back, then served up enchiladas.

"Back hurting tonight?" Drew asked behind her as he nuzzled her neck.

"Hmm?" Gabrielle turned with spatula in hand. "Oh, yeah." She grimaced. "My pants don't fit. I need to break down and buy some maternity clothes."

Gabrielle lifted the hem of her shirt and showed Drew the rubber band she had wrapped around her jeans button in order to give her belly more room.

Drew chuckled. "I think you've *popped*. That's what my sisters call it when a woman finally starts to show."

He ran his hand along her belly, then leaned down to kiss it.

"Hey, Mom and Dad." Jack hopped into the kitchen on one foot. "I'm starved. When's dinner?"

Drew poured drinks at the counter. Gabrielle smiled at the dark-haired boy who levered up onto one of the island stools.

"Dinner's ready, Jack. I'm just dishing it up now."

As they sat down to eat, Gabrielle glanced around the dinner table at her new family. She raised her glass of milk.

"A toast." She waited for Drew and Jack to lift their glasses. "To the first of many family dinners in our new home."

"To family dinners," Drew agreed.

"To family." Jack grinned. "Let's eat!"

# CHAPTER TWENTY-TWO

The September wind blew leaves across the street as Gabrielle drove Jack to school. She pulled into the drop-off line and shifted the SUV into park.

"Bye, Mom," Jack called as he threw open the door.

"Don't forget your lunch, Jack." Gabrielle held up his superhero lunch box.

"Thanks!" He snatched the lunch box from her hand and hopped out of the vehicle.

"Have a great day at school."

Jack waved as he went to line up with his classmates.

Gabrielle headed to a nearby gas station. As she levered herself out of the seat to fill up her tank, a twinge gripped her back. Absently, Gabrielle rubbed the pain with one hand as she watched the dollars add up.

After the tank was full, she climbed back into the SUV. Gabrielle reached to start the vehicle, and the pain in her back turned into a spasm. She breathed through her mouth until the spasm let up.

Gabrielle shook her head. She couldn't be in labor. Right? She wasn't having any contractions. It was just a little backache. Maybe she better stay close to home just in case.

Back at the house, Gabrielle called the store. "I'm not coming in today, Phyllis."

"Are you okay, Gabrielle? You in labor?"

"My back hurts, and since I feel like a beached whale, I'm going to take it easy," Gabrielle replied.

"Gabrielle, you never take it easy. If that backache gets any worse, you call me or Drew. Understand?"

"Okay, okay. I'm not having contractions though."

"Labor doesn't always start with contractions, hon. Promise me you'll call if you need anything."

"I will, Phyllis. I promise."

Gabrielle hung up the phone. She trudged upstairs to check her overnight bag. If the baby was close, she needed to make sure everything was ready.

Andrew was finishing up with a dachshund in room four when Annabelle entered the room.

"Something up?" he asked absently as he finished typing notes in the patient's file.

Drew turned back to the pet owner. "Mrs. Williams, you'll need to pick up the prescription at the front counter. Annabelle will make sure you get the correct dosage for Libby."

"Dr. Leland," Annabelle interrupted. "Your wife is on line two."

His wife. Andrew grinned. He never got tired of hearing that.

"Why didn't she call my cell?" He patted his pocket and checked the clip on his belt. "I must have left it in my office…"

"Dr. Leland, I got the impression it was urgent. Line two."

Annabelle pointed to the phone on the counter.

Urgent!

Drew grabbed the phone and punched the button for the correct line. "Gabrielle?"

"Drew," she sobbed on the other end.

"What's the matter, honey?"

"My water broke."

He heard her gasp on the other end of the line.

"And the contractions are coming hard. You've got to come get me *now*!"

Her sentence ended on a groan.

"Okay, I'll be right there. Where are you? Work or home?"

"Home," she moaned.

"Be right there."

Drew dashed for the door. On the way out, he called to Annabelle over his shoulder, "Gabrielle's in labor. The notes for Libby are in the file. I've gotta go."

The few minutes it took to get home were the longest of his life. Drew pulled into the driveway and slammed the truck into park. He took off for the back door, only pausing to grab the keys from the ignition. When he entered the kitchen through the mudroom, the house was eerily silent.

"Gabrielle?" Drew called.

Where were the dogs? Neither Gus nor Rocky greeted him as he moved through the kitchen.

A noise that was half-keen and half-groan answered him. Drew took the stairs three at a time. Gus and Rocky sat alert inside the bedroom door. Their gazes never wavered from the master bathroom. When Drew stepped over the dogs, they whined but didn't move.

Drew spotted Gabrielle hunched in their freestanding bathtub.

"I'm here, honey. What're you doing in the bath tub?"

As he knelt next to her, Drew ran a hand along the top of her head. Gabrielle was in her nightgown, and her knees were drawn up and splayed.

Oh, God. He was going to deliver his own child.

When the contraction eased, Gabrielle gazed at him and panted. "This baby's coming too fast. No time to get to the hospital. The birthing class said to lay in the bathtub with a towel underneath if you have to deliver at ho—"

She bit off the last word and arched her back as another contraction hit.

"Did you call the ambulance yet?" he searched in the pocket of the coat he still wore.

Shit. His cell was still at work.

"Nooooooo," she ground out.

"Just keep breathing, love. I'll be right back."

Andrew stepped into the bedroom, picked up the house phone, and made the call. He threw his coat on a nearby chair, grabbed his emergency veterinary case from under the bed and hefted it into the bathroom.

At least the instruments inside were sterile.

"Drew," Gabrielle sobbed. "We can't do this. We're in a bathroom, not a hospital. There's no doctor. Oh, God…" She broke off as another pain hit.

Drew ignored his shaking hands as he scrubbed up at the sink. He laid his instrument pouch on a clean towel, then slipped on a pair of gloves. Back by the bathtub, he slid down to the ground near Gabrielle's knees.

"Shh, love. Everything's going to be fine. I'm a doctor, remember?"

Lifting the hem of her gown, Drew checked Gabrielle's progress. He blanched at the sight of the baby's head.

"You're not a doctor. You're a veterinarian," she accused. "I want a real doctor."

"You told me yourself that in the pioneer days, veterinarians were the doctors..." He stopped midsentence when she glared at him.

Gabrielle keened like an injured animal as another pain hit.

"Drew, I can't do this. I can't," she panted after the pain had passed.

He shimmied over to her head.

"Gabrielle, look at me." He waited until she swung her head around and eyed him with pain-glazed eyes. "The baby's head is crowning, and the ambulance is on the way. Hang in there, and with just a few pushes, we'll have a baby. Together, we can do this."

She nodded and clenched her teeth as another contraction hit. "I feel like I need to push," she ground out.

Drew propped her feet up on the sides of the bath tub and crouched near the baby's head.

"Okay, whenever you feel like it, go ahead," he urged.

He needed to be strong for all of them. He could do this. He was a professional. Drew repeated the mantra in his head as Gabrielle screamed in agony.

God! He wished he could soothe her and let someone else deliver the baby. But it was just them, and he had to get all of them through the birth safely. Drew glanced down. The baby's head was out. In the distance, Drew heard sirens. Another contraction hit and Gabrielle cried out again.

"One more good push, honey. Then we'll have a baby," he reassured her.

Gabrielle murmured an expletive she would never normally use. Drew tucked his chin, so she wouldn't see his smirk. He checked to make sure the cord wasn't wrapped around the baby's neck. Everything looked good.

Gabrielle groaned again, and a minute later the baby slid into Drew's hands. He clamped the cord and blew into the baby's face. She took her first breath and squawked like the newborn she was.

"It's a girl, Gabrielle. You did a fantastic job," he choked out as tears rolled down his cheeks. He swiped at them with his elbow as he bent to cut the cord.

"A girl," Gabrielle rested her head against the back of the tub. She closed her eyes and took a deep breath.

As the baby continued to wail, Drew wiped her down and wrapped his daughter in a clean towel.

When she was bundled, Drew took the baby to his wife. "Here you go, Mama."

Gabrielle's eyes flew open, and she reached for their daughter. "She's so beautiful," Gabrielle sobbed as she admired her baby for the first time.

She looked up at Drew and sniffled. "Congratulations, Dad. You were magnificent."

Drew leaned in and kissed the mother of his children. In awe, he ran his hand lightly over the baby's head.

"I can't believe she's here. You were fantastic, Gabrielle. Our daughter. What should we name her?"

"Isabelle. After my mother." Gabrielle's blue eyes pleaded with him. "Please?"

Andrew could deny her nothing.

"A beautiful name for a beautiful baby." He smiled with tenderness.

Five minutes later, the ambulance team arrived upstairs to find mother, father, and the new baby. One of the paramedics was Cole Marsden, the same man who had helped Gabrielle after the car accident.

Cole grinned at Gabrielle as they loaded her onto the gurney. "We've got to stop meeting like this. Next time, just invite me to a barbeque or something, okay?

"You'll be invited to Isabelle's birthday party every year. How 'bout that?" Gabrielle smiled and hugged the baby to her chest.

Cole chuckled and moved to raise the gurney.

"Wait. Can you take a picture of us before we head to the hospital?" Drew asked Cole.

"Sure. No problem."

Andrew handed Gabrielle's cell phone to Cole, then crouched near Gabrielle and the baby. They heard the distinctive click of a picture being taken, then Cole handed the phone back to Andrew.

"That's one for the baby book," Cole grinned. "Now let's get mom and baby to the hospital."

Elaine Leland was in the process of slicing apples for pie when a text message chirped on her phone. She washed the stickiness off her hands, then picked up the phone. It was a message from Gabrielle. With an exclamation of surprise, Elaine opened the message and saw a picture of Drew, Gabrielle, and a red-faced newborn. She scrolled down and almost dropped the phone.

"Meet your new granddaughter, Isabelle Grace Leland. Arrived at home unexpectedly at 11 am. At hospital now to get them checked. Can you pick up Jack?"

Elaine confirmed she would pick up Jack, then asked when they could visit.

"Will let you know. Thanks Mom!"

Elaine checked to see that Gabrielle's family had received the same photo. Reassured, she went to work. Within minutes, the picture of the Lelands' newest grandchild was posted on a variety of social media sites. Celebratory texts came in from Bob, Eden, Grace, and many of the town council members.

A steady stream of visitors arrived at the hospital as soon as the new family was settled into their room. Pop and Grand-Père arrived first. Phyllis would come later, after the store closed.

When Gabrielle placed the baby into Pop's arms, a tear leaked from the corner of his eye. It was only the second time Gabrielle had ever seen him cry.

"She is beautiful. Just like her namesake. Your mother would love her, Gabrielle. She'll be the baby's guardian angel and watch over her from heaven."

Emotional anyway, Gabrielle wiped at tears and smiled. "I think Mom *will* watch out for her, Pop. No one could do it better."

Grand-Père held Isabelle next. "My first great-grand-daughter." He gazed at the little bundle. "Bienvenue, ma jolie fille." *Welcome, my pretty girl.*

Pop and Grand-Père stayed for half an hour, then took their leave so Gabrielle wouldn't tire too quickly. Elaine and Bob arrived after school got out, with Jack in tow.

"Dad! Mom! Let me see my new sister!" Jack ran into the room.

He climbed onto the bed next to Gabrielle, who held Isabelle tucked against her.

"Careful, Jack! Mom's a little sore." Drew cautioned.

"Why's she sore?"

Drew grimaced. He wasn't sure how to answer that question.

Gabrielle stepped in to rescue Drew from an awkward explanation. "Jack, do you want to hold your sister?"

"Yeah. What's her name?" Jack asked.

"Her name is Isabelle. Here, Jack. Get down and sit on the couch. Then you can hold your sister," Drew urged.

"Why Isabelle?" the boy wondered as he sat on the couch.

"That was my mom's name," Gabrielle replied. "She died a long time ago and went to heaven. Remember?"

"Yeah, just like my first parents," Jack responded, unfazed. He held out his arms for the baby.

"She's really light," he exclaimed as his eyes lit up. "And small. I better protect her like a good big brother. Right, Dad?"

Elaine sniffled and Bob wiped moisture from his eye.

"That's what big brothers do, Jack. You're already a pro." Andrew smiled.

Jack grinned at Andrew, then shifted his gaze to Elaine. "Okay, I'm done. You can hold her now, Grandma."

Jack passed the baby back to Drew, who had never actually let go of her. He scooted off the couch, then returned to Gabrielle's side.

"Tommy, at school, says it hurts moms to have babies. I'm sorry you're hurt, Mom." He stroked her hand.

Gabrielle smiled. "It's all right, Jack. I'll be better soon. Why don't you reach into my bag? See that blue package? Yes. Grab it."

"Is it for me?" Jack eyed the square object wrapped in his favorite superhero paper.

Gabrielle nodded.

"Look, Grandpa." Jack took the package to Bob. "I get a present and a new sister all in one day."

Jack tore open the paper. The box contained a whole team of his favorite superheroes. He played with the action figures until it was time to leave.

"Can I take them with us?" the boy asked Elaine and Bob.

"Sure. Let me help you pack them up," Bob responded.

A few minutes later, Andrew's parents took Jack home.

Grace and her family showed up after dinner. They admired the newest addition to the Leland clan, then herded the kids home to bed. Eden, and then Thomas, appeared right before visiting hours ended.

As Thomas held the baby, he grinned at Gabrielle. "Another beautiful Isabelle in the family. Hopefully she keeps her looks and doesn't grow up to look like Drew." He shot Drew a teasing look.

"What's wrong with looking like a Leland?" Eden asked in mock anger.

"Why're you upset?" Thomas asked. "You don't look like a Leland either."

"That's true." Eden grinned. "I look more like the O'Brien side, red hair and all. Either way, Isabelle will always be beautiful, whether she looks like a Leland or a Martin."

A few minutes later, the nurse came in and shooed everyone out for the night. Gabrielle sighed in relief, then rested her head against the pillow. For the next couple of hours, she dozed on and off.

Late that night, Gabrielle pretended to sleep as Drew held their daughter. The awe she saw on his face mirrored hers whenever she looked at the little miracle they had created. Isabelle was perfect. Healthy. The most beautiful baby in the world. Gabrielle smiled because that was every mother's first impression of her child.

Drew caught her watching him and grinned. Pride shone from his eyes like a beacon.

It was the same for a father, Gabrielle decided. A baby validated his masculinity, his ability to procreate. Every new father strutted around like he was the first man to make a baby. And that was beautiful too. It was as it should be.

Drew strolled over and slipped the baby back into Gabrielle's arms. He moved onto the bed next to them and rested his head against hers.

"Gabrielle, if we ever have more children, it's got to be in the hospital. I was scared to death delivering her. What if something went wrong?" Drew shuddered.

"You could have fooled me." She eyed him. "You were all business. You showed me no sympathy the whole time I was in labor."

Drew traced Gabrielle's forehead. "I couldn't, love. Otherwise, we both would've let fear get the better of us. We had a job to do."

Gabrielle laced the fingers of her free hand through his and gazed at the baby in her arms.

"Together. We did it together, and we accomplished a miracle."

Drew squeezed her hand, and she looked up at him.

"Being together *is* the miracle. A perfect miracle. I promise to remember that every day."

Gabrielle kissed him with tenderness. "And so will I."

# ABOUT THE AUTHOR

Katrina Alexander's writing inspiration began in childhood when she and her older brother used to write stories and exchange them. At family reunions, she would bring her current stories and read them to her cousins, who patiently put up with her. Katrina lives in Michigan where she enjoys all four seasons, but finds winter a little too long. In order to make it through the gray skies and subzero temperatures (which sometimes last into April), she likes to curl up with a good book, her dog at her feet.

CPSIA information can be obtained
at www.ICGtesting.com
Printed in the USA
BVHW051708231219
567575BV00019B/906/P